A lover of fairy tales and history, **Lauri Robinson** can't imagine a better profession than penning happily-ever-after stories about men and women in days gone past. Her favourite settings include World War II, the Roaring Twenties and the Old West. Lauri and her husband raised three sons in their rural Minnesota home and are now getting their just rewards by spoiling their grandchildren. Visit her at laurirobinson.blogspot.com, Facebook.com/lauri.robinson1 or X @LauriR.

Also by Lauri Robinson

The Lady's Stand-In Groom
A Courtship to Fool Manhattan
A Dance with Her Forbidden Officer

The Redford Dukedom miniseries

Captivated by His Convenient Duchess
Winning his Manhattan Heiress

Southern Belles in London miniseries

The Return of His Promised Duchess
The Making of His Marchioness
Falling for His Pretend Countess

The Osterlund Saga miniseries

Marriage or Ruin for the Heiress
The Heiress and the Baby Boom

Twins of the Twenties miniseries

Scandal at the Speakeasy
A Proposal for the Unwed Mother

Discover more at millsandboon.co.uk.

DARING TO DREAM OF THE DUKE

Lauri Robinson

MILLS & BOON

All rights reserved including the right of reproduction in whole or in part in any form. This edition is published by arrangement with Harlequin Enterprises ULC.

This is a work of fiction. Names, characters, places, locations and incidents are purely fictional and bear no relationship to any real life individuals, living or dead, or to any actual places, business establishments, locations, events or incidents. Any resemblance is entirely coincidental.

Without limiting the exclusive rights of any author, contributor or the publisher of this publication, any unauthorised use of this publication to train generative artificial intelligence (AI) technologies is expressly prohibited. HarperCollins also exercise their rights under Article 4(3) of the Digital Single Market Directive 2019/790 and expressly reserve this publication from the text and data mining exception.

® and TM are trademarks owned and used by the trademark owner and/or its licensee. Trademarks marked with ® are registered with the United Kingdom Patent Office and/or the Office for Harmonisation in the Internal Market and in other countries.

First published in Great Britain 2026
by Mills & Boon, an imprint of HarperCollins*Publishers* Ltd,
1 London Bridge Street, London, SE1 9GF

www.harpercollins.co.uk

HarperCollins*Publishers*, Macken House, 39/40 Mayor Street Upper, Dublin 1, D01 C9W8, Ireland

Daring to Dream of the Duke © 2026 Lauri Robinson

ISBN: 978-0-263-41875-0

03/26

Printed and Bound in the UK using 100% Renewable Electricity at CPI Group (UK) Ltd, Croydon, CR0 4YY

To Gary and Sharon in honor of our Taco Tuesdays!

Chapter One

1878

A sense of urgency filled Rosemary Crofton as she hurried along the sun-filled corridor, past the many landscape paintings and ancestral portraits decorating the wood-paneled walls of Turnbill Manor. Even knowing that Nora was sure to be looking for her, she couldn't stop the childhood memories that entered her head and filled her with a joyfulness that she hadn't felt in a long time.

The manor was more than a house. At one time it had been a formidable castle, complete with battlements and alures. Some of those remained, giving the property the magnetism of yesteryear, a history imbued with the bravery and courage of those fighting against tyranny.

Over the centuries, areas of the castle had been removed, the bricks used to create other structures in the nearby village, while remaining parts had been remodeled, turning the estate into an expansive family residence instead of a massive fortress protecting the inhabitants from enemy invasions. She'd always considered Turnbill an amazing place, and though it had been over seven years since she'd last stepped foot on the property, the grandeur of it had remained embedded in her mind, and in her heart. The estate itself felt like an old friend, one she had greatly missed.

The stone exterior gave the impression of safety to all those within. Inside, meanwhile, beautiful wooden floors, ornate woodwork, and walls covered with shimmering wallpaper and patterned plasterwork, all brightened with natural light shining in through numerous windows, provided the hospitality of a home where people lived and loved, and welcomed guests.

In their younger years, she and Nora Knight had raced through the maze of long corridors, run up and down the many staircases of all four stories and played in the oval-shaped rooms of the turrets on each of the house's four corners. Her mother and Nora's mother had been close friends since childhood, and they had relished the friendship that their daughters had formed. They had encouraged regular visits and extended stays that had thrilled mothers and daughters alike.

Time spent with Nora, pretending to be everything from kidnapped princesses awaiting rescue, to queens overseeing their kingdoms… Those were some of Rosemary's favorite memories, and thinking on them emphasized the poignant changes that had occurred since her mother's death.

The creation of all such memories had stopped completely then.

Rosemary let out a sigh. There were times when it felt as if it had been more than nine years since that devastating day when she'd been informed of her mother's death. She hadn't understood how a scratch from a rusty nail had turned deadly. But it had, and it had changed Rosemary's life. A year and a half later, her life had changed again when her father remarried.

It was easy to understand why her father, as the Earl of Havenshire, would want to remarry, want a son, an heir, to carry on the family legacy and title that had been bestowed upon him for his faithful commitment to the royal family when he'd been a young man.

As a child of twelve when her father's second marriage had happened, Rosemary had hoped for a return of the happiness her family had once known. Had hoped for the sadness to leave her father's eyes and to have a stepmother who might alleviate some of the pain she'd still felt over the loss of her mother.

This hadn't happened. Maud was not the loving stepmother Rosemary had hoped for, and she had quickly learned to avoid her stepmother as much as possible. Two years later, her stepbrother, Thomas, had been born, and Rosemary had discovered that Maud wasn't even capable of loving her own child.

She'd found that devastating, for Thomas has been nothing but a joy from the moment of his birth.

Looking back, Rosemary now saw how her stepmother's need to have all the attention focused on her had been apparent from the start. Maud cared little about the family's past friendships. Those connections, therefore, had slowly disappeared, even the one between Rosemary and Nora, which was renewed only when an event in London would bring the girls together for a short while.

However, Maud was also very astute in hiding the sides of her that others saw from her husband, and out of pure, deep love for her father, Rosemary would never let him know that the Maud he saw shower both of his children with moments of affection was a fraud. That when he wasn't around, Maud was more set upon making life miserable.

It had become more pitiable during the past few years. Maud's dissatisfaction of having a stepdaughter coming of age and gaining attention had evidently turned her aversion into something stronger. Rosemary trod carefully to avoid igniting Maud's jealousy, but a large portion of that jealousy came from the love and attention Rosemary had always received from her father. He bestowed that same devotion upon his son, which should make Maud happy. That wasn't the case. Rosemary witnessed the same loathing in Maud's eyes when Thomas received their father's attention as when she did.

That never failed to sicken Rosemary, and that was the one area where she didn't tread carefully. She showered Thomas with love, making sure he knew he was as cherished as her own mother had cherished her.

Those memories, too—those of having the unconditional love of a mother—were as prized as those she had about Turnbill.

As her mind shifted, Rosemary sighed, knowing no memory of Turnbill was complete without the inclusion of Michael Knight. Whenever she and Nora played their make-believe games, Nora's older brother had always been at hand to provide the necessary strength to move a piece of furniture for them or to open a heavy door in the rarely used north wing of the castle. He had also been their protector or extra courage when they'd explored other dark and hidden unused areas of the massive structure.

Now that Rosemary was older, she surmised Michael hadn't been afraid of those spaces like she and Nora had been simply because he'd explored them long before they had. He was five years older than both she and Nora, so while they'd been playful youngsters, he'd already outgrown child's play in many ways. Yet he had always been willing to fulfill their requests.

Even in later years, when he'd been growing into a handsome young man of fifteen and sixteen and had already been given responsibilities to complete, he'd always come to their aid when they'd asked, without so much as a grumble. In her younger years, Rosemary had wished for an older brother just like him, but as time had gone on, she'd come to dream about growing up and marrying him.

Foolish thoughts, she knew, but a child's mind was often filled with silly thoughts. Her adored Thomas was proof of that. At six, he had a delightful imagination, one that she encouraged, just like his love of the London Zoo and the animals there, which Rosemary took him to visit as often as possible.

Her thoughts came to a stop at the same time as her feet, and she pressed a hand to the front of the bodice of the pale pink and burgundy gown she'd chosen to wear upon leaving London this morning for the five-hour trip to Turnbill. With the square neckline and short sleeves, it was perfect for the warm spring day, and for the party that was already underway outside on the elaborately groomed yards and gardens of Turnbill.

The party was the first one hosted by Michael since he'd inherited the title and role of the Duke of Turnbill four years ago. Rosemary had feared Maud would manage to convince her father that they couldn't attend, but much to her delight, her father had insisted they would attend. Not just today's party, but the entire weekend. Maud had gotten her way in one thing—her claim that such an extended visit would be too much for Thomas. The saving grace for Rosemary in that instance had been Joelle, Thomas's governess, who was as competent as she was caring.

Rosemary had been the one to hire Joelle while Maud was away in Paris earlier that year. Her stepmother had believed that a wardrobe of Parisian gowns would increase her popularity during this year's season and had spent two months there, making purchases. Prior to her departure, Thomas's previous governess had accepted an offer of marriage and left their employment. Like with most everything else that concerned the house or family, Maud wasn't about to let anything interrupt her plans, and upon her return, she hadn't shown any interest in the new governess. She'd been too thrilled by her shopping expedition and visions of how much she would shine at each and every event this year.

Rosemary had her doubts about that, because new clothes didn't change the person beneath them.

Nonetheless, she was overjoyed with the prospect of spending the entire weekend at Turnbill and in rekindling the friendships she held so dear.

She had rarely seen Michael since he'd become the Duke of Turnbill, and had spoken to him only in passing, for he hadn't attended as many London events as Nora had over the past few years.

Today, however, she had to speak to him. Had to express her concerns about Nora and the man she had set her heart on marrying—Geoffrey Burrows, the Viscount of Bellview. Rosemary had firsthand knowledge of the Burrows family. Maud had been the widow of Geoffrey's uncle prior to marrying her father. Rosemary didn't know the rest of the family like she did Maud, and that was where her greatest concern arose.

This past winter, Maud had suggested a liaison of their families, as in marriage, between Geoffrey and Rosemary herself. Rosemary had refused to even consider it, and luckily her father had refused the suggestion, too. If Rosemary knew one thing, though, it was that her stepmother did not want the best for her, and that meant Geoffrey was *not* the best.

Rosemary's gaze shifted from the door before her to the end of the hall, where sunlight was streaming through the stained-glass window, causing colorful beams of light to dance across the floor. A smile formed on her lips as she remembered how she and Nora used to believe those beams were woodland fairies and had concluded that if they could catch one, all their wishes would come true.

Oh, how simple life had been back then.

She turned, faced the door of Michael's study again and drew in a deep breath before knocking upon the solid wood.

"Enter."

The sound of the baritone voice that filtered through the door put a flutter inside her stomach—nerves, perhaps, or anticipation.

Rosemary twisted the knob and, pushing the door

wide, she crossed the threshold. It was her heart that fluttered then.

Michael's back was to her, and it was a glaring reminder of how the young man she'd used to count on for heavy lifting and protection in dark, hidden rooms had grown into a tall, broad and formidable man.

"Forgive my intrusion, Your Grace," she said.

Michael turned from the window that had been holding his attention and looked at her with a slightly quizzical expression.

His eyes were the same dark blue as she remembered, his face as starkly handsome as ever, and his black hair still fell across his forehead, just a bit unruly...

Rosemary breathed in another deep breath and released the doorknob, then performed a small curtsy. "I would like to request a moment of your time."

A smile turned up the corners of Michael's lips, and he stepped away from the window. "I do not believe either of us can remember a time when you didn't use my given name, Rosemary. Nor when you would feel the need to ask permission to speak to me."

He was older, his voice deeper, but like his handsomeness, his affable attitude was still the same, which instantly eased her nerves. "That may be correct, Your Grace, but you are now a duke."

The curl of his lips increased. "And you are a lady."

"Not according to some." She pinched her lips together. That had slipped out without a single thought.

"Oh?" he asked, lifting a single brow that was as dark as his glistening hair. "Pray tell?"

His blue eyes still had a twinkle in them that made him as approachable as ever, which she appreciated. Yet, at the same time, it also brought forth a flurry of thoughts, silly memories of dreams about him and reminders of how much her life had changed since then. They made it impossible for her to continue to meet his gaze, especially after what she'd just said.

Eyeing the window instead of him, she closed the door behind her, crossed the room, and skirted around the large desk to stand before the glass, which was flanked by heavy brown drapes. Below was a yard full of guests. Some mingled about, some sat in lawn chairs and on concrete benches near flower beds in full bloom, while others were playing a variety of yard games—croquet, hoop rolling and such.

"Are you not going to tell me who doesn't consider you a lady?" Michael asked, stepping up to the window beside her.

It wasn't like Rosemary to disrespect her family, so she attempted to make light of the situation. "My stepmother for one." She tried to add in a small laugh, but it fell flat. "She's very good at convincing others to go along with her beliefs." She flinched at the second part of her response, yet had to admit that was where her confidence was the most bruised, and her heart. Maud had all but convinced her father, and many others, that Rosemary's prospects for marriage were few and far between, considering she had so few talents.

All Rosemary could surmise was that all the time spent on silly dreams in her childhood had brought forth the failures of the present that were constantly pointed out to her.

"Well, considering I have known you longer than your stepmother, I believe my opinion is more accurate, and I believe you have grown into a remarkable and graceful lady."

"One who can't sing or play a musical instrument, can barely thread a needle or hold a paintbrush." It would help if she had an interest in any of those things. She'd tried, but it just wasn't there for her. She'd much rather spend her time entertaining Thomas by reading the various tales he loved hearing or taking him to the zoo or the park or cheering for him as he learned to tie a bow and other childhood accomplishments.

Michael's chuckle was low, yet cheerful sounding. "I do not believe those are requisites of being a lady."

"You may be the only one who thinks that way."

"I don't accept that, but I do believe that you know that I would never lie to you."

The sound of his sincerity caused her to look at him. Of all the people she knew, he had to be the most honest. Always had been. "I do know that," she said.

"Then you must agree with me that you have exceptional talent in many other things."

She shook her head but asked, "Such as?"

"Chasing fairies comes to mind, as well as creating stories about damsels locked in castles. And we mustn't forget your ability to win at hide-and-seek."

She tried but was unable to keep herself from cracking a hint of a smile. His teasing about such things brought back even more wonderful memories, yet she tried to remain serious. "Those are the talents of a child, not of a lady."

"Are they?"

Her smile grew and became complete in response to the sight of the same mocking expression he'd used years ago. "Yes, and you know it, so quit teasing me."

He chuckled. "I knew that smile was still in there somewhere."

She wrinkled her nose at him for drawing out her smile. He had always been able to do that, and he knew it. So did she, and that thought momentarily tickled her insides.

Her life truly had been filled with happiness back then.

He laughed again. "It's very good to see you, Rosemary, and allow me to offer an apology. Had I been made aware of your arrival, I would have been downstairs to welcome you."

"It's good to see you, too, Michael, but there is no need to apologize." Using his given name was as easy as it had been years ago. It was the prospect of her next statement that caused her to momentarily pinch her lips together. She had to stop herself from putting blame on Maud, who had dawdled endlessly this morning and then had insisted upon stopping at a roadhouse to quell her hunger along the way. "Due to a delay in leaving London, we only arrived a few moments ago. Our luggage is currently being delivered to our rooms. Allow me to extend our gratitude for being invited."

"You have never, nor will ever, need an official invitation to visit Turnbill."

The authenticity in his tone made her smile again. "Thank you."

"Now, tell me, why would you wish to speak to me when you could be outside enjoying the beautiful weather and the garden party? Is something amiss with your accommodations?"

"No, not at all." Rosemary's nerves began jumping beneath her skin, making her question if she was doing the right thing. Michael might have already determined that Geoffrey—the Viscount Bellview—was a suitable match for Nora and could consider her concerns quite inappropriate.

"Clearly something is on your mind," Michael said. "Something of great concern if I'm not mistaken."

She let out a sigh that was so deep her cheeks puffed as the air seeped through her lips. "I must be frank with you."

"I expect nothing less."

"I'm concerned about Nora's choice of a potential

husband," she said in a breathy rush, with a sense of relief at having said it aloud.

His only move was the twisting of his head, to gaze out the window again.

"I haven't said anything to Nora because she knows the difficulties I've experienced with Maud and that Geoffrey is Maud's nephew. The family's reputation is somewhat lacking, but my concerns lie in Geoffrey himself. It's rumored that he is…" She let her words fade away, growing more convinced that she should have kept her concerns to herself by the way Michael seemed to stiffen.

"A rake," he said.

"Yes," she admitted. "Nora is my oldest and dearest friend, and I don't want to see her hurt."

"Nor do I, Rosemary," he said.

She couldn't say what washed over her. Some of it was relief that he agreed with her, but the shiver going down her spine was caused by the tone of his voice. He sounded despondent, and she'd never heard him sound that way.

Rosemary's gaze burned into the skin on Michael's cheek, yet he didn't turn to face her. Didn't elaborate on his concerns. It was common knowledge that he was protective of his younger sister. From the moment Nora had been born, it had been instilled in him that girls and women needed to be protected. He'd only been five then, so he couldn't remember the exact words his father had said to him, that first time he'd seen Nora. But the message of his father's words—that being an older brother meant doing whatever, whenever, it took to keep his sister safe—had found a home inside him, and it was still alive and well.

He was sincerely concerned about the man Nora claimed to have fallen in love with and whom she was vying for approval to marry. Hence the reason for the very party that was now taking place. He'd agreed to host the event as a consolation to his sister after he'd said he wasn't prepared to give his consent until he knew Geoffrey Burrows better than he currently did. Burrows was the Viscount of Bellview, a title and position that had recently been bestowed upon him and brought along a fair amount of family baggage. Geoffrey's late father had been known as a rake; he had been married three times, each wife younger than the last, but none of them had kept him in her bed. There were rumors of illegitimate children and proof that he had gambled and outright squandered funds. Now it had been reported that Geoffrey was following in his father's footprints.

Michael would be the first to admit that each man was his own person and should be judged by his own character and actions rather than those of his family members or those he chose as friends. Therefore, when Nora had voiced her interest in Geoffrey, Michael had followed his duty of protecting her and obtained information on Burrows. So far, what he'd learned wasn't as thorough as he'd wanted. After the death of his mother, Geoffrey had chosen to live in Birmingham with her family rather than in London with his father, and though it was known that Geoffrey visited gaming halls and gentlemen's clubs now and again while in London, his interactions there were not equal to his father's, nor were his interactions with women.

Little information was available about Geoffrey's years in Birmingham, and he'd only moved to London a few months ago, after his father had died and he'd taken over the properties and business interests that came along with the title. However, it had been confirmed that there was practically a haram of young women secretly living at the family's estate, a day's ride south of London.

Despite everything, even if he couldn't obtain more information, Michael needed to decide whether or not he should give his blessings to Nora, and he could only do that by making his own assessment of Geoffrey.

His attention circled back to the woman standing beside him. Rosemary Crofton had been Nora's best friend since the two of them had been born within months of each other. Though they had once scampered about Turnbill hand in hand, the two of them hadn't seen each other regularly since Rosemary's father remarried, and Nora had been ecstatic when their confirmation of attending the weekend's event had arrived. That hadn't surprised Michael, but having Rosemary seek him out and express her concerns did. A part of him was seriously questioning whether she was here, in this room right now, because Nora had asked her to convince him to give his blessing. The two of them had done similar things in their younger years, teamed up to convince him to help them, and they both knew that he'd rarely, if ever, denied either one of them in a request.

Rosemary was also intelligent enough to not start any such campaign by singing Geoffrey's praises. Not because she was sly, but because she had sense and knew that wasn't the way to convince him of anything.

"When was the last time you spoke with Nora?" he asked.

"Almost two months ago, at the Pribbles' ball," Rosemary replied. "I've been unable to attend many events lately, but we've written regularly."

"Been unable to attend or chosen not to?" he asked, knowing full well that she was often absent from social events. Nora claimed it was due to her stepmother, Maud, whom she'd described as a loathsome woman. Michael had met Maud Crofton himself a few times, and during each encounter he'd been confused as to why Ralph Crofton, the Earl of Havenshire, had married her. She was as different from Amelia, his first wife and Rosemary's mother, as a woman could be.

Unless of course, he wasn't seeing a side of Maud that Havenshire did.

"Both," Rosemary answered.

He didn't ask her to elaborate. She was quite devoted to her younger brother, Thomas, and was just as devoted to forgoing any engagement where her father was unable to attend.

"How well do you know the Viscount Bellview?" he asked, shifting his attention back to his sister and her whirlwind courtship.

"Not very. I met him once prior to encountering him at the Pribbles' ball, when Maud invited him to join us for the evening meal."

"When was that?"

"Around Christmastime, shortly after he'd moved to London."

"What did he do during either of those encounters to arouse your concerns?"

Her cheeks pinkened as she cast her big, brown eyes towards the floor, gazing at a spot near the hem of her ruffled pink skirt. "Nothing."

She had always looked charming, and her eyes, surrounded by long and thick lashes, had always been easy to read. Today was no different. Although, Michael would have to classify her as beautiful now, rather than just charming, for she had grown up considerably from the days when she used to stay here for weeks on end. Her hair was still honey colored, not quite blond but not brown, either, and right now, the sun was catching on the coiled-up tresses not concealed by the brimmed burgundy and pink hat atop her head. Her voice was the same as he remembered, too, uniquely soft and even toned, yet it always held a sense of joy. Just like her. She'd always been so pleasant, a delight to be around.

"So," he said. "We are in the same position."

"Excuse me?" she asked, eyeing him cautiously.

"Geoffrey hasn't done anything definite to arouse my suspicions, either, yet I am concerned that Nora could be making the wrong choice, simply because of what I've heard."

"You, too, have heard the rumors?" she asked.

"Everyone has probably heard the rumors," he replied. "To my knowledge, Geoffrey hasn't attempted to quell them." That was a significant detail that troubled him.

"Maud has made mention that he's following in his father's footprints."

"Has she witnessed it or is merely speculating?"

She sighed. "I don't know. Maud speculates about everything."

He believed that, and he didn't need to speculate himself to know that the enchanted childhood Rosemary had once known had changed greatly when her father remarried. She hadn't changed, though, and he now felt a sense of guilt that he'd assumed she'd come to see him to convince him that Nora had made the right choice. Rosemary had always had a heart of gold, and he believed she still did. Today was no different from the times years ago, when she'd sought his assistance for heavy lifting, exploring the unused north wall, saddling a horse or numerous other tasks. "So, what should we do?"

"I don't know that, either. I just felt inclined to share my concerns with you. I'm sure you are aware of how often money and status are the motives behind a marriage, and I was fearful that perhaps Geoffrey was experiencing some financial difficulties. I wouldn't want that to be the reason he's interested in marrying Nora."

"Nor would I." Michael had experienced that very situation himself. He'd also experienced how easy it was to overlook such things when a person's heart was involved.

It had been over a year now since he'd broken ties with Martha Grossman. He'd been prepared to ask her to marry him, believing she had fallen in love with him as deeply as he had her. He'd even lost a close friend over it. Drake Taylor. He and Drake had been childhood friends, and that friendship had continued after Drake had "hit the sea," as he called it, sailing around the world on his family's cargo ships.

Drake had spoken of doing just that from the time they'd been young, and each time he'd set ashore in London, they'd seen each other. Until the time, over a year ago now, when Drake had recognized Martha and commented that he'd seen her at the docks, providing services to a particular sea captain. Michael had insisted that Drake was mistaken, that Martha was a lady, the daughter of an earl, and though her father was deceased, the Earl of Beachford had provided well for his family.

A week later, Drake had proven otherwise, and when Michael had confronted Martha, she'd admitted that she visited the docks, visited a sea captain. She'd insisted that she'd had to do it, in order to have the funds to keep her in fashionable gowns and the other things needed to hold her status in society. She had assured him that it would all end when they married. In his distracted state, Michael had almost believed her, almost accepted her betrayal, until he discovered that none of what she'd said was true. Her family wasn't lacking money, and the sea captain was but one of many trysts that had started long before her father had died.

She'd then offered that he could have affairs, too. That they could still wed, that she could still be the Duchess of Turnbill. He'd pointed out that he hadn't asked her to marry him, nor would he make such an offer.

It had been an ugly ordeal, but luckily, only a few knew the grim details as to why their relationship had ended. Shortly thereafter, Martha's mother had sent her to live with an aunt in Manchester, and Michael had no idea if she was still there or not.

Nor did he care.

However, the lessons he'd learned through that ordeal were ones Michael would never forget. Not only about love but about friendships.

He hadn't seen Drake since their disagreement, and he regretted that. Drake had simply been looking out for his best interests, which was what he was doing now for Nora.

"I'm worried by how quickly she fell in love with Geoffrey, too," Rosemary said. "They met at the Pribbles' ball, so it's barely been two months, and she's already thinking about marriage? That doesn't sound like Nora."

Michael nodded. "I agree, and I'm glad you shared your concerns with me," he said. "I don't want to ask you to betray Nora, but if you hear something, learn something, something of significance concerning Geoffrey or their whirlwind romance while you are here this weekend, I would appreciate if you'd share it with me."

Chapter Two

Rosemary was not only relieved that Michael agreed with her, she was grateful that he was as interested in learning more about Geoffrey as she was. She didn't get the opportunity to tell him that she would share anything she heard with him, however, because the door flew open.

"Michael!" Nora exclaimed while entering the room. "Have you seen Rose—" She stopped talking and let out a screech, then rushed forward with such speed her black ringlets bounced off her shoulders. "There you are! I heard you'd arrived and looked everywhere for you!"

Rosemary hurried around the desk, meeting Nora in the center of the room, where they embraced each other as excitedly as they had as young girls.

"It's so good to see you," Rosemary said as the hug ended. She took a moment to scan Nora's lovely features. Like her brother, Nora had black hair and blue eyes, but where Michael could look serious, Nora's lips were always slightly curled up, as if she was ready to laugh at any given moment, and she often did. Life was a joy for Nora. Rosemary could remember a time when it had been that way for her, too, and that was one of her greatest concerns. That Nora could lose the joy that radiated off her. Most assuredly she would, if she married wrong.

"I'm so happy you are here! It's going to be just like when we were young! And your dress! It's beautiful, and you look adorable, as always." Nora's brows knit together slightly. "But why are you in here, with him, instead of searching me out?"

"Never fear, little sister," Michael said. "Rosemary merely wanted to thank me for the invitation. Naturally I assured her there was no need, because she doesn't need an invitation to visit Turnbill."

"Of course she doesn't!" Nora initiated another hug, then hooked her arm around Rosemary's elbow. "Come, I have so much to tell you!"

"There's so much I want to hear about," Rosemary replied, before she glanced over her shoulder at Michael while being led to the door. "Thank you, Michael."

"You're welcome, Rosemary," he replied. "I look forward to seeing you throughout the weekend."

He was smiling, but it was the way his smile didn't reach his eyes that she noticed the most. It reminded her of the times when she and Nora had been young and used to ask for his help. He'd known then by a simple look from them that they'd needed his help, and right now, he was displaying that same look they'd worn, asking her for help.

She wouldn't let him down. Nor would she let Nora down. When her mother died, she'd learned how quickly joy disappeared from life—and how a marriage affected the entire family. She didn't want that to happen to the Knights.

"I look forward to seeing you, too, Michael," she said.

"Of course you two will see each other," Nora said, pulling her from the room. "You're going to be here all weekend, and it's going to be so much fun! Willette Burmingham will perform this evening. She has such a beautiful voice. And tomorrow there will be horse racing during the day and a troupe of Scottish dancers will perform during the ball, complete with bagpipe musicians. Then on Sunday afternoon, a magician will perform magic acts before everyone departs. Michael let me plan everything. I do wish you'd been here to help me with it—we would have had so much fun."

"Well, I'm here now," Rosemary said, glancing back to the doorway of the room they'd exited. "And I can help with anything you need."

"Mother is handling the finer, last-minute details," Nora said. "So there's nothing for you to do but have fun! I'm so excited for you to get to know Geoffrey." Nora lowered her voice. "Then you can tell Michael that Geoffrey and I will be extremely happy together. For some reason, he doesn't believe me and insists upon getting to know Geoffrey more before he'll agree to an official engagement."

"He's your brother and has always looked out for you."

"I know, but I can't conceive of why he doesn't like Geoffrey. I know *you'll* like him."

"Perhaps Michael is concerned because you haven't known Geoffrey very long. Only a couple of months, in fact."

"I fell in love with him the moment I met him," Nora replied. "You'll soon see why. He's so handsome and smart and sincerely kind."

"Hmm." Rosemary purposefully kept her reply vague so she wouldn't have to voice her thoughts. Those about how often people disguised their true selves and their true ambitions.

"You'll see," Nora insisted. "He'll arrive in time for the performance this evening. Getting his investments in order has been very time-consuming."

"Has it?" Rosemary asked, again merely to assure Nora she was listening.

"Oh, yes. He owns a large textile manufacturing business that his father had failed to manage efficiently." Nora stopped walking and, with a serious expression, stated, "He's not like his father. Those are simply rumors. Gossip. Geoffrey hadn't lived with his father since his mother's death when he was a child. I know you'll like him, and I know you'll help me convince Michael to like him, too."

A knot formed in Rosemary's stomach. She didn't want to betray Nora in any way, but she didn't want her friend to make a decision that could prove disastrous, either. It made her feel as if she was stuck in the middle, which was beyond bothersome, but bothersome was *far* better than disastrous.

Nora let out a long sigh. "It's hard for you to think the best of Geoffrey because Maud is his aunt, isn't it?"

"No," Rosemary answered. "I would never base my opinion of someone on their family alone. I look forward to getting to know him better this weekend, but I'm more excited to be spending time with you. It's been so long."

"Oh, I agree!" Nora gave her arm a solid yank to pull her down the hallway again. "I have so much to show you and tell you. Including that Willow had a foal this spring, and she's adorable!"

"I must see her!" Rosemary took the lead in rushing along the hallway. The stables at Turnbill had been one of her favorite places, and riding was something she missed intensely. The horses here were magnificent animals—spirited but not unruly—and Willow had always been her favorite one to ride. "Now!"

After a long visit to the stable, where Rosemary fawned over the adorable brown-and-white foal and reacquainted herself with Willow, who was as gentle and loving as ever, she and Nora joined the activities happening in the courtyard. There, she reacquainted herself with people she used to know and hadn't seen in several years, including Nora's mother, Beatrice Knight, the Dowager Duchess of Turnbill. Upon spying the dowager, Rosemary separated herself from Nora to greet their hostess.

Moments later, her eyes stung with unshed tears as the dowager duchess pulled her into a loving hug and expressed how much she'd been missed.

"I've missed being here," Rosemary admitted, "and I've missed all of you very much."

The only thing that had changed about the dowager was that her black hair was streaked with a few gray hairs, otherwise she was as lovely as ever, and as kind. Being hugged by her brought forward so many wonderful memories.

"You must find time this weekend for us to visit," the dowager said as they separated. "I want to know how you've been and how Thomas is doing. I do wish you would have brought him with you."

"He's doing wonderfully, thank you," Rosemary replied. "Growing fast, as adorable as ever, and still loves the zoo. I wish he could have joined us, too, but—"

"Where have you been?" an intruder asked.

Rosemary pursed her lips at the interruption and the annoyance in Maud's voice. In preparation to reply, she drew in a breath of air through her nose and began, "I—" only to be interrupted again.

"Is that mud on your skirt?" Maud asked as she grasped Rosemary's upper arm in a firm hold. "Good heavens, you are worse than Thomas!"

Her stepmother never missed an opportunity to embarrass her, and Rosemary should have been prepared for it now, knowing that it would happen at some point this weekend. She glanced down at her skirt and, unfortunately, noticed a small smear near the hem. If it had been on the burgundy material, it wouldn't have been noticeable, but it was on the pink material that was sewn in a V shape up the center of the dress. She should have been more careful in the stables.

"I highly doubt it's mud," the dowager duchess said. "The grounds were impeccably groomed for the weekend's events. I'd propose it's merely dust from traveling."

Maud's attitude didn't change as she ignored the duchess. "You were in the stables, weren't you?" she asked, loud enough that others around were sure to hear. "Honestly, Rosemary, how many times must I tell you it's not appropriate for you to be so interested in horses? Nor is it appropriate for you to be traipsing about covered in mud like a schoolgirl. You're supposed to be a young lady, one, I might add, who is disintegrating her chances of ever finding a suitable husband by appearing so disheveled in public."

Of course, Maud would add that. She'd been pointing that out for years, as well as a never-ending list of Rosemary's shortcomings. Still, familiarity with her stepmother's rudeness didn't make Rosemary any less appalled by her crude remarks. She was contemplating leaning down to see if she could brush off the smear on her dress or possibly going inside to change, but right then, Michael stepped up beside his mother.

"Oh, Your Grace," Maud said, her voice suddenly sugary sweet. She also released Rosemary's arm in order to run a finger along her exposed collarbone and then touched her expertly fashioned golden hair, resplendent beneath the red fabric hat made specially to match her dress. "Allow me to extend our sincere gratitude for the invitation this weekend."

Besides being sickened by her stepmother's instant change of attitude, Rosemary was also embarrassed by Maud's obvious attempt to draw Michael's attention to the low neckline of her dress.

Michael gave Maud a nod. "You are thanking the wrong person," he said, flashing a smile towards the dowager duchess. "My mother was in charge of the invitations."

Maud's smile wobbled slightly, a sign that, in her eagerness to make disparaging remarks about Rosemary, she hadn't recognized the dowager duchess. Or perhaps she had and had simply been attempting to make herself appear superior, especially when it came to her stepdaughter.

"However, we all would have been greatly disappointed if Lady Rosemary hadn't been able to attend," Michael added.

"Oh," Maud gasped, once again pressing a hand to the exposed skin above the neckline of her dress. "We wouldn't have dreamed of not attending." Letting out a soft sigh, she continued, "Rosemary is in need of the influence of respectable young ladies if she has any hope of finding herself a husband someday."

Mortified but not surprised by her stepmother's continued remarks, Rosemary bit her lips together to hold her silence as she always did. It irritated her greatly that Maud was already ruining what had promised to be a wonderful weekend by doing her best to embarrass her, but it was even more vexing that Maud was choosing to do so in front of such very dear friends.

The dowager cleared her throat and settled a rather unfriendly gaze upon Maud. "Rosemary has always had a large number of admirers, far more than others I know."

Rosemary flinched and held her breath, fearful of Maud's response.

A response that didn't have time to be voiced because Michael spoke. Smiling at Rosemary, he said, "I agree, and include myself as one of her admirers. If you ladies will excuse us, I have something that I'd like to show her."

"Of course, dear," the dowager duchess said, taking

a step backwards to provide walking space between their small group.

As Rosemary stepped forward and rested her hand on the bent arm Michael was holding towards her, she had to bite her lip again at the dowager's next move.

"I, too, have something to see to," the dowager said. "Excuse me, Lady Havenshire."

Rosemary didn't glance backwards to witness Maud's reaction to being left alone. Instead, she walked away with her hand hooked around Michael's elbow and sought a way to apologize for Maud's behavior. But when she glanced at Michael, the stern set of his lips made her seek a way for him to excuse himself instead. It was obvious that he'd merely stepped in and given her a reason to leave Maud's company. Unable to think of anything else, she said, "If you are taking me to see Willow's foal, I've already been there."

"Is that where you got the smudge on your dress?"

Heat rushed to her cheeks as she glanced down at her skirt. "I'm afraid so. Is it really that noticeable?"

"No. In fact, I do not see a smear, I merely overheard your stepmother," he replied.

That was exactly as she'd surmised, and once again she sought to give him an excuse to leave her side. "Perhaps I should go change." Regrettably, her wardrobe for the weekend was limited to a few gowns, and changing now would mean wearing the same one twice later, which would again be noticed by Maud.

Her father had insisted that new gowns were brought home for her, too, from Paris, and though Maud had complied, the gowns were quite hideous. Rosemary had had a few of them altered, but most of them were made from such drab colors and were so unflattering there wasn't much that could improve them.

"I see no reason to do that," Michael said, "unless of course, you feel the need to appease her."

"It makes things easier," she admitted.

"I do not recall you as someone who takes the easy route."

"You knew me when I was much younger. Things have changed since then."

"I am aware of that," he said. "I'm also aware of the fact that if you were only looking for what's easy, you wouldn't be worried about Nora making the right decision. Going against her can't be easy."

Rosemary released a long sigh. Michael would know exactly how difficult that was, because it was difficult for him, too. "It's not easy, but it's something I must do. I don't want to see Nora hurt. I only take the easy route when it comes to Maud because she is my stepmother, and my father—" She stopped herself from saying that her father loved Maud. That was something she just truly couldn't believe. Her father wasn't naive nor foolish, but he *was* married to Maud…

Instead, she simply said, "I love my father, and I love Thomas."

* * *

Everyone who knew Rosemary knew how much she loved her father and brother, just as they knew how much Michael loved his mother and sister. However, he knew more about her than most. He not only knew how much she loved his sister, he knew how easily her feelings could be hurt. His need to protect Rosemary was as strong as his need to protect his mother and sister. That was his reason for joining their group in the first place, and why he couldn't get her and himself away from her stepmother fast enough.

There was truly nothing admirable about Maud Crofton, and her not-so-subtle actions to draw attention to the cut of her gown was nothing shy of bothersome, to put it kindly.

The woman was as close to being loathsome as anyone Michael had ever encountered. He'd nearly bitten through the tip of his tongue to keep from telling Maud just what he thought about the way she was chastising Rosemary in front of so many. For no reason than to draw attention.

Nora had told him about such things before, but he hadn't noticed it, namely because he rarely attended social events. Now, though, there was no doubt in his mind that Maud was jealous—that she disliked having a stepdaughter who was much younger, much prettier and certainly more personable than herself.

Once again he questioned Havenshire's choice for a second wife. Especially when he knew how much

Ralph Crofton loved his daughter. He'd spoken to Havenshire a short time ago, and the man had seemed very happy that Rosemary would be here, spending the weekend with Nora.

"You don't have to pretend to show me something, Michael," Rosemary said. "I understand what you did, and I appreciate it, but please don't feel obligated to entertain me."

It was no surprise that she understood his goal had been to get her away from her stepmother's rudeness, yet he really did have something to show her. "Is that your way of telling me that you don't want to see the grand hall?"

A frown took over her face. "Why? What happened to the hall?"

He shrugged. "If you don't want to see it, that's fine." Next to the stable, her second favorite place was the grand hall in the north wing. She and Nora had spent hours on end playing there. Now the huge hall had been refurbished, and judging by Rosemary's expression, Nora hadn't yet told her about it.

She put a stop to their progress across the lawn by grasping hold of his arm with both hands. "Michael. Tell me what happened to the grand hall. Are you tearing down the north wing?"

"No, we are not tearing it down." He watched how her eyes widened, but it was the bright shine filling them that made happiness rise inside him.

"You're refurbishing it?" she asked but didn't wait for his answer. "Why didn't Nora tell me that?"

"Perhaps because you were too busy visiting Willow's foal," he suggested.

She tugged on his arm as she started walking again. "Well, I'm not too busy now! When will it be completed? Are you changing much about it? How long have you been working on it?"

Several other such questions were asked in succession, all without enough room between them for Michael to reply, making him chuckle. Once they rounded the corner of the massive structure, Rosemary's speed increased, which caused him to break into a jog that quickly turned into a sprint, because she was as fast a runner as she had been years ago. His father used to say that she could leave a fox in the dust.

More memories like that one came flooding back, things Michael hadn't thought about in years. Like how much Rosemary loved flowers and peaches. She'd pluck the fruit off the tree as soon as they started to ripen. She was the reason there were two peach trees in the greenhouse, so there would be peaches even after a harsh winter.

"I'm so excited to see it!" she shouted. "I never imagined that you'd refurbish it!"

"You used to talk endlessly about how beautiful it could be if refurbished," he reminded her while running at her side.

"That was just a silly girl's dream," she replied, skidding to a stop near the large, arched wooden and iron door that had once been the main entrance for those protecting the fortress.

Michael came to a stop beside her and reached for the knob in the center of the door. "A dream that has perhaps come true."

The excitement on her face made him smile as he turned the knob and pushed the door open, but the way she gasped as she stepped over the threshold made him feel as if he'd won an award of some sort.

Truth be told, he'd thought about her regularly while the renovations were taking place. Nora had been excited about the painstaking work that had transpired over the last month, but mainly because it was for today's party, whereas he'd known that Rosemary would be excited about it because the actions were restoring the hall to its former glory.

"Oh, Michael," she said, sounding breathless. "It's even more beautiful than I'd ever imagined."

The work crew had done a tremendous job of bringing the large rectangle-shaped room back to life. Every inch had been washed, polished or repaired. Overhead, the arched center of the ceiling was a full story higher than any other room in the house and supported by thick, solid beams that had been sanded and now shone with new coats of varnish.

"You even repainted the ceiling," she said, looking in the same direction as him.

The spaces between the solid beams hosted various painted patterns of fruits, flowers and emblematic scenes. "There were a few areas where the paint needed to be touched up, but for the most part, it was simply cleaned," he explained.

The heels of her boots clicked on the mosaic stone floor as she walked farther into the room. "It's so beautiful. It's…" She sighed. "It leaves me speechless."

Following her, he teased, "I don't know if I believe that could ever be possible."

She giggled. "Perhaps not, but I am truly in awe."

"Does that mean you approve of the changes?" he asked, again teasing.

Spinning about, she shook her head at him while she stepped closer and playfully slapped his arm. "You know I do."

There was a definite shine in her eyes and a wide smile on her lips. He'd always liked her, always thought she was sweet, but at this moment, the feelings inside him seemed deeper, somehow.

Perhaps that was because he was fighting the desire to brush a wayward lock of hair away from her face, tuck it behind one of her ears. He might well have done that years ago, or might not, because it wouldn't have been any more appropriate back then than it would be right now.

Pushing aside the desire, and in an attempt to ignore whatever was flickering inside him, he gestured towards the tables that had been set up on the far side of the room. "As you can see, the staff are still putting things in order for the ball tomorrow night."

Pivoting about on the toes of one foot, she nodded. "Nothing more than a few vases of flowers and table linens are needed. Any more than that will take away from the beauty of the room, and that would be shameful."

He had no idea what his mother and sister had planned as far as decorations but agreed with her opinion by providing a nod.

"I can't believe the ceiling wasn't repainted," she said, looking up again. "The colors are so vibrant, yet I seem to remember barely being able to make out the pictures in the past."

"Well, decades of unuse and before that, decades of smoke from the fireplace had dulled it considerably."

While swirling about yet again, she exclaimed, "The fireplace! Look it at!"

The stone fireplace took up a large portion of one wall, tall and wide enough for both of them to step inside of it. Now cleaned of the years of soot, it stood out like a shrine, complete with the family crest painted on the wall above the huge log mantel.

"It's so beautiful and even larger than I remember, and the wood smells wonderful." She moved closer to the hearth and gestured to the freshly cut logs that had been stacked in the alcoves on either side. "Can't you just imagine this room filled with soldiers who had just returned from battle? Wearing their armor and sharing tales of how they'd succeeded in overturning the enemies."

She sounded much like he remembered, full of fairy tales, whereas he was more true to life and knew that celebrations of men returning from battles would not have been as pleasant as she was imagining. Yet, he wasn't about to shatter her whimsical visions. "And you'd be the queen," he said, recalling her and Nora's play, "showering them with praise and honor for their achievements in securing your lands."

Her giggle echoed off the high ceiling as she spread her arms wide and gave him a regal but modest bow of her head. "Of course."

He gave her a feigned frown. "I don't recall you ever mentioning a king."

She sighed and shrugged, giving him a sidelong glance. "He was killed in battle, leaving me to rule the kingdom."

"Oh? He had no brothers or sons? Or were you the queen, and he was merely a prince?"

"Oh, he was a king." She waved a finger at him. "Fantasies don't have rules that need to be followed."

He laughed, finding her company as joyful as it had been years ago and realizing he'd missed it. Missed her.

"There you are!"

Michael turned towards the sound of Nora's voice

and watched his sister rush into the room just as she had in his drawing room earlier.

"I turn my back for a minute, and you disappear," Nora continued, talking to Rosemary. "And here I find you with Michael again."

Noticing the flush that appeared on Rosemary's cheeks, Michael said, "I knew she'd want to see the hall, and since you were busy, I took it upon myself to show her."

Rosemary shook her head. "That's not completely true. Michael was kind enough to rescue me from Maud's disappointment at how I'd managed to get a smudge on the hem of my dress."

Nora joined them near the fireplace. "I know all about that. Maud cornered me and proceeded to inform me of just how unladylike it is to visit the stables during a garden party. Does that women have a kind word to say about anyone?"

"I'm afraid not," Rosemary replied. "And I'm sorry I wasn't there to rescue you."

Michael wondered how often Rosemary needed to be rescued from her stepmother and what happened when no one was there to do so. If she was anyone else, that wouldn't be any of his business, but Rosemary was different. Practically family, which explained the sense of responsibility he felt towards her.

"Don't be," Nora said, with a sly grin. "I pointed out that a section of lace was coming loose on the hem of her sleeve, and she hurried off to find her maid."

"Oh, dear," Rosemary replied, clearly distraught. "Poor Helen will hear about having not thoroughly examined the gown during cleaning."

"It was fine during cleaning," Nora said. "Actually, it was fine until I noticed a loose string and gave it a discreet little tug while she was holding on to my arm and questioning me on where you and Michael had gone." Not fazed by admitting her somewhat devious actions, Nora gestured towards the room surrounding them. "What do you think about the changes to the hall?"

"It's beautiful," Rosemary said. "More beautiful than I'd ever imagined."

"I know!" Nora replied. "I knew you'd be surprised. For the ball tomorrow night, the orchestra will be over here, and…"

Michael chose to leave them to discuss the ball, the decorations and whatever else they might converse about. He had his own thoughts to contend with, and those thoughts were centered on both of these young women. Nora would expect an answer from him by the end of the weekend. Like it or not, he needed to be prepared to give her one.

He was also questioning whether asking Rosemary to help him this weekend had been the right thing to do. She had her own troubles. Everything about her seemed to have heightened his senses, and it seemed only logical that the reason for that was his growing concern about what her life had become with Maud as her stepmother.

At the moment, all he could conclude was that it was going to be a long weekend.

Chapter Three

Rosemary tried to focus on what Nora was saying, but watching Michael quietly leave the hall tugged at something inside her. She couldn't put words to it, but there was something very different about how he made her feel. There was something very different about him. Something she couldn't put her finger on.

"You haven't heard a word I've said, have you?"

Turning her gaze to Nora, Rosemary shrugged, and knowing her friend would see through a lie, she replied, "I'm sorry, I just feel bad for the way Michael felt he had to rescue me from Maud."

"Why would you feel bad about that? He's been coming to our rescue our entire lives. You're as much of a sister to him as I am. He's always been as committed to defending you as he is to me. To him, we are just two little girls who need his protection. No matter how old we get, that won't change."

Rosemary questioned that—whether that was how

Michael viewed her and what it meant. It was true that he had always been watchful over both her and Nora.

"Furthermore," Nora continued, "he hates these kinds of things. Hates parties of all kinds, and only agreed to this weekend in order to put off answering my request for him to give Geoffrey permission to formally court me."

The thoughts of Michael that were still swirling in Rosemary's head temporarily stalled. "Geoffrey hasn't asked you to marry him?"

Nora let out an exaggerated sigh. "Not yet. He insists we follow protocol, which in itself should make Michael approve." A smile then lit up her face, and she tugged on Rosemary's arm. "But he will ask, and I will say yes. Come now, I have so much more to show you. Michael even had some of the rooms in this section refurbished for guests. Mainly because that's where Geoffrey will be staying. As far away from me as possible."

Arm in arm, they left the great hall and entered the corridor that would take them to the second story of the North wing. "That truly wasn't necessary," Nora continued as they walked. "I know there will be too many watchful eyes for Geoffrey and me to have a midnight rendezvous."

"A midnight rendezvous?" Rosemary asked, fearful of the scandal that would occur if guests learned about such an event, especially Maud. "Surely that's not something you would have considered."

"Of course it's something I've considered," Nora replied. "Why wouldn't I?"

Flabbergasted, Rosemary asked, "Why would you?"

"Because I'm in love, and he's all I can think about. That will happen to you one day, too."

Rosemary shook her head. Not even love would make her lose her common sense.

Nora sighed. "You'll see. Someday, you'll fully understand, and trust me, if I thought it would help, I'd do more than one rendezvous."

"How on earth can you imagine that would help anything?"

"Oh, you know," Nora said while shrugging her shoulders and rolling her eyes, "things might move quicker if my virtue was at stake. But Michael would never see it that way. Rather than force Geoffrey to marry me, he'd most likely forbid us from ever seeing each other again."

"It wouldn't be fair to put Michael in such a position," Rosemary pointed out. "Most certainly not while you have a house full of guests."

Nora stopped as they reached a stairway to the second floor, with a frown that encompassed her entire face. "What about the position he's put me in? As my friend, I'd think you'd care more about that."

Rosemary's heart constricted. "I do care about you. That is why I'm here. I've always cared about you, and I always will. There is nothing I want more than for you to be happy."

"I'll be happy when I'm married to Geoffrey. Michael doesn't understand that because he thinks the only reason people consider marriage is for money and power. Geoffrey isn't like that, but no one will give him the chance to prove it because of his father's reputation."

"That's why Michael agreed to host this weekend," Rosemary said, taking a hold of Nora's hand and giving it a squeeze in an attempt to ease her friend's obvious frustration. "I'm looking forward to getting to know Geoffrey."

"I'm looking forward to you getting to know him, too." Nora let out a long sigh. "I'm just so afraid that Michael isn't going to like Geoffrey and what will happen then."

A shiver rippled over Rosemary's shoulders. "What do you mean? What will happen then?"

"I'll leave. I'm going to marry Geoffrey whether I have my family's blessings or not. I love him, and he loves me. Nothing will change that."

Overcome with worry, Rosemary bit down on her bottom lip. There had been numerous times when Nora's determination could have gotten them in trouble, or worse, if Rosemary hadn't encouraged a time for rethinking. This was indeed one of those times.

"Listen to me, Nora Knight, and listen well," Rosemary began with a no-nonsense tone that she rarely used. "Everything is going to turn out exactly as it's supposed to. You are going to marry a man you love and one who loves you in return. And you will have your family's blessings. You just need to be patient and not do anything rash."

Nora didn't say anything for a long moment, then she stiffened slightly. "I won't do anything rash, at least not this weekend, so you can stop worrying about that. But I will marry Geoffrey. You can mark my word on that."

Rosemary took a moment to consider her next action. She definitely didn't want to argue with Nora, which was what would happen if this conversation continued. Therefore, she chose to give it all some time—herself time to think, and Nora's determination time to cool off. "Come," she said, pulling on Nora's hand and beginning to climb the stairs. "Show me the rooms that have been refurbished and tell me again about all the activities that will be happening."

Nora paused momentarily, then joined her on the steps. "You're right. We've been separated too long to spend even a moment arguing over anything."

Choosing to not verbally respond, because there were just too many thoughts that might escape if she opened her mouth, Rosemary nodded as they hurried up the stairway. She hadn't expected Nora to be so emphatic about being in love with Geoffrey. That had been foolish. She should have known better, because Nora could be stubborn at times, and Rosemary knew that better than anyone else, yet she had dared to hope that Nora would at least be open to *questioning* whether marrying Geoffrey was the right decision.

Then there was the fact that Geoffrey hadn't even asked her to marry him yet, which was just as concerning. There were so many things to worry about. Suddenly, dealing with Maud's insults didn't seem so bad.

Thoughts continued to twist about in Rosemary's mind as they entered rooms that had been refurbished back to their original glamour just as she'd always imagined. It would have been easy to get caught up in the beauty of the woodwork, colorful rugs and furnishings and other details, as she had in the great hall, but she just couldn't silence her worries. Nora marrying Geoffrey without Michael's approval could prove to be devastating. That would be as scandalous as Nora getting caught sneaking around to meet Geoffrey in the middle of the night with a house full of guests.

Considering both scenarios left her with but one conclusion. She needed to talk to Michael.

"That's the last one we can enter," Nora said upon their exit of the fourth room. "Guests assigned to the other rooms have already arrived."

"I can imagine they are all as lovely as the ones we did see," Rosemary said. "Everything has turned out so wonderfully. Just as I imagined when we were young. Now, I really should find Helen and see if she can brush the dirt smudge from my dress." Because she didn't have her own maid—that was something Maud didn't deem necessary—her stepmother's maid Helen provided personal services as needed for Rosemary, but only if and when she wasn't occupied with Maud's needs.

"There's no need to find Helen," Nora said, hooking their arms together. "I can do it for you. We'll go to my room, and you can tell me all about Thomas. I know he is your favorite subject and that talking about him is sure to put a smile on your face."

Reading between the lines, a wave of regret washed over Rosemary. She couldn't remember a time when she and Nora had disagreed or been upset with each other, and certainly didn't want anything to overshadow the joy of them being together this weekend. A light warmth filled her heart, induced by Nora's grin and thoughts of Thomas. "He is my favorite subject," she admitted. "Next to you."

They both laughed, and the warmth inside her grew as they began walking and talking about things that continued to lighten the air. Soon, they were both laughing as hard as they had years before when sharing things with each other.

Michael was standing amongst a group of men in the main front hall, discussing a new child labor law that parliament had recently passed, when he noticed Rosemary and Nora enter the room. He hadn't seen either of them since leaving them in the great hall of the north wall hours ago. Since then, guests had taken the opportunity to prepare for the evening meal and following entertainment with either a change of clothing or a period of rest. Rosemary was still wearing the same pink-and-burgundy dress and, upon scanning the room, cast a gaze his way.

The Viscount Bellview had arrived earlier. Michael had greeted him affably enough, for he had met Geoffrey a few times in the past and had no reason to truly dislike him, beyond the as-yet-unproven rumors. Currently, the tall blond man was walking across the room towards Nora, who was smiling brightly.

Rosemary wasn't. Her smile was strained. Leastwise, that was how Michael read it. He knew that when she was truly smiling, her eyes lit up. He clearly recalled that from years ago and had been reminded of just how lovely that made her look earlier today.

As the conversation continued around them, one of the men in Michael's group, Rafael Williams, turned to him and whispered, "Who, pray tell, is that brown-eyed beauty?"

"The Earl of Havenshire's daughter," Michael answered, instantly knowing his friend was referring to Rosemary.

Rafael gave a low whistle. "You don't say." The eldest son of the Viscount Westerly, Rafael was on the hunt for a suitable wife. One well-bred and refined, ready to fulfill the role of a lady, position herself amongst the ranks of Society, and provide him with an heir. "Would you be interested in making an introduction?" he asked, with a hopeful expression as his eyes remained on Rosemary.

There would be a time when Michael would need to seek such a woman, too, but for now his first experience in the marriage mart was still too fresh inside him. Furthermore, dealing with one potential marriage within his family was enough. However, Williams's words struck a chord of protectiveness inside him.

"No," he replied without an ounce of regret as his gaze met Rosemary's and her smile grew more natural.

"That's unfortunate." Williams let out a sigh before slapping the back of Michael's shoulder. "Accept my apology, I hadn't noticed that she only has eyes for you."

"Not in the way you assume," Michael said, noting that Rosemary's smile had waned again as her gaze had shifted off him. "She and Nora have been best friends since birth."

Williams grew wide-eyed. "That's the girl who used to be here all the time when we were young?"

"Yes," Michael answered.

"Why didn't I recognize her?"

"Because we were interested in other things and didn't pay them any mind back then, which is exactly what you need to do now."

Williams laughed. "True, but you must admit that she's grown into quite a beauty."

That was undeniable. Michael had no choice but to nod.

"You also have to admit that there could be a number of men in this very room who might be interested in seducing something as beautiful and innocent as the Earl of Havenshire's daughter."

"I am aware of it now," Michael said, bristling inside. "And I expect you to warn others how I will respond to that."

"Hear, hear." Rafael emptied the remaining contents of his glass in one swallow. "In the interim, I will find a footman to replenish my thirst."

"Make yourself useful at the same time," Michael said, handing his empty glass to Rafael, then he excused himself from the group.

Rosemary watched him as he crossed the room, and the way her eyes lit up caused something to flicker inside his chest cavity. Perhaps it was just his protectiveness again: Nora and Bellview were conversing with another couple, leaving Rosemary as somewhat of an outsider, and Michael was glad to be able to offer her some companionship.

Or it could just be that she was a very beautiful woman, and he did appreciate beauty when he saw it.

The rest of the small group noticed him before he stopped next to her and welcomed him into the gathering. The conversation focused on the horse racing session that would take place tomorrow, which Bellview had agreed to participate in, and Michael participated easily in the talk, up until a footman whispered near his ear that the meal was ready to be served.

Upon telling the servant to have the announcement made, Michael offered his arm to Rosemary. "Miss Crofton, may I have the pleasure of escorting you to dinner?"

Resting a hand upon his bent elbow, she nodded, "Certainly."

They walked to the doorway, then stepped aside to wait for and greet the guests as they exited the room. Nora and Bellview stopped on the other side of the doorway and were soon joined by his mother. Michael had never had a woman besides his mother or sister stand beside him to acknowledge guests like this before, because he knew such an action could signify an alliance. Even when he had attended social events where Martha Grossman had also been present, back when he'd believed that he'd fallen in love with her, he just hadn't been ready to admit any sort of an association publicly. There were simply too many risks, too many possible consequences.

Yet having Rosemary stand next to him didn't feel risky. In a way, it felt natural.

As people filed past them, Rosemary said, barely above a whisper, "Nora claims she loves Geoffrey and will marry him even if you deny consent, even if it means running away."

Unsurprised, because he knew his sister well, Michael nodded to the guests walking past as he quietly replied, "It's not my wish to deny her love or marriage. I simply want to know that the man she marries is honorable and that he will take the responsibilities of a husband seriously."

The smile Rosemary held on her face was simply for show. "That is what I wish for, too," she whispered, "but I'm afraid that no matter what we learn or what we tell her, it won't make a difference."

Michael held in a sigh of irritation at himself for involving her in something that was truly his dilemma, and his alone. He couldn't, not in all good conscience, give his consent to Nora without fully believing she was making the best choice. But, currently, that same conscience inside him was fully aware that his action of involving Rosemary in this could damage her joy this weekend. A weekend that could very well be her last opportunity to spend time at Turnbill with Nora. For when Nora did marry, and Michael was sure that would happen at some point, mostly likely very soon, she would no longer be living here.

Casting a smile her way, he said, "Well, then, we both shall focus on enjoying the weekend as we get to know Geoffrey. I trust that Nora has found good things about him, and I look forward to discovering them myself."

Surprise filled Rosemary's eyes as she stared up at him. "You want to find good things about him?"

"Of course I do." He frowned slightly. "Did I do something in our younger years to make you think of me as some sort of an ogre?"

"No, no, not at all, and you know that." Giving a slight one-shoulder shrug, she added, "I assumed our thoughts were aligned."

"We are aligned. We both want what is best for Nora." The last of the guests had left the room. Taking ahold of Rosemary's elbow, he encouraged her to move with him towards the dining hall. "And we both are going to do our best to get to know Geoffrey, while enjoying the activities that Nora has arranged for the weekend."

Her gaze settled on Nora and Geoffrey, as well as his mother, who were walking a short distance ahead of them. "What if he is on his best behavior all weekend?"

"I expect him to be on his best behavior all weekend."

"Will you be on your best behavior, too?"

He chuckled slightly at the hint of humor in her sideways glance. "Of course."

"Even if Nora isn't?"

A tiny shiver rippled across his shoulders, and he slowed their steps even more. "What is she planning?"

Rosemary shook her head. "She's not planning anything, merely mentioned that she would encourage a midnight rendezvous if she thought it would help."

An ounce of relief washed over him, because that

was something he'd already considered. "I assumed as much." He'd not only assumed it, he'd put provisions in place to make sure his sister's reputation would not be put to question. Shifting his attention on the dining room as they walked through the doorway, he nodded towards the large table centered in the room. Two other tables had been added to accommodate the weekend guests. "I believe you are seated with the family."

A moment later, he felt as if he'd just taken a small punch to the gut upon seeing the place card hosting her name positioned atop the gold-trimmed plate next to the one intended for Rafael Williams. The man was also standing in attendance, waiting for Rosemary to be seated.

Out of politeness and attempting to keep any sort of warning out of his voice, Michael offered, "Rosemary, allow me to introduce Rafael Williams. An old friend."

"Hello," she greeted kindly.

"This is Lady Rosemary Crofton," Michael then said to Rafael, whose bold grin was enough to make his back teeth clench.

"Oh, Lady Crofton, I doubt you remember me, but I, too, used to visit Turnbill in my younger years."

"I do remember that," she replied. "You would often ride Buck, the gray gelding who received his name due to his penchant for bucking off his riders."

Rafael laughed while Michael frowned. She was

correct about the horse. Rafael was one of the only riders not to get bucked off.

"Oh, yes, such sweet memories," Rafael replied, with more charm than necessary. "I do believe some people wanted to see me lose my seat, but it never happened. Due to my horsemanship."

"Due to luck," Michael half mumbled.

"It appears I am still lucky," Rafael said, moving to take hold of Rosemary's chair for her to be seated.

Left with nothing more to say or do—leastwise nothing that wouldn't draw attention, like rearranging the seating—Michael made his way to the head of the table where he stood until the guests had all been seated, including his mother at the foot of the table. Then he gave a nod to Horace, the butler, to pass on instructions that dinner was now to be served.

It was difficult to keep his eyes from the spot halfway down the long table where Rosemary and Rafael were conversing and laughing. Genuinely laughing. From Michael's vantage point, he could see the shine in her eyes, indicating that she was enjoying the company of her seatmate. When he managed to pull his gaze away, it was just as apparent that others were similarly captivated by whatever Rafael was spouting about. His horsemanship, no doubt.

Or it could be any other number of things, for Williams was a jolly sort, well-liked and quite accomplished in many things, Michael sternly reminded himself. A man that Michael considered a friend.

An unexpected and deeply compelling thought occurred to him then. He'd lost one very good friend, Drake Taylor, over a woman and had sworn that would never happen again. There was no reason to believe it should happen, either.

He caught a glance from Rafael and gave his friend a nod in return as he raised his crystal glass to his lips, one that said *I've already warned you, so don't press the issue.*

Astute in many ways, Rafael gave a slight nod in return.

The gesture didn't ease whatever it was that was bothering Michael. Truth be told, Williams was right. Rosemary had grown from a sweet, brown-eyed girl into a beautiful woman, one many in the room might take interest in. Perhaps he was taking his old adage of protecting women too far. Rosemary did have her father to look out for her…

Still, Michael reasoned silently, he did feel a deep responsibility to her and would never forgive himself if something unspeakable were to befall her this weekend.

As his gaze once again flitted her way, he concluded that one thing was for certain: seeing Rosemary again after all this time had sparked something inside him. Whether it was simply protectiveness or something else, he wasn't all that certain.

"She has certainly grown into a beautiful young lady."

Michael's attention instantly shifted to the speaker, who was seated to his left. His Great Aunt Lettice was shrouded in black from head to toe, as she had been for almost as long as Michael could remember. Her husband, his Uncle Clarence, had passed away when Michael had been but five or six, yet to hear Lettice speak, one would think it had simply been last year. Lettice, did however, believe in making her black wardrobe look as sparkling as any other colorful gown by adding enough jewelry for three women. From the diamonds in the headband decorating her nearly snow-white hair, the pearls dangling off her earlobes, the three stands of pearls around her neck to the jeweled bracelet circling her wrist, she shone brighter than many others in the room.

Some considered her an imposing woman and were quite intimidated by the fact that, upon Clarence's death, she'd taken the reins of running a very large and lucrative farm with barely a blink of the eye. What was more, she had made it even more profitable than perhaps he would have, had he lived the past two decades, or if their marriage had provided an heir, which it had not.

Michael didn't find her intimidating, for he both loved her as an aunt and admired her greatly for other reasons. Her business savvy was remarkable, which he'd discovered years ago when she'd come to him for some advice. She also regularly informed him that upon her death, she expected him to oversee the estate in her stead, just as she had for Clarence.

"Who is that you are referring to, Aunt Lettice?" he asked.

She huffed a breath, causing a low whistling sound. "As if you don't know."

"The room is full of beautiful women," he replied. "Including you."

Flattery never affected her, nor her straight-handed manner. "Don't be obtuse. I'm talking about the one you haven't taken your eyes off since you sat down."

"You know as well as I that Rosemary Crofton is Nora's best friend and practically grew up in this house," Michael replied, knowing there was no use trying to convince Lettice that he hadn't been staring at Rosemary. Honesty was merely one vertebra in the backbone of the relationship he had with his aunt.

"I do know that, and sense you are not happy about her tablemate. I wonder why? Rafael is one of your best friends."

"I am perfectly content with her and Rafael sitting next to each other," he stated, while buttering a piece of bread so firmly it broke in two.

Aunt Lettice nodded as the first course of the meal was set before both of them, then pursed her lips, glancing across the room at one of the other tables. Picking up her soup spoon, she continued, "One thing I don't know is how that stepmother of hers hasn't managed to marry her off yet. Maud Crofton has done her best at every opportunity to push Rosemary into society, including tonight. I can only imagine that she's quite jealous. I'll never understand some men, and her husband's one of them. His first wife was so genuine and kind. As of late, this one has become barely intolerable, especially in the way she treats Rosemary. Maud walks around like a peacock, decked out in all her finery. But she's a peahen, not a peacock, and therefore has no *natural* finery. And the way she makes her stepdaughter wear gowns fit for a girl rather than a young woman, while she wears the latest styles, all tailored for her in France! I find it quite revolting. To be truthful, I find that woman to be about as useful as a boil on one's backside."

The way his great aunt voiced her opinion might be shocking to some, but Michael was used to her somewhat off-color remarks. "Rosemary's gown is quite lovely," he said, glancing halfway down the table again as he spooned soup into his mouth.

Lettice gave him a pitying glance. "*She* looks lovely, but the dress... Well, men seldom understand these things. I happen to know that while Maud was in Paris, she specifically commissioned some very unflattering gowns for Rosemary. I have to assume this is one."

"I wasn't aware of that." Women's gowns were not his specialty. Other than to notice how lovely a woman looked now and again, he knew very little about the actual details that women seemed to take as seriously as humanly possible. However, even though her gowns were always black, Lettice certainly did know fashion.

"Of course you weren't. You're as blind as a bat when it comes to some things. You could simply have listened when Nora spoke of such things. Rosemary wrote to her about it—how Maud went to Paris, leaving her home to take care of Thomas and her father."

The emotion in Lettice's voice was unusual. In all the years he'd known her—ultimately, his entire life—he'd never known her to be prone to gossip of any sort. Then again, she, too, had been close to Rosemary and her mother all those years ago. "Perhaps we should change the subject. I sense this topic is upsetting to you."

Lettice set her spoon in her empty bowl and leaned closer as if to make sure that no one else could hear, even though the others surrounding them were engaged in conversations with their seatmates. "I'll change the subject when I'm good and ready. That woman has upset me ever since she coerced Ralph into marrying her. Rosemary was like a second daughter to your mother, and the first thing that woman did was put a stop to that."

His mother had been upset over Rosemary no longer visiting and had been worried about how Rosemary would be treated by a stepmother. He'd missed her visits, too, but at that age, had had many other things to occupy his mind. Now he wondered if he, too, should have been more concerned. "I can't believe Havenshire would allow Rosemary to be hurt," he said, perhaps because he was looking for justification for himself.

"There are more ways to hurt someone than physically, and plenty of ways to hide it."

Michael's gaze once again settled on Rosemary, and this time, he didn't attempt to conceal it. Not even when she glanced up, smiled and then frowned slightly, as if wondering what was behind his stare.

Chapter Four

Rosemary ate her last bite of the steamed pudding full of preserved peaches and topped with a sweet syrup and sliced almonds. Each course of the dinner, from the savory chicken soup to the stewed fish and the main course of veal with spinach, had been delicious. Throughout the meal, her gaze kept drifting to the head of the table, where Michael not only sat but appeared to be in deep conversation with his Aunt Lettice.

She remembered him visiting Lettice at her estate, only a few miles from Turnbill. Although he'd still been young, he'd often helped his great aunt with tasks, especially when the time came to harvest her many acres of farmland and orchards.

Part of the reason why Rosemary's gaze kept going to Michael was Rafael Williams. Rafael had numerous stories about Michael that he shared, things that Rosemary hadn't known. They mainly concerned things they'd done when they were young. Like when

Michael had lost his seat while they'd been riding, landed in the creek and then ended up with a blister on his foot from having to walk all the way back home. They'd tried riding double on Buck, but the horse quickly started bucking, and rather than both of them ending up walking, Michael said he'd walk while Rafael rode.

To Rosemary, that sounded exactly like the Michael she'd always known. Generous and kind, even as a boy and then a young man. He was grown now, of course, but still held those honorable traits that she remembered. Seeing him again had reminded her exactly why she'd first wished for him to be her older brother and had then dreamed of growing up to marry him.

"That pudding was delicious," Rafael said as he set his spoon down.

"Yes, it was," Rosemary agreed, glad to change her thoughts. They'd been childish thoughts that had no bearing on reality or reason to be in her mind now.

"I have to admit that the food at Turnbill has always been a favorite part of my visits," Rafael said.

"I agree," she replied. "Especially the peaches. I loved being here in the fall, plucking and eating them right off the trees."

"Oh, yes, and having the juice run down your chin and neck made them taste that much better."

Rosemary felt a lightheartedness at the memory. It should certainly have been embarrassing, talking about such a thing as sticky peach juice covering her chin and neck, yet Rafael's bright green eyes chased away any self-consciousness, and she laughed along with him. "Oh, yes, it did indeed. It just couldn't be helped. They were that full of juice."

"Agreed," he replied.

He was still chuckling, and she giggling when the others at the table began to rise from their seats.

"I do declare, Lady Rosemary," he said while pushing back from the table, "you have been a most delightful dinner companion, and I hope we are seated beside each other tomorrow night as well."

"Thank you, Mr. Williams, I have enjoyed your company greatly," she replied, looking at him over her shoulder as he took a hold of her chair. "Will you now be attending Willette Burmingham's performance?"

"I will. I've heard she is quite an accomplished singer."

"She is." Rosemary rose from her seat. "I believe she will one day be singing in an opera house in London."

"You know her well, do you?" he asked, while pushing her chair back to the table.

"I did as a child. She and her family would visit Turnbill while I was here, and even then she was a singer. No matter what we were doing, she was singing, often making up songs as we played."

"Did you sing along with her?" he asked, offering her his arm.

She laid a hand on his elbow. "Unfortunately, I did." That had been before Maud had pointed out that Rosemary was tone-deaf and shouldn't sing. Ever. Not even in church.

"Why would you consider that unfortunate?"

"If you ever heard me sing, which you won't, you'd know why."

He laughed. "I must say, Lady Rosemary, that I find you the most remarkable young woman that I've ever met."

She laughed, too. "And I must say that I understand why you and Michael are friends, you are as charming as he."

He laughed harder. "I'm going to take that as a compliment."

"Good, it was meant to be one."

They exited the room and followed the line of other guests down the corridor to the main hall to await for the performance to begin. "Allow me to ask a question?" he asked.

"Of course."

"Did you enjoy singing along with Miss Burmingham?"

With such fond memories once again filling her head, she asked, "Dare I say I did?"

"Of course," he replied, "and *I* daresay that your singing along with her was not unfortunate because you were enjoying yourself, and that is always considered a fortune."

Something warm filled her insides. "You truly are a lot like Michael."

His dark brows furrowed together. "Tell me, does every man remind you of Michael?"

That was something she might have to ponder, for she wasn't exactly sure, nor had she been expecting such a question. "I don't believe so. It must just be because I'm here, at Turnbill, and it's been a long time since I was able to spend any amount of time with... with Nora and her family." She'd almost said Michael but stopped herself because she was now wondering if she was focusing too much on him. She couldn't remember if she had questioned Rafael about Michael or if he'd been the first one to bring Michael into the conversation.

"That could indeed be the reason," Rafael replied. "You did spend a lot of time here as a child."

"As did you."

"As did many children. It seemed this was the place to come and, well, to just enjoy being a child."

"Indeed," she said, agreeing wholeheartedly. There had been a freedom here that she'd never felt anywhere else.

Seeing Nora waving at her as they entered the hall, she let her hand fall from Rafael's arm and performed a slight curtsy. "Thank you for the escort and your companionship, but I am being summoned."

"I see that. Know it was my pleasure and honor,

and as I said earlier, I do hope for a repeated honor tomorrow evening."

She nodded and left his side to meet Nora near another door of the room, one that led to the corridor towards the music room, where Willette Burmingham would perform as soon as the servants had the time to supply more chairs for the audience to sit upon.

"Come, I told Willette we'd visit her before the performance," Nora said, hooking their arms together. "She is quite nervous, which is why she didn't join us for dinner. Says she can't sing on a full stomach. It always gives her the burps, which is most embarrassing."

"I can see how it would be," Rosemary agreed. "I'm looking forward to seeing her and to hearing her sing. It's been a long time. Remember how she used to make up songs as we played, about being queens and damsels in distress?"

"Oh, yes, that was such fun," Nora answered as they walked out of the room and into the long corridor. "Remember this one? *Deep in the dungeon, Princess Rosemary still dances like a fairy, awaiting the day of her rescue by the man she will marry.*"

Rosemary laughed while forcing herself to not sing along to the lively tune that Nora sang. "Oh, yes, and how about, *Queen Nora, Queen Nora, your king is on his way. He's been gallant and brave in battle and will be home today!*" She said it as a poem, rather than singing it, and they both laughed again.

"I hadn't thought about those in years," Nora said.

"Me, neither."

"Willette lives in London now. The two of you could visit."

"That would be wonderful," Rosemary answered, although she knew it wouldn't happen. Maud was quite particular about whom and where she could visit, and a singer would not be an acquaintance she'd approve of, out of spite if nothing else.

As soon as that thought crossed her mind, Rosemary silently chided herself. Yes, Maud was quite strict with some rules, but the truth was, Rosemary preferred staying home. It was easier than dealing with Maud's inquisitions about every detail both before she went anywhere and after she returned.

"You and Rafael where certainly laughing a fair amount during dinner," Nora said.

"Oh, yes, he's very charming."

"I know. I used to dream of growing up and marrying him."

"You did not!" Rosemary gushed, although there was no reason for Nora to lie. Nor was it out of the ordinary for her to admit such a thing. They used to tell each other everything.

"I did. It was after your mother died. He was here more often then, and without you here, I was all by myself, so Michael let me tag along with the two of them on occasion. I soon realized it was just a young girl's first infatuation. Everyone has one of those. I grew up and, of course, fell in love with Geoffrey. He's just so handsome, isn't he?"

"I suppose, I hadn't noticed," Rosemary replied, with her mind on Nora's admission. She hoped that Nora wouldn't ask if *she'd* had a first infatuation. She would then want to know who it had been, and Rosemary could never admit that it had been Michael. Not even to her dearest and oldest friend. It was simply too outrageous.

"Not noticed?" Nora asked as if shocked. "How could you not notice?"

"I guess it's just not something that I notice, but he was very charming and told me several stories about when he'd visited here when he was young."

"What? Wait! You're talking about Rafael! Geoffrey never visited here when he was young."

"Yes, I'm sorry, I was talking about Rafael, about not noticing if he was handsome." That was true, but she had noticed how handsome *Michael* was. He'd always been handsome.

Maybe there was something to what Rafael had asked, about her comparing all men to Michael. If that was the case, no wonder she hadn't noticed anyone else's looks. No one could be as handsome as Michael.

"He's looking for a wife," Nora said.

Rosemary's feet stopped dead in her tracks, and her heart nearly did the same. "He is? Who? Have you met her? Do I know her?"

"I said looking. As far as I know, he hasn't met anyone yet."

"As far as you know? He's your brother. Surely you'd—"

"Not Michael, Rafael." Nora shook her head. "I've never known you to be scatterbrained. Are you all right? First you're talking about Rafael while I'm talking about Geoffrey, then you're talking about Michael while I'm talking about Rafael."

Embarrassed and relieved at the same time, Rosemary nodded and began walking again. "Yes, I'm fine. I was just having a hard time following the conversation. Yes, Geoffrey is very handsome, and no, I wasn't aware that Rafael was looking for a wife. He didn't mention that."

"Well, he is, and Michael isn't. Not after the fiasco with Martha Grossman."

Rosemary's heart almost stopped beating again. She had fallen behind. Nora was pushing open a door, and she had to hurry to catch up in time to ask, "Who is Martha Grossman?"

The conversation with his aunt left Michael with several questions. Had Maud coerced Ralph into marriage? If so, how and why? And more than that, was Rosemary indeed being mistreated by her stepmother?

Other subjects had been discussed during the meal, including Geoffrey and the reputation that preceded him. Aunt Lettice had also wanted to know what

Michael's thoughts were about the viscount, and she wasn't shy about letting him know that by withholding his blessings, his sister could turn disastrous if he wasn't careful.

Lettice had ended that conversation by voicing that it was past bloody time that someone in their family married and started creating the next generation to inherit their wealth and title, which had gotten Michael thinking about marriage in general.

His parents had been happily married, with a love that had been apparent to all. They'd been a pair that had complemented and supported each other. While his father had pursued the financial interests of the family, his mother had pursued their happiness; their interests had been a combined quest that they both worked diligently to accomplish.

He'd heard of and seen other marriages that were simply unions formed out of duty. Where there was little fondness for one another, and each partner sought to have their needs and desires met elsewhere, with no concerns as to what the gossips shared.

There was little doubt that no marriage was the same. With his parents as a guide, Michael had determined the type he'd wanted and had thought he'd discovered one that would be close to ideal when he'd met Martha.

It might have been his assumptions and expectations that had made him jump in with both feet, and those same things that had sent him into a turmoil of emotions when it had all turned out to be a farce on Martha's side. She'd been looking for nothing more than a union to provide her with the place in society she sought—a duchess.

Which was why he was so steadfast about knowing more about Geoffrey Burrows before the wedding. Rightfully so. However, Lettice's words had made him turn his thoughts to other issues. Like what he was going to do about his own future, because he would soon have to decide and act upon that decision sooner rather than later.

A slap on the shoulder interrupted him from pondering any further on the topic.

"Lady Rosemary is more than a pretty face," Rafael said. "She is the most refreshing young lady that I've met in some time, and I voiced that sentiment to her."

"Did you?" Michael replied, glancing around the room as the last of the guests made their way to open chairs for the imminent performance. The glance was to hide that he was biting down on the tip of his tongue to keep himself from saying more. Asking more. He wanted to know what Rafael and Rosemary had discussed during dinner that had them laughing nearly constantly. He also wanted to know what she'd said or done to make Rafael believe she was so refreshing.

She *was* refreshing. And delightful. Always had been, and though he appreciated that, his gut churned at the idea of other men finding her so.

"Yes, I did, and I will gladly be her dinner companion tomorrow night," Rafael replied, lifting one brow. "All in order to fulfill my promise of keeping others at bay."

Michael shook his head. "I have nothing to do with the seating arrangements."

"Well, then, I will have to put a word in with your mother." Scanning the room, Rafael added, "There she is."

"I'm sure she can accommodate your request, but perhaps you should ask Rosemary if that is what she wants."

"True," Rafael acknowledged. "She already has. I believe because I remind her of you. Charming."

"She thinks you're charming?"

"Of course she does. I can be very charming." Rafael leaned over so their shoulders bumped. "It's far more confusing that she believes you are charming."

A flutter started up inside Michael's chest, but he had no opportunity to rebut Rafael because he was already walking past the lines of chairs, making a beeline towards the front where the dowager sat—to ask about seating arrangements tomorrow night.

Michael considered following and making an opposing request regarding seating arrangements but knew he couldn't do that. It was only when he saw Nora and Rosemary enter through the side door that he quickly made his way towards the front of the room, too.

By the time he arrived, the row of chairs was nearly

full, with Geoffrey, then Nora, Aunt Lettice, Rafael, his mother and Rosemary. The only empty seat was next to her, which was fine with him, but Rafael stood.

"Here, Michael, you can sit next to your family, I'll sit on the end."

"Never you mind," Aunt Lettice said, pulling on Rafael's arm. "You sit right back down. It's rare that I get to sit next to a handsome man who's not family. It's good to get the old heart thumping every now and again."

"Lettice," Michael's mother whispered beneath her breath.

"What?" Lettice replied loudly. "I'm old, but I'm not dead."

As good-natured as ever, Rafael shrugged, sat back down and had Aunt Lettice giggling by the time Michael lowered himself onto his seat and Willette Burmingham entered the room.

Tall and willowy, Willette gave a slight curtsy to him before she walked across the room to the piano, where a pianist was already seated, hands ready to touch the ivory keys. Michael remembered Willette from when she'd visited years before, when she was so thin that his mother had always encouraged her to have second servings at each meal. It hadn't helped. She was still very thin, with coal black hair and faded blue eyes.

"She's very nervous," Rosemary whispered. "This is the largest crowd she's ever sung in front of."

"I'm sure she'll do wonderfully," Michael whispered in return, and then followed her lead by offering the singer an encouraging smile.

A moment later, a soft, lilting and very pleasant voice began to sing. The beautiful sound floated across the room, and hushed sighs indicated that people were already enjoying the performance.

Rosemary was, too, because with both hands pressed against her breastbone, she smiled at Michael, eyes glimmering with moisture, before her gaze went back to Willette.

Michael did his best to keep his attention on the singer, but it was difficult when every one of his senses were heightened. His concentration was on Rosemary. The soft floral scent of her perfume and how she sighed or softly hummed along with the music. He was pleased that she was enjoying the performance and again struggled to understand why he'd forgotten how unique she was. She simply had a kindness, a love for other people, that was truly refreshing, as Rafael had said.

That shifted his thoughts to the two of them laughing at the dinner table again. It wasn't that it bothered him, but it did cause a reaction inside him. One that wasn't comfortable.

It had to be due to Martha and how his relationship with her had ended his friendship with Drake. That loss felt stronger than the loss of losing the woman he'd once considered marrying.

That would never happen again, for his relationship with Rosemary was simply a friendship. An old and strong friendship that he appreciated. Just like his friendship with Rafael. That had to be why he was feeling out of sorts and thinking about Martha. Prior to today, Martha hadn't entered his thoughts for months.

He drew in a deep breath, appreciating how Rosemary's soft, floral scent wasn't overpowering but rather pleasing to his senses. He allowed his gaze to shift towards her, to notice how a few curls of her honey-colored hair weren't pinned up, but instead formed corkscrews along the side and back of her neck. Her profile was exquisite, and it showed her enjoyment of the singing filling the room. Every so often, her long eyelashes flittered closed and the smile on her lips was broad enough to lift her cheeks, so the lashes rested upon her peach-colored skin.

His gaze shifted lower, past her earlobes, slender neck and the small portion of her slanting shoulder that was exposed by the neckline of her gown. A thought paused his gaze. It was imaginable that her mother would have had jewelry, ear fobs and necklaces that she would have inherited, and he wondered why she wasn't wearing any. Perhaps it was simply her choice, that she found them uncomfortable, but his mind couldn't stop from going towards her stepmother. If somehow Maud prevented Rosemary from wearing, or even owning, any jewels.

The end of the music pulled his attention back to the room, and he clapped along with the others with appreciation. When the applause ended, and another song began, his thoughts returned to Rosemary and her stepmother.

Bloody hell, he cursed to himself. As if he didn't have enough to worry about, to deal with, he was adding more to his plate. It couldn't be helped, though. If Havenshire wasn't watching out for his daughter in all ways, someone else needed to, and that someone was him.

At the start of Willette's second song, Rosemary let out a great sigh of relief for the singer. Willette had been extremely nervous and had been certain that she'd forget the words or sing off-key or some other dreadful thing that hadn't happened. Her voice was beautiful, the singing absolutely captivating, and Rosemary was convinced that everyone in the room was enjoying the performance. How could they not?

Unless they were like her, preoccupied by other thoughts. In her own defense, it was difficult to think about anything else with Michael sitting beside her. She'd tried, but he was impossible to ignore, as were her thoughts about Martha Grossman.

Nora had simply said that Martha was a woman Michael had considered marrying. There hadn't been time for more of an explanation because Willette had been on the other side of the door and very excited to see them.

When had he considered marrying this Martha woman? Why hadn't they married? Had he loved Martha? Was he still in love with her? Had something happened to her?

There were so many questions racing through her mind, and each one led to others. Some included Martha, others were simply about Michael. Why did sitting next to him make her heart beat faster? Was that what his great aunt was referring to? That it was simply natural for handsome men to make a woman's heart beat faster? Why had that never happened to her before?

As if he knew she was thinking about him, Michael glanced her way, and the smile, accompanied by a wink of one eye, sent her heart thudding against her rib cage. It continued at that heightened pace to the point that when Willette's performance came to end, Rosemary was caught off guard and the last to join in on the applause.

She rose to her feet at the same time as those around her, and when Michael laid a hand on the small of her back, encouraging her to step forward along with him and the others in the front row, she walked to Willette.

Michael's touch on her back was sparking off heat waves that traveled up her spine and then spread elsewhere, making her fear that she might not be able to speak, to congratulate Willette on an excellent performance.

To her surprise, when it was her turn, the words came easily and were genuine. "I've never heard anything more beautiful, Willette. Your singing took my breath away."

"Hear, hear," Rafael said, having waited his turn to offer his praise. "It was truly a remarkable performance, and may I offer to escort you to the hall and offer to find you a refreshment? I can only imagine you must be thirsty."

"I am," Willette said, accepting his offered arm. "Thank you."

Soon the six of them, Willette and Rafael, Nora and Geoffrey, along with her and Michael, were all standing near the large stone hearth in the main hall, sipping from crystal glasses filled with various drinks, while other guests stepped forward to congratulate Willette on her performance.

Rosemary felt her stomach tighten as her stepmother made her way towards where they all stood. Glancing left and right, she looked for the easiest escape route, but she was flanked by Michael on one side, Rafael on the other, and the fireplace directly behind her.

"Miss Burmingham," Maud began, while opening the fan that dangled off her wrist on a gold string. "Your family must be so proud of your talents. Listening to such a beautiful voice was a refreshing surprise. For, you see, our own Rosemary…" Maud made a point of waving her fan before Rosemary "…is quite tone-deaf and has been asked to not sing while we are in church."

Insults from Maud were nothing new, but she was usually more sly about it, and Rosemary couldn't remember a time when her stepmother had embarrassed her so thoroughly. She felt her legs wobble slightly, and Michael took hold of her arm.

"Lady Havenshire," Michael started but was quickly interrupted by Geoffrey.

"Excuse me, Your Grace," Geoffrey said stepping forward and taking a hold of Maud's arm. "Please allow me to escort the lady to her husband, for perhaps she has had too many glasses of wine."

As Maud exclaimed, "I certainly have not!" Geoffrey turned her about and spoke over her.

"This way," he said. "I see the earl right over there."

Maud struggled to release his hold on her arm as Geoffrey led her away, but whatever she said, and she was clearly saying something to him, was quiet enough to not make a scene as he continued to lead her across the room.

Rosemary was shocked and appalled and so very embarrassed. She was also fully aware of the repercussions that would occur when Maud caught her alone. Therefore, she felt compelled to admit, "She is correct. I am tone-deaf."

"Nonsense," Nora said.

"We all three sang the songs I made up, and I remember you having a beautiful voice," Willette said.

Rosemary shook her head, mainly because their opinions wouldn't override Maud's. She'd lost her will to want to sing. Along with the will to want a lot of other things.

"What we witnessed had nothing to do with your singing ability," Michael said. "It was Lady Havenshire's shortcomings. I suggest we not let it interrupt the enjoyment of our evening."

Rosemary appreciated Michael's attempt to smooth over the encounter but read more in the glare he was casting across the room. He was kind and goodhearted, but he was also stern, and she had the sinking feeling that Maud had taken a step too far this evening. That meant she would need to prepare herself to leave tomorrow morning. Maud would insist upon it, claiming she'd been offensively mistreated.

Rosemary tried hard not to let that overshadow the rest of the evening, but the sinking feeling wouldn't leave her.

It was still there, hours later, as she dressed for bed. Although she was in the lovely bedroom that she'd spent so many nights in as a child, with its huge fourposter bed, plush colorful rugs and tall windows that allowed vast views of a starlit sky, the familiarity of it all wasn't easing her qualms.

Maud had to be furious and would retaliate, but

Rosemary's greater fear was that Michael would retaliate against Maud. It was a frightful situation.

Just as she was crawling between the covers, a knock sounded on the door. Before she had a chance to respond, a request came through the wood.

"Lady Rosemary," a female voice said. "Lady Nora would like you to meet her in the library posthaste."

Collecting her housecoat off the foot of the bed, Rosemary put it on while crossing the room to ask why, but by the time she unlocked and opened the door, the corridor was empty in both directions. Nora must want to discuss what Maud had said. No one had mentioned the incident, even after Geoffrey had rejoined their group, and though Rosemary would much rather not, she couldn't leave her friend waiting. She had half expected Nora to come to her room, but she must be concerned that Michael would have people watching the halls for late-night visits. A trip to the library to choose a book for late-night reading wouldn't arouse suspicion.

Buttoning her housecoat to cover her sleeping gown from ankle to neck, Rosemary left the bedroom and made her way to the staircase that would take her to the third floor. Lamps were still lit along the corridors and stairway, and due to the lateness, she wasn't surprised not to encounter anyone along her way.

However, she was surprised to find the library empty. Lamps in the room were lit, casting about their golden glows, and figuring Nora would arrive soon, Rosemary scanned the many shelves of books, then chose a short novel and sat down to wait.

Chapter Five

Dressed in a light blue gown, with a white lace stand-up collar and cuffs, the following morning, Rosemary left her room and walked down the corridor to Nora's room. When her knock was responded to, she pushed open the door, only to discover Penny, Nora's maid, straightening up the room.

"Good morning, Lady Rosemary," the maid greeted. "Lady Nora has already gone down to breakfast. Is there something I can do for you?"

"No, no, thank you," Rosemary replied, backing out of the doorway. "I was just going to accompany Nora to breakfast."

"She went down a few minutes ago. I'm sorry you missed her. Would you like me to go find her?"

"No," Rosemary replied. "I will see her downstairs. Thank you very much."

The maid gave a slight curtsy, and Rosemary left the room, somewhat flustered. Last night, she'd waited in the library until a footman entered the room to extinguish the lights and had then gone to knock upon Nora's door—not very loudly, because she hadn't wanted to disturb others in nearby rooms. She had also been afraid that Nora might not be in her room; discovering that would have meant Rosemary must go look for her, which would have alerted others. Instead, she'd gone back to her bedroom, choosing to hope that wherever Nora had been, she would return to her room without being discovered

She had woken still worried about that.

Downstairs, Nora was in the dining room, sitting next to Geoffrey. Because breakfast wasn't as formal as dinner, there were no place cards, and a large buffet table held various covered dishes for guests to help themselves as they arrived.

Rosemary selected a few items for her plate, more out of respect for those who had prepared the vast selection of meats, eggs, fruits and variety of pastries than actual hunger, then carried the plate across the room and sat down next to Nora. Her sense of frustration was only heightened by the way Nora greeted her as if nothing was amiss. As if she hadn't left Rosemary waiting in the library for over an hour last night.

After returning the greeting and providing the same to Geoffrey and a few others at the table, Rosemary dared a glance towards the head of the table where Michael sat.

He gave her a nod and a smile. "Good morning, Lady Rosemary."

"Good morning, Your Grace."

"I trust you slept well."

"Very," she replied. "The beds here are of the utmost comfort."

"Hear, hear," replied Rafael, who was a seated near Michael. "I must agree."

Others quickly began sharing their thoughts of the accommodations and the castle overall, which provided Rosemary the opportunity to whisper to Nora, "Why did you ask me to meet you in the library last night?"

Nora's brows knit together as she shook her head. She then leaned closer. "Who told you to meet me in the library?"

"A maid."

"When?"

"Shortly after I'd retired. I waited in the library until a footman came to turn out the lamps, and—" Rosemary was forced to stop talking by a hand that fell upon her shoulder.

"Good morning, dear," her father said while leaning down to kiss her cheek.

"Good morning, Papa," she replied. "How are you this morning?"

"Ready to break the fast," he replied, giving her shoulder a slight squeeze, before he greeted a few others and then walked over to the sideboard to fill his plate.

Rosemary couldn't stop herself from twisting about

to see if Maud had accompanied him into the room. She still had lingering effects from how her stepmother had embarrassed her last night and was glad to not see Maud amongst those filling a plate.

"We need to talk," Nora whispered.

"I agree," Rosemary replied, her attention back on her friend.

"Eat quickly."

Considering she wasn't really hungry, and therefore hadn't put much on her plate, it wasn't long before it was empty. Nora told Geoffrey that she had to get something and asked Rosemary to assist her, giving them both a reason to leave the room.

"What maid told you to meet me in the library?" Nora asked as they walked out of the room.

"I don't know, I didn't see her. She simply knocked and told me that you wanted to see me in the library posthaste."

"I didn't," Nora whispered, because they were encountering other guests moving along the corridor towards the breakfast room. "But someone, a maid, told Geoffrey the same thing. He was quite upset with me this morning."

"I didn't see him in the library," Rosemary exclaimed.

"Because he didn't go. He opened the door to tell the maid that he would not be meeting me, but she was already gone."

"She was gone when I opened my door, too."

"That is simply too odd," Nora said. "Too odd."

"You weren't planning on a rendezvous, were you?"

"No, I told you that already, and I promised Geoffrey I wouldn't do anything that might upset Michael." Nora stopped and spun about, stared down the corridor towards the breakfast room.

"What?" Rosemary asked, knowing her friend was thinking about something.

"Michael is testing us. Testing me and Geoffrey. That's a dirty thing to do."

Although a hint of guilt rose up inside her over how she and Michael had agreed to share anything they learned about Geoffrey, Rosemary didn't believe Michael was behind last night's request. "He wouldn't do something like that."

"You don't know him like I do. He's dead set against anyone getting married after what happened between him and Martha."

Rosemary opened her mouth to ask about that, for it had been another subject that had danced in her head while she'd been waiting in the library last night and then lying awake half the night. But she didn't get a chance to speak before she heard her name and recognized the voice of her stepmother.

Drawing in a deep breath to fortify herself, she turned and greeted her warmly, "Good morning, Maud."

With a scathing look that encompassed her from head to toe, Maud asked, "How late were you up last night? You look like you barely slept." Reaching out, Maud patted Rosemary's face with both hands rather firmly. "You have bags beneath your eyes."

She probably did and probably should say that she would find a cold cloth to place under her eyes, but other subjects were far more important this morning than appeasing her stepmother. However, it was the almost inhumane growl coming from Nora that sent Rosemary into action. Not wanting to further her stepmother's ire by having yet another person step in to defend her as Geoffrey had last night, Rosemary grasped Nora's arm. "Excuse us," she said, while pulling Nora around Maud, and quickened her footsteps, getting them away from Maud before either her stepmother or her friend could say more.

Michael paced across the tiles near the front door. It had been decided that several of them would go horseback riding this morning, but that had been before Rosemary had joined them at the breakfast table. He anticipated she would want to participate, but the way she and Nora had been whispering then quickly left the room had him concerned.

He was also quite frustrated. Frustrated that it had been Geoffrey who had stepped in last night when Maud had rudely embarrassed Rosemary. While cursing himself for not promptly responding, he'd also had to admit that how quickly Geoffrey had acted, leading Maud away from the group like that, was commendable.

Damn it, Michael should have thought of that. Might have, if he hadn't been focused on how Rosemary had wobbled. She'd clearly been affected by her stepmother's words, and rightfully so; they had been nothing shy of vile and disgusting. So disgusting that he'd been afraid to open his mouth because he had wanted to lash out at the woman for her rudeness. That wouldn't have been appropriate, he understood that, and had controlled his response to be nothing but stern words before Geoffrey had interrupted him. He was still so irritated that he'd merely nodded at Maud when she'd wished him a good morning while entering the breakfast room a short time ago. He sincerely hoped he was correct that Rosemary would be joining them in riding this morning and that he would have the chance to apologize to her for not coming to her defense last night.

He also wanted to know more about how she was treated at home. If nothing else, he would be speaking to Havenshire about it.

Geoffrey and Rafael had left the table at the same time as him, and while Rafael had headed out to the stable to choose his horse, Geoffrey had gone to see when Nora would be ready for their ride. Another action that Michael had to acknowledge. Where many men would have sent a servant or been exasperated at having to wait, Geoffrey had shown a dedication to Nora by his action and by saying that the others need not feel compelled to wait for them.

Michael would wait. He was indeed progressing towards his goal of getting to know Geoffrey better this weekend, but his ability to focus on that was lacking. Rosemary had become front and center in his mind.

"The ladies are collecting their riding coats and gloves," Geoffrey said, entering the foyer. "They shouldn't be long."

Michael acknowledged the information with a nod as the man walked closer. "Very well."

"While we have a moment, there is something I would like to address," Geoffrey said.

Michael recognized a hint of defiance in the man's stance as he stopped next to him. "Certainly," he replied.

The lifting of the viscount's chin and the squaring of his shoulders let Michael know that the man wasn't afraid of confrontation. "An occurrence happened last night that has caused me concern."

Michael felt his muscles tighten as his frustration renewed itself, but he couldn't hold anything against the viscount for bringing it up. "Lady Havenshire's actions last evening were repugnant, and I thank you for defending Lady Rosemary."

The viscount frowned slightly, as if confused or perhaps questioning something, then he shook his head. "There is no need to thank me. Lady Havenshire's behavior was unacceptable, but forgive me, because I'm afraid that I'd momentarily forgotten about that incident and probably shouldn't have."

Michael wondered uncertainly whether his continued thoughts about Rosemary had caused him to miss something Geoffrey had said. He could think of no other incident last night that might have caused the viscount to be concerned. "Excuse me?"

Geoffrey's gaze had shifted to the hallway, which was still empty, but his expression had turned thoughtful. He gave a slight nod, as if answering a silent question, before saying, "Another occurrence happened last night. After I retired to my room, a maid knocked on my door and informed me that I was to meet Nora in the library. I simply want to assure you that I would never, will never, do anything to damage Nora's reputation."

Michael found himself blinking several times, unsure of exactly what Geoffrey was insinuating, because there was something that the viscount wasn't saying. "Why did she want you to meet her there?"

"According to Nora, she didn't make the request. When I opened the door to decline, the maid was gone, and I simply went to bed. This morning when I questioned Nora about the request, she said that she had not been in the library last night and certainly hadn't sent a maid, nor asked anyone to tell me to meet her there."

"So someone else did, someone you think was trying to spy the two of you together late at night and inform me," Michael said, voicing his own thoughts aloud.

"I do, and until a few minutes ago, I wasn't sure who might do such a thing."

A shiver coiled around Michael's spine. "Lady Havenshire." It wasn't a question, because he believed Maud would want retribution for what Geoffrey had done last night, and he was sure that was what the viscount had just determined as well.

The sounds of footsteps had both of them looking towards the corridor leading to the foyer. As they watched Nora, Rosemary and the Earl of Havenshire enter, Geoffrey quietly agreed. "Yes, I believe it very well could have been Lady Havenshire. I'd thought the maid had said Lady Nora wanted to meet me, but they could have simply said a lady. Right now, I'm not so sure which it was."

"We'll finish this discussion later," Michael said just as quietly, before stepping forward to greet the approaching group.

"I've decided to join you for a ride," the earl said. "It's been a long time since I rode for enjoyment."

"Excellent," Michael replied as he gestured for the butler to open the door.

During their walk across the manicured front lawn and around to the west side of the stone house, Michael felt his sister's eyes on him. It was a spiteful glare, leaving him with no doubt that she thought, as the viscount had, that he'd somehow been behind the request for Geoffrey to meet her in the library. It didn't sit well with him that she'd think he was capable of such a thing, but considering he hadn't yet accepted her request to wed and that he'd wouldn't put it past her to arrange a late-night rendezvous, he couldn't say that he was shocked.

He was troubled by what had happened and by who may have tried to set up a rendezvous that could have damaged her reputation. The culprit, whoever they were, was probably quite upset that their well-laid plan hadn't worked. Judging from what Geoffrey said, Nora had never gone to the library last night. Michael's first instinct was to have his valet, Gilbert, check into it and concluded he'd do just that after their ride this morning.

If his instincts were correct, he would have a discussion with both the Earl and Lady Havenshire later today. Such underhanded deceit would not be tolerated in his home, nor anywhere else.

They reached the stable and entered through the wide double doors. Inside, there was a bevy of activity taking place. A soft sigh had him glancing over his shoulder to where Rosemary stood, eyes closed and breathing deeply. The air was filled with the scent of horseflesh, fresh-cut hay and the oiled leather of riding gear, and he grinned, knowing how much she enjoyed the stables.

Her father noticed the same thing. "She's always

loved this place," the earl said. "And has missed being here the past several years."

"We've missed having her here," Michael said.

Rosemary's eyes popped open, and her face turned a lovely shade of pink as she walked forward between him and her father. "I can hear both of you, and yes, I have missed being here."

Along with the earl, Michael chuckled. Just as he'd expected, she walked directly to Willow's stall. The dapple gray mare instantly stuck her head over the stall gate for a pet, and nickered softly when Rosemary obliged in stroking the horse's elongated face.

"You can ride her," Michael offered. "The foal will follow."

"No, that would be too much for one still so young," she answered with her cheek pressed against the horse's. "I will ride Shadow instead, if no one else has chosen her."

"If they have, they can choose another one," Michael said, snapping his fingers to signal a groom to saddle the black mare that was both gentle and surefooted.

The activity increased, with grooms saddling several horses and conversations going back and forth between the group of riders. There were ten of them. Besides Rafael, the earl and the viscount, there were four other men. Nora and Rosemary were the only two women, and Michael found himself paying the most attention to the conversation happening between Rosemary and her father.

She was pointing out a chestnut-colored horse with a black mane and tail. "His name is Charger, but don't let that intimidate you. He's spirited but well-mannered. See how he holds his head and the slope of his shoulders? He's proud, dignified but not boisterous."

"How do you know all that?" the earl asked.

"Because that's how he was as a colt, and I have no reason to believe that he's changed."

"What about this one?" the earl asked, pointing to another bay that wasn't being saddled but watching the activity going about him intensely.

"That is Sampson," Rosemary replied. "Notice his four matching black socks and black nose? He's quite handsome and knows it. In his younger years, there wasn't a horse that could compete with him in speed. Due to his long and sleek legs. He was the duke's horse and was officially retired upon the duke's death. However, he is still the king of the stable."

"Rightfully so," Havenshire replied.

Michael felt a tug in his chest at the thoughts of his father and how she knew, or remembered, that Sampson had been his father's horse and how he'd been retired. Then again, that was how she's always been. Noticing the small details that others missed or felt were insignificant.

"Well, Charger it is," Havenshire said, stepping over to take the reins from the groom.

"You'll enjoy riding him," Rosemary replied as she took Shadow's reins.

Michael took the reins of Atlas, the solid black horse with one patch of white on his forehead that he'd raised from a colt, to lead him out of the stable. The others followed, leading their mounts, and once everyone was in their saddles, they rode away at a slow pace.

"I can't remember the last time I rode across Turnbill property," the earl said.

"I'm pleased that you could join us this morning," Michael replied, riding beside the earl. "I'm also sure that you'll notice that not much has changed."

"I was hoping as much. I recall a grove of silver birch just over that ridge."

"It's still there. We can ride through it, if you'd like," Michael offered.

"Actually, if you wouldn't mind, I would prefer to ride over there alone. Amelia and I used to ride up to that grove on our visits here, and I'd like to spend a few moments remembering that. Remembering her."

"Certainly."

"Thank you, and uh…" Havenshire nodded at where Rosemary was riding next to Nora ahead of them. "I trust you'll keep an eye on my daughter."

Michael nodded. "I won't let her out of my sight."

"Thank you, and please remind her that she hasn't ridden very often lately, so to take it slow until she gets her bearings back."

Michael was glad to see firsthand how tenderhearted the earl still was concerning his daughter. "I will."

"Thank you, again. I'll let her know where I'm going. She'll wonder if I don't." Havenshire nudged his horse into a canter until he caught up with Rosemary. After speaking with her for a moment, he separated himself from the group.

As soon as that happened, Rafael rode up beside Michael. "Are we heading as far as the caves?"

Turnbill had two large working coal mines that he oversaw, but there were also several old caves on the property that had been part of a mine that had played out years ago. As children, even though they'd been warned not to, they'd explored them endlessly. Now as an adult, having been inside working mines, Michael understood the dangers of that. "Yes, Nora wants to show them to the Viscount Bellview, but we will not be entering them."

Rafael laughed. "Afraid you'll end up in the creek again?"

It was a moment before Michael remembered that he'd lost his seat in the saddle when they'd been riding away from the caves one time, and he'd landed in the creek. "No, I'm not afraid because I will not end up in the creek again, nor will I get blisters from having to walk all the way home."

"Lady Rosemary enjoyed hearing that story last night," Rafael said.

"That's why the two of you were laughing at the dinner table?"

Rafael nodded.

"Did you tell her that you'd thought you'd seen a ghost and that's why we were racing away from the cave?"

Lifting a brow, Rafael shook his head. "No, she wasn't interested in my part of the story, only yours."

"Because she knows me better than she knows you," Michael justified.

"That she does." With a chuckle, Rafael nudged his horse and trotted up to beside Rosemary.

Unable to ignore the twinge of irritation at Rafael's ease of befriending Rosemary, Michael nudged Atlas forward. He wasn't exactly sure if he made room between her and Rafael or if they both moved. Either way, he was positioned between her and Rafael as they rode onward.

Glancing his way, she whispered, "We need to talk."

He knew why she'd said that, and he knew why he agreed, "Yes, we do." His reason was to apologize for his failure to intervene after dinner, and hers was to tell him that Nora blamed him for whoever had been trying to cause trouble last night. "And we will. I'm sure there will be time during our ride." He'd make sure of that.

The opportunity happened a short time later when Rafael and the other four men rode off ahead, and

Nora and Geoffrey stopped so that he could adjust the reins of her horse.

"I'm sorry about last night," Michael started, wanting to broach that subject first. "I should have interrupted Lady Havenshire when she misspoke."

Rosemary's smile was soft, almost agreeable, even as she shook her head. "There is no need to apologize. Nora explained that because Maud is his aunt, Geoffrey felt it was his duty to, well, see to her. He apologized, too, a short time ago, but the truth is, neither he nor you are responsible for Maud." She shrugged a shoulder. "That's just how she is. How she's always been."

"Your father allows it?"

"I don't believe he knows or sees certain things. She's a different person when he's near and usually isn't so outspoken in public. Most of the time, it's just a comment or two that she easily explains. I quit hoping that he'd see through her acts years ago, and simply ignore them for the most part."

Michael didn't like it but was inclined to silently admit that there wasn't much he could do about it. Other than to say, "Well, I do hope that after last night she understands that such behavior will not be tolerated this weekend."

Her smile had completely disappeared, leaving him wishing he'd kept his mouth shut.

She glanced behind them, making sure that Nora

and Geoffrey were still out of hearing range. "There is something else I wanted to tell you about."

"Oh, yes," he said, trying to sound playful to lighten the mood. "The mysterious midnight library meeting."

Her eyes widened. "You know about it?"

"Geoffrey mentioned it while we were waiting for you and Nora to collect your riding gloves."

"What he didn't mention, because he didn't know until a few minutes ago, was that someone knocked on *my* door last night, asking me to meet Nora in the library, too."

Michael's spine stiffened. "Who?"

"I don't know. When I opened the door, no one was there, and when I questioned Nora this morning, she told me about Geoffrey getting the same message. I'm afraid to say that she believes you may be behind it. I told her that you'd never do such a thing."

"Thank you—I wouldn't. But why would someone want you and…" He let his question trail off because the answer came to him. He had more reason to believe Maud was behind it now. She wanted Rosemary and Geoffrey to get caught together. The woman truly was spiteful and vengeful to want to put her own stepdaughter in the middle of a scandal.

"I have no idea why anyone would have done such a thing," Rosemary said. "It doesn't make any sense."

It did to him, but he couldn't convict someone without proof. "Did you go to the library?"

"I did, and I waited for Nora until a footman entered the room to douse the lamps. I knocked on her door on my way back to my room, but she didn't answer because she was asleep. I didn't knock very loudly. I didn't want anyone else to hear."

"You didn't see anyone else in the library or in the hallways?"

"No, no one."

He nodded, then gestured towards Nora and Geoffrey who were trotting their horses towards them. "It's time to get the truth out of Nora."

Rosemary's eyes grew wide. "She wouldn't have lied about it."

"I hope not," he admitted. If his sister hadn't made the request, it had to have been Lady Havenshire, which goaded him to no end.

Chapter Six

Rosemary was truly enjoying riding again, but it felt as if she'd lost her confidence. Years ago, she'd felt as comfortable on the back of horse as she had walking, and within minutes of mounting would have been galloping across the fields, but today, she was glad that no one had suggested going faster than a leisurely walk.

All of that could be because her mind wasn't on riding. She was glad to know that Michael hadn't been behind the late-night meeting in the library. Just as she'd suspected. She was also glad that, when Michael had brought up the subject with his sister, Nora admitted that she hadn't really believed he'd been behind it, either. She insisted that she was telling the truth about not requesting anyone to meet her in the library.

After the discussion, Michael suggested that no one should leave their rooms tonight if such requests came again.

All three of them, her, Nora and Geoffrey, had

agreed to Michael's suggestion. The oddity of the occurrence still puzzled her, but she had trust that Michael would get to the bottom of what had happened. It was easy for her to have such confidence in him, considering how long they'd known each other and how seriously invested he was in providing for his family in all aspects.

The subject had changed then, and along with it the tension she'd sensed before, her lack of self-confidence about being in the saddle eased. Shadow's gate was smooth and even, and soon, she was galloping along beside the others. The sense of freedom it gave her, one that she hadn't experienced in years, was like a breath of fresh air on a spring morning. It simply filled her entire being.

They ventured all the way to the caves, a place she'd never been before because it had been forbidden when she was young, due to dangers of getting lost or a tunnel collapsing. Truly, they were old mine shafts. To her, they still looked genuinely dangerous. The boards on the entranceways were rotted and falling down in places, and the caverns themselves looked dark and scary.

But when she said as much, Nora admitted that she'd been inside the caves before to no ill effect.

"So, I'm the only one who obeyed the rules," Rosemary stated.

"It was when I was older," Nora justified. "After you stopped coming for visits."

Rosemary shook her head, smiling at Michael, who had already admitted that he and Rafael, as well as other friends, had been in the shafts many times. "I suspect it was when you were older, too?" she asked.

He chuckled. "I've always been older than you."

"And you always will be," she replied tartly.

They were all walking along the ground in front of the tunnels, while the horses were tied to nearby trees, except for Mr. Wayne and Mr. Shepherd, two of the other men that had joined in the ride. They had climbed the hill and were exploring up there. Mr. Hillman and Mr. Buckholder were up ahead with Rafael near another tunnel entrance, while she and Michael, along with Nora and Geoffrey, were still near what had been described as the main tunnel, merely peeking inside the dark cavern and exploring the entranceway. She'd never met the other men before, but like Rafael, they were all congenial and friends of the Knight family.

"True," Michael replied.

Something in his grin, or maybe it was the way their eyes met and neither of them looked away, she wasn't sure, but one or the other caused her heart to skip a beat. A needed beat because suddenly she couldn't even remember what they had been discussing.

He was so very handsome. Those silly thoughts of yesteryear, of growing up to marry him, reasserted themselves. Back then she used to picture herself living at Turnbill full-time, eating peaches every day and of having Michael kiss her. Which was the silliest thing of all for a young girl to imagine. Yet, here she was now, thinking about that very thing.

Feeling a blush rising upon her cheeks, she managed to look away and forcefully reminded herself that he was nothing more than a trusted old friend. Trusted by her father, too, because before he'd left to explore the birch grove shortly after the ride had begun, he'd told her that Michael had promised to keep an eye on her. He'd also reminded her that she hadn't been in the saddle for a long time and should be cautious.

She'd assured him that she would, and remembering all of that brought her back to the conversation. "Which caves have you gone inside?"

"All of them at one time or another," Michael replied. "Which we won't be doing today."

"Because you've suddenly decided to obey the rules?"

He touched the tip of her nose with one finger. "I am now the one who makes the rules."

"Oh, are you?" she asked, even though she knew the answer. It was just fun talking to him like this, in a teasing way. It had every part of her tingling with happiness.

"Yes." Grinning, he gestured to where Rafael was walking. "What Rafael chose not to mention while being so amused at telling you about me losing my seat in the saddle and ending up in the creek, was that he had become convinced that he'd seen a ghost and that the tunnel was haunted."

"A ghost?" A tiny thrill zipped through her. Unlike some, she wasn't fearful of the possibility of ghosts. The idea intrigued her. Always had. "What had he seen?"

Michael shook his head. "Don't be getting your hopes up with the idea of seeing one. I recall you being quite taken with the idea."

"You do?" She was taken aback that he'd remember such a thing about her.

"How could I not?" His grin grew. "You were giddy with excitement at the possibility of seeing one while exploring unused areas of Turnbill."

As long as he was sharing things he remembered, she said, "And you, of course, knew we wouldn't encounter one because you'd already explored those areas yourself."

"Indeed I had."

The idea of Rafael seeing a ghost still intrigued her. "So, what did Rafael see?"

"Most likely it was a beam of light coming from a hole in the ground overhead."

"Most likely, but you aren't one hundred percent sure," she concluded.

He laughed. "No, I'm not one hundred percent sure. I didn't see what he saw, but I did see a shaft of light."

"Did you see a hole in the ground?"

"No."

"It could have been a ghost if you didn't find a hole in the ground."

"I didn't look for a hole in the ground because I didn't have the opportunity. Rafael ran out of there so fast he was already on his horse, racing away by the time I exited the tunnel. I didn't catch up with him until he was near the creek, which is when Atlas stumbled, and I lost my seat. I hit the ground and didn't stop tumbling until I landed in the water. Being much younger, and a bit more unruly than he is now, Atlas kept right on running all the way to the stable."

Rafael's telling of the story last evening had been humorous, but now she found herself concerned. "You weren't hurt, were you? By the fall or landing in the creek?"

"No. The walk home gave me blisters because of the wet boots, but those healed quickly, so no sympathy is needed."

Confused, she frowned.

He laughed again. "It's written all over your face, and I'd much rather see you smiling as you were when Rafael told you about it last night."

"That was because of the way he told the story. He was laughing so hard it was impossible to not laugh with him." That was true, but so was something else. "I had asked him if you were injured, and he said no, but that you'd gotten the blisters because Buck refused to be ridden double."

"That is true. We considered riding double, but

Buck's reaction when I attempted to climb on behind the saddle quickly led us to believe that me walking seemed to be a better plan than both of us taking a tumble. Rafael offered to ride ahead and catch up with Atlas, but I knew the horse would already be at the stable and unsaddled by a groom."

"How could you know that?"

"Because that wasn't the first time he'd unsaddled me and raced home, nor would it be the last."

"But you were never hurt?"

"No, I was not, so you can stop worrying and find something to smile about instead." He bent down and plucked a tiny flower from the ground and handed it to her.

It was just a weed flower, one she didn't know the name of, but it was a pretty little white-and-yellow blossom, and it made her smile. "Thank you." She wrapped the flower stem round one of the buttons of her dress, just below her chin.

He reached over and straightened the flower, then touched the bottom of her chin with one knuckle. "You're welcome."

Between his smile and the way her chin felt as if it was on fire, her breath caught somewhere between her lungs and her throat. While struggling to merely breathe, she also attempted to ignore the thoughts rushing into her mind again. At first they were about kissing him again, but they quickly changed course. To him and Martha.

After they'd escaped Maud this morning, she'd had the opportunity to question Nora about Martha. Nora had said that she didn't know exactly what happened. Only that she and her mother had thought Michael and Martha would marry, then the relationship abruptly ended, and he was suddenly dead set against marriage. Which now included hers to Geoffrey.

Rosemary wondered if Michael had always been against marriage and that was why he'd ended the relationship with Martha, but she hadn't had the opportunity to ask Nora. Geoffrey had found them, and they'd needed to quickly collect their riding gloves in order not to keep everyone else waiting.

That was certainly a sad thought—Michael never wanting to marry. His kindness and generosity would make him a wonderful father. Surely he wanted children. A son to carry on the family legacy. That was the main reason her own father had remarried.

Her heart skipped a beat. What if Michael had discovered Martha was similar to Maud? Could that be it? That he believed she wouldn't have treated his family kindly? Or was she just looking for excuses? Because a part of her was joyous that he hadn't married Martha. That he hadn't married anyone.

That was most likely because she didn't want him to be miserable. But what if *not* getting married had made him miserable? Nora was convinced that whatever had happened with Martha had changed him. Changed his attitude towards marriage.

"Why are you against marriage?" Rosemary instantly clamped her lips together, ashamed and embarrassed that she'd asked such a forward question.

He eyed her curiously. "Is that something else Rafael told you?"

"No, Rafael didn't," she admitted. It had to be true, though, if that was his answer. "I'm sorry, but I—" Thinking quickly, she added, "I was referring to Nora and Geoffrey."

Nodding, he lifted a brow. "I believe we've already discussed that. I merely want to make sure he is the right choice for Nora, and for her sake, I'm hoping to discover that he is by getting to know him better."

That was all true, which added to her embarrassment at speaking without thinking. And for letting her thoughts run wild. It was just that his handsomeness, charm and personality, things she'd been captivated by so many years ago, had remained unchanged and were captivating her all over again. A silly thing to happen and something she must stop. His friendship, Nora's friendship, were things she cherished. She cherished their entire family, which was why she was so worried about Nora, just as he was. She was merely getting that all confused with childish memories and dreams.

"What are you thinking so hard about?" he asked.

She shook her head. "Nothing."

He shook his. "You are not a good liar, Rosemary. Never have been."

She huffed out a breath, because that was one more thing that he remembered about her. Which wasn't so hard to imagine, considering all the things she remembered about him. "Marriage," she admitted. "I was thinking about marriage and how it can be a wonderful thing when it's the right person and miserable when it's the wrong."

"You're speaking from experience?"

She nodded. "My father was so happy when he was married to my mother, and now, married to Maud, he's a different person. Not all the time but often enough that... Well, I don't like seeing the sadness in his eyes."

"That's why you try so hard to get along with Maud."

She shrugged. "I can't say that I try to get along with her. For the most part, I try to ignore her, just keep my distance from her. I don't want to be the cause of more sadness for my father."

"It's been that way since they were married?"

"Yes, and because of that, I don't want to see Nora marry the wrong person or anyone else that I know. I don't want to see anyone that unhappy."

"It's difficult," he said, catching and holding her gaze, "seeing someone we care about being unhappy."

The sincerity in his voice and expression made her ask, "You know someone who is unhappy due to marriage?"

"Yes, I do, through no fault of their own."

He could be speaking about a family member or friend that she wasn't acquainted with or perhaps he was speaking about himself and what had happened with Martha. Before she could think of a suitable reply, he took hold of her hand.

Pulling her towards the horses, he said, "Come, now, I must find a way to cheer you up. I've seen that frown simply too many times today, and I seem to be the one putting it there."

Amongst the chaos taking place inside her due to the warmth of his hand firmly wrapped around hers, a flash of guilt struck, making her regret bringing up the subject of marriage. Quickly searching for a more palatable subject and a way to make him smile, she said, "We could look for a ghost. Unless you're afraid."

The topic worked. He laughed aloud. "Nothing you can say will convince me to let you inside any of these tunnels."

"Because you're afraid."

"No, it's because it's dangerous."

They were still holding hands, and she leaned over and bumped his upper arm with her shoulder. "You're afraid of ghosts, and danger."

"Those tunnels could cave in at any time."

"That never stopped you when you were young."

"Young and foolish, neither of which I am now."

"No," she disagreed, both in her heart and mind.

"You were never foolish. I remember you being adventurous."

"Adventurous?"

She nodded.

They had arrived at the horses, and he assisted her into the saddle, before laying a hand on her knee and smiling up at her with sparking eyes. "That's how I remember you, too. Someone who woke up excited and eager to make the most of every day."

"That's because I was here, at Turnbill."

"And where are you today?" he asked.

A buoyancy rose up inside her, a happiness that she hadn't felt in a very long time. She was here, at Turnbill, and suddenly felt a long-lost sense of adventure. A feeling that here, at Turnbill, her life could be anything that she wanted it to be. This was her haven for dreams and adventures. Fun and excitement. What Michael had said was exactly how she used to feel every morning, and it had felt wonderful.

It was also something she wanted to feel again. Tugging on the reins, she steered Shadow around and urged the horse to quickly find a smooth gallop.

"Wait up!" Michael shouted.

Feeling playful, she shouted in return, "Join me, if you're not afraid of adventure!"

Within moments he was riding next to her. "What's the adventure?"

"I don't know yet," she admitted, "but it's going to be wonderful!"

* * *

A mixture of emotions filled Michael. On one hand, he was happy to see Rosemary enjoying herself. She'd been so serious and unsure since arriving. Very unlike herself, leastwise the person he'd once known. Her explanation of her father's marriage to Maud explained a lot of that. It also confirmed a lot of what he'd assumed. Now, witnessing the way she was handling the horse, riding carefree across the countryside, reminded him of her years ago. Confident in the saddle and excited for whatever was about to come.

On the other hand, he was still concerned about her home life and the way she was treated by Maud. It was as if all of the happiness, all of the life inside her, was instantly sucked out of her every time she encountered or spoke about her stepmother, and he knew what he was seeing right now wouldn't last. He not only regretted that, it saddened him.

At the same time, he couldn't help but feel a thrill rising up in him at how she continued to laugh as the others caught up with them. It was as if her excitement was contagious and quickly spread to those around her.

"Where are we going now?" Nora asked.

"To the orchards," Rosemary shouted.

Michael laughed at how her shout had sounded like a battle cry and at how her love of peaches hadn't waned. However, it was quickly confirmed that he wasn't the only one who knew about that.

"Where we will eat some peaches," Rafael shouted.

"Hear, hear!" she replied.

"And let the juices run down our chins!" Rafael added.

Her laughter filled the air, but in the next moment, Michael's heart leaped into his throat. A rabbit shot out of the tall grass, and startled Shadow.

Rosemary appeared to quickly get the horse under control, but he was already reaching for her, wanting to catch her before she fell. His action was what caused just that to happen. He pulled her out of the saddle and embarrassingly lost his own seat in the process when Atlas bolted sideways, undoubtedly because the material of her skirt covered the horse's face.

Michael wrapped his arms around her and twisted, taking most of the shock with his own body as they hit the ground and kept her firmly against his chest as they rolled. Not once but several times, then he had no choice but to acknowledge that he hadn't realized how close they'd been to the creek until they landed it in.

The water wasn't deep but still chilling, and they were both instantly soaked. His heart was pounding and regret swirled through him as he released his hold enough to rise to his knees and pull her into a sitting position. "Are you all right? Hurt anywhere? I'm sorry, I—"

Her laughter cut him off. As did the way she plucked a stringy wet weed off his shoulder. Dropping the weed into the water, she shook her head. "Well, this was not the adventure I expected, but it certainly was a shocking one."

"Are you two all right?" Nora asked from the bank of the creek.

"Yes," Rosemary answered, then frowned as she looked at him. "I am, are you?"

"I'm fine," he said, other than his pride. It was wounded. Trying to save her had created the opposite. Pulling up what dignity he had left, he stood and helped her to her feet. "You're sure you aren't hurt anywhere?"

"Yes, I'm sure," she replied. "Just a little wet."

He held on to her arm as they waded to the shore, where the others all stood, with expressions that said they were unsure how to react. Laugh or simply stare, which was what they were doing—staring, with hidden smirks.

With a giggle, Rosemary reached down to wring the water from her skirt. "I'd always wanted to know what it felt like to fall into a creek."

The others laughed. Michael didn't. He was too busy cursing himself. She was an accomplished rider and would have been fine if he hadn't interfered. Their horses had been collected, and while the others joined in on her laughter and in retelling what they'd seen, he helped her onto her horse. Her dress, shoes, even her hair and hat, were dripping wet, causing his stomach to sink lower.

"I'm sorry," he said. "It was all my fault."

"I said I wanted an adventure and am not disappointed." Still smiling, as if being soaked through was no inconvenience, she said, "Except for not seeing the ghost first."

"There is no ghost." Only a very foolish man who had been intent on protecting her.

"You don't know that for sure," she said, taking the reins of Shadow in hand.

Yes, he did but chose not to reply and instead informed the others that he and Rosemary would be returning to the house.

While the others agreed to return with them, she shook her head. "No, please, there's no need for everyone to return. You go see the orchard and bring me a peach."

Rafael and Nora both promised peaches before riding towards the orchard, while he and Rosemary took the shorter route home. Try as he might, Michael couldn't find any words to express the sorrow he felt. He'd failed her. Failed in his promise to keep her safe from harm.

"It was simply an accident, Michael," she said after they'd ridden a distance in silence. "It could have happened to anyone."

"I should have kept a closer eye on you," he said. "I know how easily horses can get spooked."

"So do I," she said. "You warned both Nora and me

about that from the time we started riding. I'm just grateful that you won't end up with blisters this time."

The remorse inside him was turning dark. "You should be taking this more seriously. You could have been hurt. Severely hurt."

"So could you, but we weren't, and I'm choosing to be grateful for that rather than worrying about what could have happened."

Her cheery attitude, the one he'd always admired and had wanted to see again, was misplaced in this incident. In fact, she should be angry with him. Women needed to be protected, and he'd failed. More than failed, he'd been the reason that she could have been seriously injured.

"We will ride directly to the house," he said. "And I'll request a bath be prepared for you."

She looked at him for a long moment, so long he found himself wanting to look away, because now she had to be seeing how he'd failed her, how he was the one to blame.

Without a word, she simply nodded, and they rode the rest of the way to the house in silence.

Michael had a bath prepared for himself, too, and after washing away any remnants of creek water, dressed. With his mind still filled with a flurry of thoughts, he walked to the window and looked out to the courtyard where the preparations for the picnic luncheon were well underway. He was far from over the anger he felt towards himself.

Why hadn't he noticed they were riding next to the creek? Why had the fact that Rafael knew how much she liked peaches bothered him? It had. The moment before her horse jolted, when she and Rafael had been laughing about eating peaches, he'd recognized the feeling that had overcome him. Jealousy. Recognized it because he'd felt that way before. When he'd learned about Martha and the sea captain.

At first, he hadn't believed Drake. Had thought it was all a mistake. That Drake had been wrong. Before it had been proven that he was the one who'd been wrong, jealousy had struck him like he'd never known. It had been that same jealousy that had turned into anger. A dark, all-consuming anger. When he had learned the truth, that Martha had indeed been seeing more than the one sea captain Drake had known about, that uncontrollable anger had overridden everything else. It had blurred his thinking, his common sense, his life.

He'd ended the relationship with Martha and with Drake.

Drake had sent messages, right up until he'd set sail again, but by then, Michael's jealousy had turned to embarrassment, which had kept him filled with anger. He'd been embarrassed that he'd been so foolish and blind to Martha's true goals, blind to everything except for visions of marriage with the perfect wife he thought he'd found. Unable to think about anything except for the next step he was expected to take in his life.

Marry. Have children. A son to take over the dukedom and family. Those expectations had been embedded into his mind as early and as deeply as protecting women had been.

The fact that Martha's father had died, that she'd needed someone to take care of her, protect her, had been what drew him to her. He'd thought he'd been in love with her. Thought he'd been the only one who could provide for her, protect her, and had been jealous at the idea that he wasn't.

He couldn't walk down that path again.

He wouldn't.

Rosemary didn't need him. She had her father. Her home life was none of his business. She was none of his business. Furthermore, he'd just proven that he couldn't protect her from harm. His own insecurities were what had almost gotten her injured.

Nora. His sister. Her marriage to Geoffrey was what he needed to concentrate on. So far, Bellview appeared to be all that Nora insisted he was—a good, caring man. There was still that rumor about the women at his country estate, and the only way to know the truth about that was to confront the owner. Depending upon what Michael discovered, he could approve or not approve the marriage and move on to the next step—whatever that might be.

He started to step back from the window, but his attention was caught and held by someone entering the yard directly below his window. For several long moments, he was transfixed, wondering how Rosemary had bathed and dressed so quickly. How had her hair, which was now styled and pinned up beneath a small brimmed hat, dried so quickly? The hat matched the emerald dress she now wore, one that fit her so perfectly, her feminine shape was clearly defined.

He watched as she slowly made her way across the lawn. She was a strikingly beautiful woman. Even her walk, the way her skirt swished about her feet, was elegant. Her posture was poised, her head held up with confidence. Anyone seeing her wouldn't believe that a mere hour ago, she'd been waist deep in creek water. And laughing. Laughing about being pulled off her horse, tumbling onto the ground, then rolling into the creek. Laughing at how it had been an adventure.

She had chosen to be grateful that they weren't hurt, and he was, too, especially grateful that she hadn't been hurt in any way, but that didn't ease the anger at himself over how it all came to be. Yet, he had to admit that he admired the way she had handled the situation. Many a woman would have been in tears, sobbing, upset and filled with embarrassment. She'd never reacted in such a manner, not that he could remember. Even at times, during their younger years, when Nora had thrown a tantrum, Rosemary hadn't.

She'd remained calm and done her best to quietly comfort Nora.

Still watching her, Michael felt a tightening inside him as he noticed her steps shorten, her stance droop slightly. Then he noticed why. Maud was on the other side of the lawn, but heading towards Rosemary, with an expression that made his hands ball into fists.

Pivoting about, he left his room in a solid, hurried march. By the time he hit the hallway, he was jogging, and then bolted down the stairs and out the door.

Chapter Seven

Michael espied Rosemary upon his arrival in the backyard, as well as her stepmother who was waggling a finger mere inches away from Rosemary's nose. His march forward was as purposeful as when he'd left his room, and he felt no sense of regret when he stopped next to Rosemary and leveled a fixed stare on Lady Havenshire.

"Allow me to extend my sincere apology for what happened earlier today," he stated, having no qualms about interrupting their conversation. "I can only imagine how worried you must have been to hear of the mishap. As with all mothers, your first concern would be for Rosemary's safety. I, too, was concerned and feel fortunate to express my assurance that your daughter was not injured."

Lady Havenshire's mouth opened and closed, as if she didn't know how to respond before her lips formed into what she must have considered a beguiling smile. "Oh, how gallant of you, Your Grace. Thank you." She pressed a hand to her breastbone while continuing, "I was greatly concerned. I've told her many times that horse riding is far too dangerous for a lady."

"On the contrary," he retorted, with his ire growing even stronger. To his way of thinking, the woman's shallowness was made more apparent by her limited acting skills. "Rosemary is a skilled rider. The entire mishap falls on my shoulders."

"I simply can't believe that, Your Grace," Maud replied, lying a hand on his arm.

"I can't help what you believe, Lady Havenshire," he said, taking a hold of Rosemary's elbow. "If you will excuse us, I would like Rosemary to accompany me as I express an apology to the earl, for he had put her in my care." Michael made a point of pulling his arm from beneath her hold and pointed to where the Earl of Havenshire was standing several yards away, speaking with Rafael.

"There's no need—"

"Yes, there is," Michael stated, cutting off Maud's protest.

Rosemary fell into step beside him as they walked away, and as soon as Maud was out of hearing distance, she asked, "So are we talking to each other again?"

His brows tugged together tightly as he glanced down at her. "I wasn't aware that we weren't talking to each other," he said, wondering whether she had made such a proclamation and he didn't recall it.

"Weren't you? You barely said anything the entire ride to the house and then ordered servants around like I wasn't even standing next to you."

No one had ever made him feel as incompetent as she just had. "My apologies. I fear I did not handle the situation very well today. My only defense is that I wanted to get you home and dry as soon as possible."

She stopped walking and stared at him. "Why? For fear of catching a cold? It's a beautiful day. Full of sunshine and warmth. I was hardly in danger of catching pneumonia." Shaking her head, she continued, "You don't need to feel obligated to come to my rescue continuously. It was simply an accident, and accidents happen."

He did feel obligated and wouldn't apologize for that. "That may be true, but I was responsible for your safety. I had given my word to father to look out for you, and I will apologize to him for failing. I'm sure he's just as concerned about you as your stepmother was."

With a sigh, she said, "Maud wasn't concerned about the accident. She's mad because your mother loaned me this dress. Nora insists that I keep it, which I won't. It's far too lovely."

He'd noted how perfectly the dress fit her from his window, but now, standing closer, saw how it truly accented her figure, including the low cut of the neckline that exposed the swell of her breasts. Swallowing against the thickness forming in his throat, he said, "It certainly looks lovely on you."

"Yes, well, I suppose it's not a style that Maud approves of." She hooked her arm through his. "It appears father is waiting on us."

Every dress that he'd seen her stepmother wear had shown off far more skin than the green one Rosemary was wearing, and that alone gave Michael full understanding of why Maud wouldn't approve of it. The woman was as jealous as the day was long, for neither her looks nor figure compared to that of her stepdaughter.

Maud had arrived at her husband's side, and Rafael was still standing on the earl's other side when Michael and Rosemary arrived.

Rafael was the first to speak. "Lady Rosemary," he said, with a slight nod. "I do hope you received the peaches I had sent up to your room."

Michael fought against the tension rising inside him by pressing his heels deeper into the ground. He had no right to feel any sort of jealousy and wouldn't. Simply wouldn't.

"I did, thank you very much," Rosemary replied, "I already ate one. It was delicious."

"I'm very happy to hear that," Rafael said, before he took a step backwards. "If you will excuse me."

As Rafael made his exit, the earl stepped forward, arms held out to his daughter.

"Oh, sweetheart," he said, embracing Rosemary in

a hug. "The others told me about your tumble when I met up with them in the orchard. I'm grateful you weren't hurt."

"Not at all, Father," she replied as the embrace ended. "Thanks to Michael. A rabbit hopped out of the weeds and startled my horse. Michael caught me before I slipped all the way out of the saddle. However, my dress startled Atlas when it covered his eyes, and both Michael and I ended up on the ground and then rolled all the way into the creek. I can only imagine what a humorous sight it had been to watch." She covered her smile with one hand as she added, "It was quite an adventure."

"I'd say it was quite an embarrassment," Maud said dryly.

The earl cast a disparaging look his wife's way.

"She was soaking wet when she arrived at the house," Maud said in a justifying way.

"Which no one saw," Rosemary said, smiling at him. "Thanks again to Michael. He escorted me all the way to the back door and ordered a bath prepared posthaste. The dowager duchess kindly loaned me one of Nora's dresses, so I won't be short on gowns for the weekend."

Michael felt a sense of pride welling in his chest. Not because of the way Rosemary had made him out to be the hero, but how she was standing up for herself in front of Maud.

"That was indeed kind of Michael and his mother,"

her father replied, "but with all the gowns Maud recently brought back from Paris, I can't believe you'd be short on clothing."

"Well, one could consider that to be my fault," Rosemary answered. "To save space in the carriage, I only packed one traveling trunk, so I didn't bring any extra day dresses, and the ball gown I plan on wearing this evening isn't appropriate for day wear."

Along with a smile, the earl shook his head. "I daresay, Michael, I will never understand women's fashion. Will you?"

"I would never proclaim such a thing," Michael admitted, "for surely I would soon be found to be wrong."

"I attest to that," the earl replied. "And thank you for taking such good care of my daughter. I knew I could trust you. I always have, even when you were just a lad—you were always looking out for her."

Michael gave a nod of acceptance before saying, "Please accept my apologies that such a mishap took place under my watch."

The earl waved a hand. "Fully accepted. Our goal for this weekend was for Rosemary to reconnect with old friends, and it warms my heart to see her being so happy in doing just that."

Michael knew he could have left the conversation right there, but the disdain in Maud's eyes simply wouldn't let him. "As long as we are speaking of mishaps," he said. "Something occurred last night that has me concerned."

The flash of shock or perhaps disbelief in Maud's eyes told him that she was afraid that he would mention one of two things: her vile remarks about Rosemary's so-called inability to sing or the unexplained invitations to visit the library.

"Oh, what is that?" the earl asked.

Michael chose his words carefully, not wanting to let Maud know all that he knew. At least, not all at once. "Someone knocked on Rosemary's door last night, asking her to go to the library."

Havenshire turned to his wife. "Was that you?"

"Heavens, no."

"But you went to the library last night, while I was climbing into bed. You said you were going to get a book to read."

Maud fidgeted both her hands and her feet as she replied, "And I did, but I was only gone for a few minutes. You wouldn't know that because you were asleep when I returned to our room."

"Did you see anyone else in the library?" Michael asked her.

"No." Shaking her head in a chaotic way, Maud added, "I was quick in my selection."

Havenshire nodded before asking Rosemary, "Who knocked on your door?"

"I don't know," she answered. "Whoever knocked—I'm assuming it was a maid—wasn't there when I opened the door. They'd told me Nora requested me to go to the library, but this morning, Nora told me that it wasn't her. That she hadn't requested me to meet her there. I did go to the library but didn't see anyone else there, so I went back to my room."

"I heard about the incident this morning, from both Nora and Rosemary," Michael said, "and as you can imagine, it concerns me to have someone sneaking about the house, knocking on doors in the middle of the night."

"I hardly imagine it was the middle of the night," Maud said.

"The actual time is of little consequence," Michael replied. "It's the action itself. I wouldn't want to believe that any of my guests are aspiring to make mischief, but considering what I've learned, I will have servants keeping a watchful eye out tonight. I want everyone to enjoy their time spent here, and that includes not having their sleep needlessly disrupted."

"I agree," Havenshire said before he asked Rosemary, "Did it frighten you, sweetheart?"

"No, Father, it did not," Rosemary answered. "It was just the oddity of it, because when Nora wants to speak with me, she simply comes to my room."

"True." Havenshire, then addressed him by saying, "Thank you again, Michael, for always looking out for Rosemary. I believe you have it all under control and doubt that there will be a repeat tonight."

"I sincerely hope there isn't," Michael replied before he gestured towards the tables, glad for a reason to escape the couple. "It appears that lunch is ready. You are welcome to sit at any of the tables outside or inside, and there are blankets available for those who would like to have a picnic in one of the gardens."

It wasn't until hours later, long after the noon meal, the horse races and numerous yard games, that Rosemary had the opportunity to think about the conversation between her father and Michael about who had knocked on her door the night before and why.

At the time, she'd noted that Michael hadn't mentioned that someone had knocked on Geoffrey's door as well. She'd assumed it had been because he didn't want her father to be further concerned. However, now, while sitting at the dressing table, eating a light repast that had been delivered to her room to tide her hunger over until the late-night meal would be served, after the performance by the Scottish dancers and the ball, that she questioned all parts of the conversation.

Maud was not a reader. She didn't even read to Thomas. Therefore, her visit to the library made no sense whatsoever. In the gut-churning way that happened too often when it came to her stepmother, Rosemary knew that Maud had wanted her to get caught in the library with Geoffrey. There wouldn't have been a better way to put a wedge between her and Nora, and Michael for that matter.

That angered Rosemary clear to her bones. She

hadn't come to that conclusion, that surely correct conclusion, until she'd retired to her room to prepare for this evening. The emerald gown that she'd worn today was so pretty, so elegant, that she hated to swap it out for the ball gown that had been pressed and was lying on her bed. Although the gown was a lovely shade of pink, like most of her other gowns, it buttoned all the way up to her chin. Granted, the one she'd worn last night hadn't had a collar, but the neckline had barely shown the tips of her collarbones. Nothing like the neckline of the green gown from today that swooped much lower. Nor did the pink gown fit her as tightly as the green one had—it hadn't been tight, just tailored to show off the curves of her sides, and the flatness of her stomach. The pink gown, like all of the gowns she usually preferred, hung loose on her and didn't define any portion of her body.

She would be lying if she didn't admit that what she'd liked most about wearing the green gown was the way Michael had looked at her. There had been appreciation in his eyes. She might not have noticed or understood it if not for his Aunt Lettice. During the horse races this afternoon, dressed in black as always, Lettice had taken reprieve from the sun under the same tree branches as Rosemary and Nora. That was when she had commented on how lovely the green gown was and how she wasn't the only one to notice how spectacularly it fit.

"Even from a distance, as he sits upon his great

steed, his eyes are filled with interest as they cast nowhere but directly at you," Lettice had whispered in Rosemary's ear, while pointing to where Michael sat upon Atlas, awaiting their turn to be called to the starting line. "You should wear that dress every day, every hour, that you are here."

At first, Rosemary felt little more than a hint of embarrassment at Lettice's remarks, for she'd feared that Lettice might somehow know about the long-ago thoughts that still filled her mind about growing up and marrying Michael. Until, later, when Lettice commented that there was nothing like the right gown to make a woman feel beautiful and a man to take notice.

It was then that Rosemary had admitted, at least to herself, that she did feel beautiful in that gown, and she still did, while sitting alone here in her room.

That was what had made her think about Maud and how angry her stepmother had been about the borrowed gown that fit her too tightly and showed off too much skin, even though it was far more modest than many of the gowns Maud wore.

Furious, Maud had approached her as soon as she'd walked into the yard earlier today, shaking her finger in her face for almost getting hurt, then wanting to know why she wasn't wearing one of her own dresses.

Before they could discuss it, Michael had approached them and planted the seed of suspicion that was now growing in Rosemary's mind. Maud had been behind the midnight knocking. Rosemary had no doubts about that now and was growing angrier by the second, thinking about how her stepmother wanted to ruin her dearest, oldest friendships.

Whether it was because she was here, at Turnbill, a place she'd always loved and had empowered her imagination or because she was so tired, so fed up at being under Maud's thumb, Rosemary wasn't sure, but when she lifted her head and met her own reflection in the mirror, she saw something she liked in herself.

Call it determination or defiance, for she felt both, she liked it and was going to use it. They'd be going home tomorrow, so this could be her one and only chance to truly be herself. The self that longed to return, to thrive, as it once had.

She rose from the stool, gave the dress lying on her bed a final look of contempt and walked to the door.

A short distance down the hallway, she knocked on Nora's door and was instantly granted access to enter. Nora, too, was eating from the tray that had been sent to her room and smiled broadly as Rosemary crossed the threshold and closed the door behind her.

"Good, you are just in time," Nora said, rising from the chair before the small table holding her tray of food. "I'm having a hard time deciding what to wear." She pointed to her bed where three gowns, all pressed, were lying across the mattress. "The yellow, the red or the purple."

Rosemary crossed the room, eyes focused on the purple gown. It was made from shimmering taffeta material, with three layers of skirt, all trimmed with wide black lace. The sleeves were short and puffed, and the neckline came to a V in both the front and the back and trimmed with more of the same delicate black lace that was on the skirts. A wide black ribbon encircled the waistline, and a gorgeous white cameo was sewn to the top of the bodice, right where the V neckline met in the center of the front of the dress.

"This one is absolutely stunning," Rosemary said.

"Yes, I like it, but I'm drawn to the red one," Nora said, picking up the red one, which was more of a deep burgundy color. "I love the back of it. All the layers."

There were numerous layers of material that cascaded one upon the other from the waistline to the floor, whereas the front had but one layer of material. "It, too, is beautiful," Rosemary admitted. "And that color would go perfectly with your black hair. Because of the way the layers of material fall, it almost looks black in places."

"I'm thinking that's the one I'll wear, although I do like the yellow one, too. It's so shimmery."

Rosemary nodded, taking a closer look at the yellow. It, too, had short sleeves and a V neckline, like the other two, but the bodice of the yellow one also formed a V where it met the waistline, and the skirt was pleated numerous times all the way around the waist. There were also layers of white lace on the hem and pink roses made of silk sewn onto the neckline at the shoulders. "You would look lovely in that one, too. It certainly is a hard choice."

Nora laid the red one back on the bed. "What color is your gown?"

"Pink. Maud either insists upon dull grays or browns or pink." Rosemary let out a sigh as she looked at the purple dress again. "I have a few light blue dresses, too. None are vibrant colors like these."

"Because Maud doesn't want you to outshine her," Nora said.

"I know," Rosemary admitted. "That's why I'm here."

Nora frowned.

"I believe it was she who either knocked on my door last night. Either that, or she had Helen, her maid, do it."

"That's what Geoffrey thinks, too," Nora said. "She wanted to ruin this weekend for you."

Meeting Nora's gaze directly, Rosemary said, "Ruin it for you, too, and I'm not going to let that happen."

A sly grin appeared on Nora's face. "What are you thinking about doing? I know it's something. And I want to be a part of it."

"I'm not going to wear the pink dress." Glancing at the bed, Rosemary said, "I was hoping you'd loan me one instead. I want her to see that I'm not the little girl that she's been bossing around since the day she married my father."

Nora let out a little squeal. "I've been waiting for the day you finally stand up to her. That's the girl I remember, and my best friend." While talking, she walked to her bureau and pulled open the top drawer. "And I have just the things to help make it even better."

"What is it?"

"These!" Nora held up two small white oval things that looked like miniature pillows of some sort.

"What are those?"

Nora held them under her bosoms. "You put them in your corset, and they push everything up. Makes it appear as if things could fall out of the dress at any moment."

Rosemary flinched slightly, because she didn't want to embarrass herself. Looking down at her own bosoms, she asked, "But *things* won't fall out, right?"

"Of course not, but it will make Maud turn green with envy."

With excitement rising, Rosemary pushed aside any worries. "Where did you get those? I've never heard of them."

"Aunt Lettice," Nora replied. "I'll tell you more about the things she's shared with me while we change. Penny will be up shortly to help, but we can get started without her. Turn around, and I'll unbutton your dress."

By the time Rosemary left Nora's room, she was confident that nothing would fall out. She had jumped up and down with her hands over her head, twisted in every way imaginable, and bent over, touched her toes, several times in a row. All the while, the low neckline had remained secure, while displaying an ample amount of cleavage enhanced by the white cameo sewn onto the purple dress.

Wearing the red dress, which showed off just as much bare skin, Nora walked beside her, with their arms hooked together. "I can't wait to see Maud's eyes pop out of her head," Nora whispered.

Rosemary was getting a smidge nervous, because besides the wrath she could encounter once they returned to London and Maud cornered her alone, she was worried about how Michael might react to the dress. Perhaps he'd think showing so much skin was inappropriate. She didn't want to alienate him while trying to get back at her stepmother.

As if reading her mind, Nora whispered, "The men are going to love it, too. Be prepared to dance all night."

"Do you think Geoffrey will like your dress?" Rosemary asked, not interested in dancing or drawing the attention of other men. Only Michael's, but she couldn't admit that.

"Oh, yes, I know he will."

"He won't think you're exposing too much, well, skin?"

Nora laughed. "You and I have been apart too much over the years. If only we had more than a weekend together. There is so much that I've learned, and so much that you haven't because you've been stuck under Maud's thumb."

Rosemary didn't doubt that.

"Men like seeing skin, as you called it, yet they also like when things are left to the imagination."

Considering all that Nora had shared during their dressing time, Rosemary asked, "Is that something else Aunt Lettice told you?"

"Yes, it is. She is one wise woman."

More than a flicker of hope rose up inside Rosemary as she recalled what Lettice had said about wearing the green gown. With any luck, this purple one would be just as appealing to Michael.

Because most of the attendees had been at Turnbill all weekend, there were no formal announcements as people entered the grand hall, which looked absolutely stunning with the late evening sun shining in through the stained-glass windows. She and Nora entered the room side by side, and though Rosemary could have paused to simply take in the grandeur and beauty surrounding her, Nora was on a mission and didn't slow a single step in crossing the room to where Geoffrey was standing near the massive fireplace.

To Rosemary's disappointment, Michael was nowhere to be seen, but Rafael was next to Geoffrey, and if his expression was anything to go by, the purple gown would not go unnoticed.

"Lady Rosemary, I declare that I've never seen you

looking more radiant," Rafael said as he reached for her hand, then placed a small peck on the back of it.

"Thank you, Mr. Williams," she replied, "and may I say you look overly charming tonight as well."

"Charming, is it?" Rafael asked. "Not dashing or extraordinarily handsome or a debonair gentleman?"

She laughed. "Oh, yes, you are all of those as well."

He gave an exaggerated sigh as he waved a hand overhead as if speaking to the heavens. "My life is complete. I can now die a happy man."

Laughing harder, for it was impossible not to, she declared, "You are truly too extravagant, and please, don't speak of your own death. Life would be miserably boring without your wit in it."

"Aw, there you have it, I can't die tonight after all, for I cannot bear to think of a boring world." He then leaned a hint closer and said, "Might I suggest, dear lady, that you turn about, so the good duke can stop scanning the room for what he seeks."

She frowned slightly while deciphering his words. Rafael twirled a single finger, indicating she should spin about, then he raised a hand in acknowledgment.

Pivoting on one heel, Rosemary nearly stumbled before coming to stop as she espied Michael walking towards them. He was always so very handsome, but tonight, wearing a black frockcoat with tails and shimmering gold buttons, matching vest and a ruffled white shirt, he looked extraordinarily debonair. Her heart took to pounding so hard, she wondered if it could be that repeated impact, coming from the inside with such force, that caused *things* to pop out over the top of the dress's low neckline.

Michael's walk was purposeful, his strides long, and that alone was enough to signify his station in life. Although she knew how gentle and kind he was, his appearance proclaimed him a formidable man, a duke, who was not only proud and righteous but also not one to be trifled with, leastwise not without repercussions. At this moment, Rosemary knew that whatever happened tonight as far as her stepmother was concerned, she herself was safe and secure. For Michael would be there to protect her.

He was still crossing the room, coming closer with each step, and her eyes met his. In that moment, something she couldn't define happened inside her. It was as if the rest of the world didn't matter. Her feet moved, walking towards him, and before she realized it, she was standing directly in front of him. Gazes locked as if neither of them could or wanted to look away.

"Lady Rosemary," he greeted with a slight bow.

She curtsied. "Your Grace."

He took her hand, and as Rafael had done, he kissed the back of it. Unlike Rafael's peck, the touch of Michael's lips sent a warmth up her arm that spread throughout her body, making her eyes close momentarily in the wonder of it all.

"You look absolutely stunning this evening," he said.

"Thank you, I shall say the same about you."

"Might I suggest that you wear purple more often?"

Although she was ecstatic that he approved of the gown, she cautioned herself about putting too much weight in it. Needing to keep her wits about her, she leaned closer to whisper, "I borrowed it from Nora and must warn you that Maud might not be too appreciative."

He nodded. "Well, that is her loss."

"I think she is the one who knocked on my door last night. If not her, she had her maid do it. She wanted to ruin the weekend."

He was still holding her hand and tucked it under his arm as he moved to stand by her side. "I have come to the same conclusion, but that is not something we are going to concern ourselves with his evening. Let us join the others near the fireplace."

Chapter Eight

If Rosemary hadn't already believed Turnbill was a place that encouraged one to believe in magic and fairy tales, she would have been convinced of it that night. The evening was so very enchanting that she wondered if she was dreaming.

The restored ballroom was captivating in itself, even after the sun no longer shone through the stained-glass windows. The flickering light from the chandeliers overhead not only illuminated the room with a golden glow, but also caught upon the paintings on the ceiling, making it appear as if the room itself was alive. Shortly after all of the guests had entered the room, the Scottish dancers began their performance. Every song the kilt-wearing bagpipe musicians performed was lively and made more so by the truly amazing dancers dressed in colorful plaid costumes. Their dance steps were unbelievably fast. She'd never seen anything like it.

The true joy for Rosemary came from watching

how much the musicians and the dancers were enjoying themselves. The way they laughed and smiled and teasingly interacted with one another had the audience laughing along with the performers. Including her.

It was simply impossible not to get caught up in the joy and laugh and clap or tap a toe along with the music, and all of that was even more fun when Michael would nudge her and make a game out of clapping along with others.

When each and every song ended, the room filled with exuberant rounds of applause that lasted until the music began again.

Most of the guests, at least those she could see, were standing, unable to sit due to the music that was not only filling the room but filling their very souls. That was what it felt like to Rosemary, and she could have listened and watched the performance all night. She truly thought nothing could be better.

When one of the musicians announced the last song was for everyone to dance and encouraged guests to find a partner, she didn't even question her actions as she turned and faced Michael. Her heartbeat increased, and her entire being grew warm as one set of their hands clasped together, the others resting upon one another in a classic dance stance.

The music began, and rather than the fast lively tunes that had been played, this one was slow, the bagpipes sounding almost haunting, yet also tender and reverent. Michael easily led her around the dance floor, never taking his eyes off hers, and the dreamlike state that she found herself in grew deeper and deeper.

"I'd never seen bagpipe musicians before," she said, trying to keep herself embedded in some semblance of reality. "Or Scottish dancers."

"They were exceptional," he replied.

"Yes, they were." She closed her eyes just for a moment and let the music fill her, but the next thing she knew, the music had ended. With a sigh, she opened her eyes and was met by Michael's smile.

"I've never seen anyone who enjoyed music so much," he said.

"I've always enjoyed music, but this was truly exceptional."

"I agree that Nora made an excellent choice for the entertainment tonight." His hand released hers as he took a step back, then held out a bent elbow to her. "Shall we have a refreshment while waiting for the orchestra to get set up?"

A sudden bout of insecurity struck Rosemary at the prospect of seeing Maud amongst the guests. That hadn't happened prior to the performance and was sure to occur now.

Michael lifted a brow. "Come now, your efforts tonight cannot be for naught."

She frowned. "What?"

"Wasn't that dress meant to show someone you've grown up?"

Heat rose up into her cheeks. "Maybe I just wanted to look pretty."

"You are pretty no matter what you're wearing, and this dress is meant to be a statement. One that your stepmother won't be able to miss, because the moment I leave your side, you are going to be surrounded by men."

Afraid that her plan might not have been as clever as she'd thought, she wrapped her hand around his elbow. "I am?" That wasn't what she wanted.

"Indeed, but no need to worry, because I don't plan on leaving your side." He grinned and patted her hand. "Shall we get a refreshment?"

Back to feeling safe and happy, she nodded. "Yes, please."

Michael drew in a deep breath, needing some sort of fortification as they walked towards the edge of the dance floor. The dress that Rosemary was wearing was exactly as he'd told her: a statement intended to provoke a response. And he'd responded. From the moment he'd seen her standing by the fireplace, his body had been lit on fire, and it was continuing to burn with flames so hot he imagined he'd still be smoldering weeks from now.

Damn her. Taking his eyes off her had already been hard enough, now it was impossible. Add in her enjoyment of the music and dancing, and the jealousy he'd once worried about was but a drop in the bucket compared to what he felt right now.

The other thing he'd told her was also true. That the moment he left her alone, she would be surrounded by men who had no idea just how sweet and innocent she was beneath that purple gown that made her appear to be a temptress.

He wasn't about to let that happen.

Nor was he about to miss Maud's reaction to seeing how she truly compared to her stepdaughter. As he had been earlier today, he was proud of Rosemary for taking a stance. She'd been belittled and smothered for too long.

Nora met them at the edge of the dance floor. "Weren't they wonderful?" she asked, meaning the musicians and dancers.

"Oh, they were fabulous," Rosemary answered. "I've never seen anything like it."

"Geoffrey told me that he liked bagpipe music," Nora explained, "So I asked Aunt Lettice, and she contacted them."

Michael released a soft chuckle. There wasn't anything that Lettice didn't know or couldn't find out about, all while living in the country hours away from London.

While the women continued to talk about the music, he signaled a footman and collected two glasses of champagne and handed one to Rosemary, while Geoffrey did the same for himself and Nora.

It wasn't long before the Earl of Havenshire and his wife approached, and just as Michael suspected, Maud's expression was filled with fury.

Etiquette dictated that, as a duke and their host, he should be greeted with a respectful bow or curtsy. He didn't expect it from Havenshire, having known the man since he'd been a young lad, yet, accepted it with a nod when the earl gave a slight bow. He felt a bit of concern at how obviously it pained Lady Havenshire to complete a quick dip; it was clear she didn't approve of the way that, by standing next to the duke, Rosemary had one more thing over her. He hoped that didn't increase the woman's wrath. The dress alone was accomplishing enough.

Although her own dark blue dress exposed as much flesh as Rosemary's, Lady Havenshire was also once again displaying an array of jewels dangling from her ear lobes and around her neck.

"Hello, darling," Rosemary's father said, kissing her cheek. "You look lovely this evening."

"Thank you," she replied. "Did you enjoy the performance?"

"Very much," he replied.

"And you, Maud?" Rosemary asked. "Did you enjoy it?"

In Michael's opinion it was impossible not to notice the resentment in Maud's eyes as she once again eyed Rosemary from head to toe. Nora noted it, too, because his sister bristled visibly, as if ready defend her friend should Maud make any sort of disparaging comment.

"Well, it was certainly different," Maud replied. "Perhaps a bit too brightly colored for my taste."

"I find everything about tonight to be perfect," Nora instantly piped in, obviously unable to stop herself from making some sort of comment. "Especially all of the colorful gowns. Some are simply gorgeous."

Michael held his silence as Nora's and Lady Havenshire's glares were locked as if in a standoff.

"Perhaps the orchestra will be more to your liking," Rosemary said to her stepmother.

"Speaking of which," Michael interjected while looking at Rosemary, "they are ready to begin. Shall we?"

"Yes, thank you."

As Michael led her away, he heard her father say, "It's so nice to see Rosemary enjoying herself."

"I agree," came from his sister. "It's been too long."

Rosemary heard the exchange, too, because she looked up at him. He smiled and continued to lead her to the center of the floor, which was the signal for the guests to know the dancing was about to commence.

They danced for three dances before he suggested taking a rest. His nerves needed one. Actually, it wasn't his nerves as much as it was his restraint. Having her body so close to his, her floral scent filling his nostrils and her joyous laugh tickling his ears, had every part of his body humming with desire.

Never in his life had he wondered so deeply about what lay beneath a woman's gown and how it would please him and how he would please her. The low-cut V-shaped neckline of the gown gave him a spectacular view of the swells of her breasts and that was more than enough for his imagination to run wild.

His sister was again at the edge of the dance floor and instantly requested that Rosemary accompany her for a moment of reprieve. While Geoffrey stated he'd escort the women to the hallway, Michael retrieved a glass from a footman who was thankfully close at hand and downed the contents of the glass in one swallow.

The liquor burned all the way down to his gut, but that wasn't a big enough distraction for him to pull his gaze off Rosemary as she made her way through the crowd. The back of the gown was as enticing as the front, exposing her shoulders and portion of her upper back, and he felt a silent groan rumbling in the back of his throat.

A low mumble had him pulling his gaze off Rosemary and turning to his left. "Would you care to repeat that?"

"Repeat what?" Rafael asked, with a smirk.

Michael was close to his breaking point and considered ignoring Rafael but knew his friend too well. Rafael wouldn't go away on his own. "Whatever it was that you mumbled under your breath."

"Oh, that. I was merely admiring—"

Cutting him off, Michael said, "I suggest you find someone else to admire."

Rafael slapped his shoulder, "But I've always admired you, my friend."

Michael leveled a solid stare that spoke for itself.

Letting out a low chuckle, Rafael said, "I was admiring the way you can't keep your eyes off a certain young lady and the fact that you aren't as made of stone as you claim to be."

"She's a family friend and—"

"You don't need to repeat it to me, unless of course it will help you believe it."

"It's the truth."

"Can't help the truth," Rafael said. "Not when it's also the truth that your family friend has grown up to be a beautiful woman."

Michael couldn't deny that, nor could he think of anything viable to say about the condition he currently found himself in. Desire had never consumed him like this.

"Tell me, old man," Rafael said in a low voice, "if you truly are not interested in Lady Rosemary becoming more than a family friend, is it fair to her or to the rest of the men in this world to keep her all to yourself?"

Michael nearly crushed the crystal glass in his hand as his fingers tightened. A passing footman saved the glass from being turned into shards, but nothing could save him from knowing Rafael had indeed spoken yet another truth.

* * *

Like something caught in a tree branch, too far up to reach and waving at you like it knew you couldn't do anything about it, Rafael's statement hung in the back of Michael's mind. Not only during the rest of the ball, where he remained at Rosemary's side, danced with her, laughed with her and enjoyed the time more than he probably should have, but long after the meal had been served when most of the guests, tired and full, had retired to their rooms.

He'd gone to his room, too, but wasn't able to sleep because that waving flag in the back of his mind kept getting bigger and bigger. The part of him with its common sense still intact told him that she could never be more than a friend. The part of him that was on fire with desire told him that he already wasn't thinking about her as a friend.

There was yet another part of him that was sincerely worried about her. The Earl of Havenshire was happy that his daughter was reconnecting with old friends and enjoying herself, but his wife was not. Her glowers at Rosemary had not only become darker as the night had gone on, Maud looked as if she almost had a smile on her face. As if she was plotting something.

Regrettably, he had no idea what to do about that. They'd be leaving tomorrow, and with the earl busy with his commitments to the Royal Army, there was no doubt that Rosemary would be alone in their London home with her stepmother.

Such thoughts kept him up until the wee hours of the morning, and after only a few hours of restless sleep, he climbed from his bed. Within the hour, he settled himself in his study, not quite sure if he was hiding or taking the more prudent route of distancing himself from Rosemary.

In his estimate, it would be hours before guests began to rise from their beds, and hopefully, by then, he'd have some semblance of a plan for how he should go forward.

There was a knock on the door. Assuming it was a servant, perhaps Horace, the butler, or his valet, Gilbert, Michael granted entrance without looking up from the ledger that he had been staring at but not reading for some time.

"Excuse me, Your Grace, I would like to request a moment of your time."

Recognizing Geoffrey's voice, Michael looked up and nodded. "Of course, come in."

"Thank you." The viscount entered and shut the door behind him. "I know it's early, but it's likely that I'll be busy until it's time for me to leave later today."

Michael waved to a chair on the other side of his desk. "Nora did manage to schedule events for every moment of the weekend."

The viscount settled himself onto the chair. "She

did. Thank you for your hospitality. I've enjoyed the time spent with your family and friends."

"We've enjoyed having you here." Michael leaned back in his chair. Bellview was likely here now to ask for permission to officially court Nora, with the understanding that an engagement and wedding would soon follow. Though he felt that he had learned more about Bellview this weekend, Michael still hadn't made a decision about giving his permission.

With the same confidence and conviction that he'd displayed several times over the weekend, Bellview sat back in his chair. "I understand this weekend was also to give you the opportunity to determine if my pursuit of your sister is genuine and sincere. Yet we have not had the opportunity to actually talk, discuss questions that I believe you have for me and ones that I have for you. I was hoping we could do that now."

"I appreciate that." Michael gave a nod. "Please, ask any questions you might have."

"I'll start by asking what you expect from a husband for Nora."

"I expect an honorable man, one who will respect her and her wishes. I'd like him to have a sense of humor, because she loves to laugh. I want him to be generous, not only in providing for her but in allowing her to provide for others. Nora is committed to seeing that all people have their needs met and has worked alongside my mother with several charities. I also would like to see her married to a man who won't try to stifle her free will. She is an intelligent woman who speaks her mind, and that should be embraced rather than smothered." Leaning forward, Michael planted his elbows on his desk. "But most of all, I want her to be loved. Loved first and foremost. I have no doubt that is how she will love in return."

Bellview's smile grew broad. "Everything you have mentioned are things that I admire about Nora and would never want to see any of it change. Nor would I want her dedication to change. If she's your friend, she'll be your friend for life. Just as she'll be your sister for life. She's dedicated to you, her family, and I find that honorable. She told me that she wants to marry me despite what you say, and I told her no. That we won't get married without your blessing, because I don't want her to have to give up anything for me, especially not her family. Not having your approval will sadden her, and I will do anything, everything to never see her sad or hurting in any way. Her beauty caught my eye the first time I saw her, but I fell in love with her when I came to understand that she's just as beautiful on the inside."

Michael had to admit that Bellview certainly had the right answers and was quite comfortable talking about his convictions. "How do you know it's love?"

"I just do. I've never felt this way before and know I never will again." Bellview leaned closer. "I want to be near her all the time and can't stop thinking about her. I want to protect her, encourage her, share everything with her. It's hard to explain, but deep down, I know it's love, and I feel lucky to have found it."

Impressed in many ways but mostly by Bellview's unashamed honesty, Michael nodded, in part for himself. Would he ever be at the point where he was so sure of himself again that he'd be open and accept the possibility of love? It seemed highly unlikely. He was grateful that Nora would never betray Geoffrey the way Martha had him.

Rosemary would never betray a man, either.

Needing to keep his mind off her for the time being, he said, "There is something that has concerned me that we need to discuss."

"My reputation."

"Yes."

"Well, allow me to say that I would be a fool to think that you haven't already led an investigation to know all there is to know, and I would expect no less."

"I have," Michael said.

"Except you couldn't find out the truth about one thing."

"It appears as though you want people to believe the rumors."

"The only person I've told the entire truth to is Nora."

Michael said nothing, merely kept eye contact. Bellview didn't look away, either.

"After my mother died," Bellview began, "I went to live with her family because my father had remarried and his new wife wanted nothing to do with me. It was mutual. I was a young boy of ten and didn't want a lot to do with her, either. I didn't want a new mother, I wanted to remember my old one."

Michael nodded, understanding that was how a child could feel.

"My mother's family was good to me," Bellview continued, "and I had no intention of ever leaving. Not even when my father died, and I inherited the title and all that went along with it. Until my cousin came to me. She is my mother's sister's daughter, and we are as close as brother and sister in many ways. Her name is Sarah, and Sarah has a heart of gold. As a young girl, she took in every stray or injured animal she found. She'd heal them and set them back in the wild. The ones she knew wouldn't survive without her, she kept, and as she got older, she started doing that with people."

"People?"

Bellview nodded. "Young girls. Ones that society had failed. In situations that…" He shook his head. "You can imagine. Sarah kept it secret, because more than anything, these girls just needed a safe place to heal. She was renting a house outside of Birmingham, but it had become overcrowded. The Bellview estate would fit her needs, so I accepted the title and holdings. Upon discovering how poorly my father's business had been run, I made changes, brought in new management, which caused some to be disgruntled.

Rumors began circulating, but I was too busy getting things in working order to worry about it. When word of the young women living at Bellview spread, I ignored that, too, simply let people think I was following in my father's footsteps, a rake and womanizer."

"All to keep Sarah, your cousin's, secret safe?"

"To keep the girls safe. They deserve the opportunity to heal and learn. Sarah has implemented training programs, and several have obtained legitimate employment. Up until I met Nora, I was content to let people believe what they will, but that is no longer the case. My father owned another piece of property, near Newport. I'm having it renovated, and Sarah will move the girls there once it's completed. I've told Nora that the move will happen before we wed, so that she will not be entering into a life overshadowed with a scandal."

"Won't it be unsettling for Sarah to move the girls again?" Michael asked, quite impressed by Geoffrey's willingness to help others, even though it damaged his own reputation.

"Sarah agrees that moving would be best. She doesn't want her passion to interfere in my and Nora's life."

"I can understand that justification but feel obligated to point out that without the truth being revealed, in the view of much of society, Nora would be marrying a man with a damaged reputation. Which is a something that she is willing to overlook, but as her guardian, I must take it into consideration."

"I am well aware of that, which is why I wanted you to know the truth. Had I known months ago that I would meet Nora and fall in love with her, I would have made different choices. At least I want to believe I would have, but some of Sarah's wards have been so injured in the past that every man scares them, and I've been glad to help in any way possible."

Michael's status in life and wealth hadn't shielded him entirely from some of the worst of the worst situations. He knew that certain areas of major cities were crowded with the unfortunate that society overlooked, how easily those people were taken advantage of and how dearly safe places were needed by anyone lucky enough to escape. What Geoffrey and his cousin were doing was admirable, and he could see Nora wanting to be a part of it.

He found himself in a quandary. If he was honest with himself, he had to admit that he had already been half convinced by Geoffrey's scandalous reputation. It had been his goal to protect his sister from a rake and a womanizer by uncovering the truth about him and forbidding the marriage. But that "truth" had turned out to be a falsehood, one that couldn't be revealed for the safety of others. What could he possibly do about that?

Chapter Nine

For as amazingly wonderful as last night had been, the morning was dreadfully sad for Rosemary. Every step felt as if she had heavy rocks tied to her ankles, and she had to keep blinking away tears as she placed items into her traveling trunk. She didn't want the weekend to be over or cut short, but had no choice. Helen had personally delivered a message from Maud stating that they would be leaving prior to the noon meal.

Rosemary considered arguing, or at least asking if they could stay to see the magician's performance, but knew better. It was easier to comply.

Letting out a long sigh, she closed the lid of her trunk. This had been the best weekend of her life, and she was going to miss being here more than ever. Miss the people here more than ever.

Last night had truly been like the fairy tales she used to dream about. Dancing and laughing and being on the arm of the most gallant, most handsome man of all. Michael had noticed the purple gown and had looked at her with appreciation, just as she'd hoped, but for what gain? Michael would never see her as more than an old friend. The little girl who used to stay with them for weeks on end because their families had been friends for years.

Had she hoped for more?

That would be as foolish as her dreams used to be when she was young. Michael would never fall in love with her. Never marry her. Nora insisted that whatever happened between him and Martha had changed Michael's view on marriage forever.

She could understand that, because she knew how marriage changed everything. How miserable it could make people and everyone around them.

Would there ever come a day when she didn't feel that way? When she would want to marry and raise a family of her own? Parts of her could imagine that. The same parts of her that used to dream about growing up and Michael. About living at Turnbill and attending balls like last night.

The older, wiser parts of her knew the foolishness of such dreams and knew that just as she'd packed her clothing in her traveling trunk, she needed to tuck those dreams away and go back to London. Back to where her life was dedicated to making sure her father's home was run efficiently and that Thomas was taken care of and loved.

A nauseating swirl overtook her stomach at the

thought. Home was sure to be worse than ever. Maud wouldn't forget what happened last night. The purple grown had more than irritated her.

Rosemary sat down on the bed. Why had she not thought through the repercussions? Had she truly believed that one night of freedom, of feeling beautiful and enchanting, would be worth the wrath? Furthermore, what was the use of wanting those things when they couldn't last? Without Michael at her side, she didn't have the courage to stand up to Maud.

A knock on the door startled her, and she had barely risen to her feet when the door flew open.

"You aren't going to believe it!" Nora exclaimed, gleaming with excitement.

"What?" Rosemary asked.

"We're going to London!" Nora replied. "Michael, Mother and I. Michael has some work to do and said that we'll leave this afternoon, after all the guests have departed. And we'll be in town for the rest of the month!"

"That's wonderful." Rosemary was truly excited at the idea of Nora being nearby. "Will you have time for us to visit?"

"Yes! I'll have time to see you regularly and to join you and Thomas for a trip to the zoo. I know how much he enjoys you taking him there."

Rosemary's heart swelled at the thought of her brother. The weekend had been busy, but she'd still thought about Thomas being at home without her.

"Oh, he does, and he'll love telling you about all of the animals."

"I'll love hearing about them and love being able to do so many other things with you." Nora hooked their arms together. "Come help me pack. It's been so long since I've spent longer than a day or two in London."

Although it had consumed a large portion of her thoughts while helping Nora pack, Rosemary hadn't asked why Michael needed to go to London. He tended to visit the city only when his work required it and then didn't remain there long. The exact opposite of her father. Due to his need to be near those he commanded, the soldiers who guarded the Royal Family, her family rarely left the city. When there was the opportunity to visit their family estate, Havenshire, Maud always reminded her father of how much she despised the country, and they would end up staying in London.

The fact her father had put his foot down and insisted they attend this weekend had been a true surprise to Rosemary. That thought made her stomach grow sick again. Her behavior last night, acting so out of character in wearing the purple dress, might have assured that her father would never get out of the city again. All because of her.

Pressing a hand against her churning stomach, she continued along the corridor towards the grand hall, wanting one last look at the restoration before the noon meal was served and her departure would happen.

That was what she told herself, anyway. That she wanted to see the restoration and not simply bask in memories of dancing in Michael's arms. Despite the repercussions she was sure to face, last night had been a dream come true. One she would cherish for the rest of her life.

Although the hall was a skeleton of what it had been last night, with the tables stripped of their linen cloths and bouquets of flowers and the stage removed, the room still held an inherent beauty. Sun was again shining through the stained-glass windows, casting sparkling, fairylike lights on the walls and floors.

Her footfalls echoed in her wake as she crossed the room all the way to the fireplace, where she stopped and stood in the very spot that she'd been standing when she'd turned about and seen Michael walking across the room.

This time she didn't turn around but instead closed her eyes, letting the memories rush back. She could almost hear the bagpipe music that the musicians had played during her first dance with Michael. The memory was bittersweet, because she knew it would never happen again.

In that moment, she determined that wearing the purple dress had been worth whatever might come once she was back in London. It had created memories that no one could ever take away from her.

"I thought I might find you here."

Her eyes flew open, and she spun around. Her heart thudded as Michael walked closer. He wasn't wearing the black frock coat and ruffled shirt as last night but looked just as handsome in the white shirt covered by nothing more than a red-and-gold vest. It was a moment before she found her voice. "I wanted a final look at the restoration."

"I'm confident that you'll see this room again."

She wasn't but smiled nonetheless. "Nora told me that you'll be traveling to London with her and your mother."

"That's why I was looking for you."

"Have your plans changed?"

He stopped in front of her. "No. We will be going to London later today. The reason why is what I'd like to discuss with you."

"Oh?"

"Yes. I've determined that I need more information before I can grant my blessing to Nora and Geoffrey."

A tremendous wave of disbelief washed over Rosemary as she realized she'd forgotten about their purpose this weekend. It hadn't been for her to live out a fairy tale; it had been to determine if Geoffrey's wish to marry Nora was honorable. Not once had she questioned Geoffrey's actions, nor had she shared anything about him with Michael. Every secret she'd shared had been about herself and, unfortunately, her stepmother.

Drowning in guilt, she bowed her head and whispered, "I'm sorry that I wasn't more helpful to you."

His finger touched her beneath the chin and forced her to look up at him. "There's no reason to apologize. You have been helpful, and I'm hoping you will be again while we're in London."

Despite how awful she was feeling a moment ago, her heart leaped inside her chest. "Of course, if I can."

He smiled. "Thank you. We'll be staying at the London town house, so will only be a short distance from you."

The Knight family's impressive four-story brick home in London was near the park, and she walked past it every time she took Thomas to see the swans and other aquatic birds swimming in the pond. Rosemary found that she couldn't say that, because looking at Michael made speaking too difficult. There was something in his eyes, the way he was looking at her, that was stealing the air from her lungs. Making it hard to breathe and impossible to look away. It felt as if time stopped. As if the world forgot to keep turning.

She had the strangest sensation that he wanted to kiss her. Or maybe those were her thoughts. For that was exactly what she wanted. With every part of her body.

His finger was still beneath her chin, and his thumb was caressing her cheek and sending a thrilling heat through her face, down her neck. Her lips were tingling, her heart was pounding, and the rest of her had the greatest desire to rise on her toes so her face was closer to his.

She'd never wanted something so badly. So completely. An unusual excitement was growing stronger and stronger at the mere idea of kissing him. Of his lips touching hers. She could imagine that it would be better than dancing with him. Better than anything she'd ever known.

Just as she was giving in, about to rise onto her toes, a piercing sense of reality struck. This was Michael. The one man she'd always dreamed of kissing and the one man she couldn't kiss. Couldn't ever let him know about the dreams she'd had for years. He'd merely been being kind to her this weekend, watching out for her, because as Nora had mentioned that first day, he thought of her as another sister. Someone he had to protect. Nora had said that would never change, and he certainly hadn't done anything to make Rosemary believe otherwise.

She'd been the one wishing it would change, and she shouldn't have. It wouldn't matter what she wore—he would never see her as a woman he could be interested in for something more than friendship.

Coming to her senses, she jerked her head backwards, and knowing that wasn't enough, she took a step backwards, too, all the while struggling to catch her breath.

The hand that had been touching her face fell to Michael's side, and it suddenly felt like she'd lost something precious.

He stared at her for yet another stilled moment, and she wished with all her might that she could read his mind. She couldn't, so all she could do was hope that he hadn't realized how badly she'd wanted him to kiss her.

With a slight nod, he took a step back, too. "All right then, I have some things to see to before the noon meal will be served."

The ability to speak still wasn't within her grasp. The most she could do was nod.

They walked from the room side by side, without touching, without saying a word. Her heart was still pounding, her knees felt weak and wobbly, and she wondered if she'd ever be able to face him again. If his silence said anything, it was that he knew.

Knew exactly what she'd wanted him to do.

Michael entered his study and closed the door firmly behind him before letting out a sigh that emptied his lungs. What was wrong with him? Had he lost every last ounce of the common sense he'd been graced with at birth? Or had he been pretending to have common sense all this time and suddenly realized that he didn't have any after all?

If Rosemary hadn't stepped away from him, he would have kissed her. Kissed her thoroughly and completely. She knew it, too. The look of shock in her eyes had nearly gutted him and was filling him with regret so deep he sank into a chair.

He owed her a sincere apology. It wasn't her fault that he suddenly found her irresistible. That was all on him, and there was no explanation as to why it had happened, either. He was perfectly content without a woman in his life. Perfectly content to let that state continue for at least a few more years. Yes, he was putting off the inevitable, but the alternative had too many possible repercussions that he wasn't willing to experience again.

Somehow, he'd forgotten all that over the weekend. He'd let other things cloud his mind. Things he must remedy.

As it turned out, that would take longer than he'd expected. By the time he'd gone in search of Rosemary again, to apologize and explain that she didn't need to assist him while he was in London, she was gone.

Her family had left for London, prior to the noon meal and the afternoon entertainment. Although he hadn't needed confirmation, he now had proof that his actions had made her uncomfortable and that she couldn't wait to get away from him fast enough.

"Evidently, Lady Havenshire was worried about her son," his mother said. "It appears that Thomas had the sniffles before they left."

Michael considered that a likely excuse, for despite what had happened and all that he now understood, he hadn't forgotten how infuriated Lady Havenshire had been last night. In his mind, their early departure had nothing to do with the Havenshires' young son.

"I offered to allow Rosemary to travel to London with us later today, but she declined," his mother said.

Of course she'd declined. He was the reason.

"Oh, and Lettice has decided to join us in London," his mother added.

Michael nodded, more concerned about what Rosemary could be facing than who would be joining them in London. With the earl in the coach, he doubted that Lady Havenshire would say or do much of anything, but once she had Rosemary alone, the woman could seek retribution.

He should have spoken to Havenshire this weekend, shared his concerns about Rosemary. That would have been the best thing to do, but he hadn't done that. Instead, his need to protect her had kept her at his side, an act which had been unfair to her. "I believe I'll leave for London now," he told his mother. "Get an early start on the work I need to complete. Please make my excuses to the guests."

"Of course, dear," she replied. "I'm sure that Geoffrey won't mind escorting us to the city."

He nodded and took his leave.

Within an hour, he and Atlas were on their way to London. During his ride, he formulated his plan to pay a visit to Havenshire this evening and, if the opportunity arose, to apologize to Rosemary. He'd also let her know that her assistance was no longer needed.

That was where his other plan came into play. Geoffrey's reputation needed to be made right, and the best way to do that was by the word of influential people.

He would introduce Geoffrey to those people. People who, once they got to know Michael's future brother-in-law, would put a stop to the rumors about him. His plan had been to do that by attending a few social events, and having Rosemary attend with him would have made things easier. On him. Attending social functions alone would make it appear as if he was looking for a future duchess, which simply wasn't true.

His thoughts continued along those lines as he rode, of his nonexistent search for a future duchess, of righting Geoffrey's reputation and of Rosemary.

She was nothing like Martha. The two had no resemblance in personality or looks. Nor in their goals for life. Martha had wanted to become a duchess. Wanted the prestige and money and had been willing to do anything to get it. Whereas Rosemary had no desire for such things. She merely wanted the opportunity to be herself again. Free to laugh and dream and live. Everything that was currently being stifled.

He'd wanted to help her find those things again this weekend but had failed. Failed because his baser instincts had set in.

That had started before he'd seen her in that purple dress. For whatever reason, seeing her as a grown woman had hit him hard. A simple dress didn't have that kind of power. It was nothing more than material. So there, too, he was simply making excuses for himself. Excuses for the powerful jealousy he'd felt.

A raindrop—actually, more than one—pulled him from his musing. It was a warm day, so a passing shower wasn't enough to slow him down, but a few drops quickly turned into a downpour. The storm then progressed to bolts of lightning, and he was grateful to be so close to a wayside inn.

It was a simple establishment, one that offered a warm meal and a clean bed for travelers en route to and from London. Josiah McMillian was the innkeeper, and Michael knew the man wouldn't mind if he put Atlas in the stable until the storm let up. He'd barely turned off the road when the stable door opened, and through the pouring rain, he saw Josiah's young son, Trenton, wave him inside.

"Thank you," Michael said upon entering the stable and dismounting.

"You're welcome, Your Grace," the lad replied. "I'll unsaddle him and dry him off. You can go on inside the inn and dry off yourself."

"I will do just that," Michael said, ducking his head as he ran back out into the rain and across the gravel to the inn. There were so many puddles he didn't even try to leap over them, and by the time he arrived at the door to the inn, the brim of his wool felt hat was collecting more rain than it was repelling. Pulling it off his head, he gave it a solid shake before opening the door and, while stepping inside, he used his other hand to push his wet hair off his forehead.

His hand paused atop his head when he noticed the other occupants of the inn. He'd hoped that Rosemary and her family had been ahead of the storm, but it appeared as if they, too, had taken shelter from the worst parts of it. Even in the darkness of the room, lit mostly by the oil lamps flickering on the table, her beauty shone like the sun.

"Your Grace," Josiah greeted. The portly man held out a towel with one hand and took Michael's hat with his other hand. "Welcome. Come in and dry off."

Shaken from his stupor, Michael said, "Thank you." He took the towel and gave his head a good rubbing. "Trenton has my horse in the stable."

"Very good, very good. We have a few others in there today, getting away from the thunder and lightning. In here, too. I believe you know the Earl of Havenshire and his family."

"I do." Michael handed the towel back to the innkeeper.

Rosemary had risen from her chair and was walking towards him with worry filling her brown eyes. "Is something amiss at Turnbill?" she asked.

"No, not at all." It was difficult not to reach out and touch her, for she was close enough. Instead, he used his hands to brush water droplets from his jacket. "I merely decided to leave for London early."

"Join our table, Your Grace," Havenshire invited.

For the first time since entering, Michael noticed other patrons seated throughout the large room. With a nod towards a few familiar faces, he followed Rosemary as she walked back to the table. "Thank you. It appears the storm caught several of us by surprise."

"It was all our driver could do to keep the horses from bolting when the thunder and lightning began," Havenshire said.

"It struck quickly," Michael said, holding the back of Rosemary's chair until she was seated, then he sat beside her.

"Hopefully, it will pass just as quickly," Lady Havenshire said. "We need to get home. I explained to your mother that our son had the sniffles before we left."

Michael couldn't miss Rosemary's frown and wasn't sure if she was hoping he believed the excuse or was afraid that he didn't. "I was informed of that and do hope Thomas is doing well when you arrive home."

"I'm sure he will be," Havenshire said. "Rosemary stated your family would be visiting London. We'd be honored to host a dinner party for all of you while you're in town."

Josiah set a plate in front of Michael filled with a hearty-looking chicken stew with peas and carrots, as well as a cup of tea. After thanking the innkeeper,

Michael said, "Not knowing their schedules, I'm not at liberty to accept invitations on behalf of my mother, sister or aunt but will certainly relay the message and have them reply." With a nod towards their half-eaten plates, he said, "Please, finish your meals. I happen to know that Mrs. McMillian is an excellent cook."

"It is very tasty," Havenshire said.

As they ate, Havenshire spoke about how much they had enjoyed weekend and his joy of riding for pleasure. They discussed a few other subjects, including the weather, while rumbles of thunder were still making the windows rattle.

The meal had long since been over and additional cups of tea had been consumed by the time a hint of sunlight gradually graced the windows. Rosemary had barely spoken, and Michael had done his best to keep his eyes from roaming to her. She was clearly uncomfortable. He knew why and didn't want to worsen the situation.

As soon as the storm had fizzled into a lingering shower, he prepared to leave. Havenshire stated they would be departing, too, and Michael took advantage of the two of them walking towards the innkeeper together. "Would it possible for me to visit your home this evening?" he asked. "I have something I would like to discuss with you."

"Most certainly. Come for dinner."

"That's not necessary," Michael said. "It won't take long."

"Very well, then," Havenshire stated. "Six?"

"I will see you then," Michael said. After paying the innkeeper for his hospitality, Michael accepted his still wet hat and exited the building. He had half a mind to ride slowly, to make sure the rest of Rosemary's trip to London was uneventful, but knew that was coming from the half of his mind that couldn't stop thinking about her. He had to get control over that. Control over other things, too.

Hours later, upon his arrival at the London house, he discovered that the messenger he'd sent to inform the household staff of their pending arrival had not encountered the storm. Everything was fully prepared for the entire family, including a room for Aunt Lettice. He thanked the staff for being so efficient and then proceeded to his upstairs bedroom to change out of the clothes that had dried on his body during his travels.

Afterwards, he retired to the back parlor to wait until it was time to visit Havenshire. He didn't want to insult the man, nor his wife for that matter, but he couldn't live with the idea of Rosemary being mistreated in any way.

Rosemary stared out the window of the coach, pretending to be captivated by the scenery as they slowly made their way towards London. She had noticed a rainbow shortly after leaving the inn, but not even the colorful display could lighten her mood or stop her from thinking about Michael.

She'd been shocked to see him walk through the inn door, and then worried, and then embarrassed all over again by her behavior in the grand hall this morning.

Once again, she wondered about Martha. If Michael had kissed her. Surely, he had. Surely, he'd kissed other women, too, for there had been a time, before he was the duke when he'd attended balls with numerous different partners. That was before she and Nora were old enough to attend, and once in a while, Maud would permit her to spend the night at the Knight town house when the entire family was in London. Nora would talk then about Michael and how their Aunt Lettice said his good looks attracted girls to him like bees to flowers.

Rosemary had forgotten about that.

Was that what had happened to her? That his good looks were simply too irresistible to women. And girls, because she'd thought he was handsome long before he'd grown into a man. Back when she used to dream of growing up and getting married. Before she knew that marriage could cause more harm than good.

She let her gaze leave the window for a moment. Her father was dozing, with his arms crossed over his chest and the back of his head resting against the carriage wall. Maud was sitting beside him, staring out the window on her side of the coach.

Rosemary turned back to the window before Maud could sense her gaze and cast yet another disparaging scowl her way. There had already been plenty since leaving Turnbill. After all these years, she should be used to them. Perhaps she was, because they no longer sent her scurrying as they once had.

At first, she'd tried to do everything possible to please Maud. When that hadn't happened, she'd learned to just avoid her stepmother as much as possible.

That had become increasingly easier once Thomas was born. Maud had been so busy basking in having delivered the perfect baby that she hadn't had time to care about what her stepdaughter was doing.

Everything changed again when Thomas grew past the age when he only ate, slept and pooped. With the nursemaid caring to most of his needs, Maud was again aware of a stepchild underfoot and started suggesting boarding school. Rosemary couldn't imagine being away from her father and focused on doing everything she could to be needed. She helped the nursemaid, the household maids and cooks. Anything Maud complained about having to see to, Rosemary would do. Not even that had pleased Maud, and it was still that way.

This was the first weekend in a long time where she hadn't worried if the menu was being followed or if the windows had been washed or if any dust had accumulated under the furniture. She didn't mind doing any of those things. In fact, she took pride in knowing the house was well maintained. She also enjoyed seeing that her father and Thomas were well taken care of.

Thomas had not had the sniffles when they'd left home, either. She wouldn't have left if there was a chance that he was ill. That had merely been Maud's excuse for them to leave early. Nora had been so disappointed, and it had been difficult to decline the dowager duchess's offer for her to ride with them to London later today.

If she hadn't so thoroughly embarrassed herself earlier, she might have accepted the offer. But she had known she needed more time before facing Michael again.

Luck, along with the weather, had chosen not to give her the time she needed. Or perhaps it was just fate's way of showing her that there would never be enough time. What was she going to do? For she would surely see him while he was in London. Furthermore, she'd already promised to continue to help him determine if Geoffrey was the right husband for Nora.

Somehow, for some truly inexplicable reason, that, too, had been another thing she'd overlooked this weekend. Nora marrying the wrong man. She shouldn't have, because that had been her strongest motive for going to Turnbill for the weekend.

When had that changed?

Why had that changed?

Chapter Ten

Thomas was overjoyed to see them and showed no signs of the sniffles, just as Rosemary had known. He talked nonstop while she was unpacking, telling her all about how Joelle had taken him to the park and that they'd seen a dog hiding in the bushes. Joelle hadn't let Thomas get close, but he was sure it just wanted to be petted and asked if Rosemary would *please* take him to the park to see if the dog was still there.

"I just arrived home, darling," she replied. "And it's too late to go to the park today."

"Tomorrow?" he asked.

"We'll have to see," she replied, smoothing the skirt of the dress she'd just hung up in her wardrobe closet.

"See what?" he asked, with a frown knitting the brows above his adorable brown eyes.

He was standing beside her trunk, watching as she lifted each gown out, then spinning around to watch her hang it in her wardrobe. Walking back to the trunk, she touched the tip of his nose. "What the weather is like for one. It might rain tomorrow." It was the only excuse she could think off at the top of her head. Perhaps because of the part the weather had played in her fate today.

"No, it won't."

"It won't?" she asked, smiling at how he was shaking his head.

"Nope."

He couldn't know that, nor could he know that her true reason was that she wasn't sure if she'd feel up to walking past the Knight house tomorrow. "Well, we'll just have to see how good you are at predicting the weather."

"What's that mean?"

"How good of a guesser you are," she answered while bending down to take the last gown out of her traveling trunk. It was the blue one she'd been wearing when she'd fallen in the creek with Michael. Penny had seen that it had been washed and dried and had put it in the trunk for her.

A sigh escaped as she lifted the dress and gave it a shake to get rid of the creases from being folded and in the trunk.

"I'm a very good guesser," Thomas said. "Remember when— Wait, what's that?"

"What's what?" she asked.

"This." He bent over and picked something up off the floor.

It was a folded piece of waxed paper, and her breath

caught as he unfolded it. Tucked between the folds of paper was the little white-and-yellow weed-flower blossom that Michael had given her. The one whose stem she'd wrapped around a button, and Michael had straightened. She was amazed the blossom had survived the tumble into the creek.

Penny must have found it and thought it precious enough to press it between the waxed paper for her.

"It's a flower," Thomas said.

"It is." She held out her hand for him to set the paper and flower in her palm, not sure why her eyes were burning.

"Why are you saving it?" he asked.

"Because it reminds me of a special day and someone special." She carried it to her dressing table and laid it next to a small bowl holding hair pins before carrying the dress to her wardrobe.

"Who?" he asked, while crossing the room to her dressing table.

"Someone as handsome as you," she answered.

"It certainly is little," he said, staring at the flower. "Weren't there any big flowers in the country?"

She walked over and ruffled his hair while kneeling down in front of him. "Yes, there were, but sometimes, the smaller ones are more precious." Pulling him into a hug that turned into kissing his cheek and tickling his sides, she added, "Like you."

When the tickling ended and his delightful giggles

stopped, he asked, "If it's not raining tomorrow, can we go to the zoo?"

"The park and the zoo?"

He shrugged. "Just the zoo. Joelle couldn't take me there."

That was a very easy request. "Yes, if it's not raining, we will go to the zoo."

"And see Drake?"

"I don't know if Mr. Taylor will be there or not, but Hugo will be."

"Yay! I love Hugo!"

"I know you do." She stood up and patted his shoulder. "Now, it's time for you to go spend some time with Papa and your Mama." She did her best to see that he spent time with both their father and Maud whenever possible. "You haven't seen them all weekend, and they've missed you dearly."

"Are you coming?"

"Not yet, I still have some more unpacking to do." At his frown, she added, "But if you mind me now, I promise that I will ask if you can sit with us at dinner."

"At the big table?"

He enjoyed that much more than eating alone in his room, and though dinner wasn't served until seven, which was close to his bedtime, she hoped that she could convince Maud that it would be appropriate for him to join them since they'd been gone all weekend. "Yes, at the big table." Then with a warning tone, she added, "That means you'll need to put on a jacket and use your best manners."

"I know!" he shouted, running to the door.

She smiled, walking to the door he'd left open, then watched him skitter down the hall to the stairway before stepping back into her room. After closing the door, she walked straight to the dressing table to stare at the tiny weed flower. Poignant memories made her eyes sting again, and knowing this, too, was something she had to tuck away, she folded the waxed paper back over the flower, then put it in a side drawer on the table.

After unpacking the small carrying bag that contained her hairbrush and hand mirror, as well as other small essentials, she made her way downstairs. Maud would be more likely to answer positively about Thomas joining them for dinner if the request was made in front of her father.

After making a brief stop in the kitchen to confirm all had been well during their absence and that dinner would be served at seven, she approached the front parlor. She could hear voices coming inside and smiled as it became clear that Thomas was repeating his dog-hiding-in-the-bushes story.

Thomas was sitting on their father's lap, explaining how he was certain the dog wanted him to pet it when Rosemary entered the room. Maud was sitting in the chair beside their father, and Rosemary walked over to the small, upholstered settee.

"Did Joelle allow you to pet it?" Maud asked.

"No." Thomas sighed. "She didn't let me get close to it. If it's not raining tomorrow, I'm going to go see if it's still there."

"Why would you think it's going to rain tomorrow?" their father asked.

"I don't," Thomas replied. "Rosemary does."

Father laughed as he winked at her, understanding that had merely been an excuse she'd made. "I see," Father said. "She might be right. It could be raining."

"I hope not," Thomas said. "Rosemary said she'd take me to the zoo! I haven't seen Hugo in weeks!"

"I believe you mean days," Father said. "As I recall, Rosemary took you to the zoo last week."

Rosemary nodded, having taken him to the zoo on Thursday to make up for being away from him all weekend.

"You certainly love that elephant, don't you?" Father asked.

Thomas nodded. "Oh, yes, it's the first one I've ever seen."

"It's the first one to be at the zoo," Father said.

"I know! That's why it's the first one I've ever seen!"

Rosemary laughed along with her father and was touched slightly at the way even Maud laughed.

"You should see him someday, Papa," Thomas said. "You, too, Mama. Hugo is humungous. That's why he's named Hugo, because he's so huge!"

It appeared to be the perfect opportunity for her to

make her request, and Rosemary smiled at Thomas. "Father, Maud, since we've been gone all weekend, and someone has clearly missed us, would it be possible for Thomas to join us for dinner in the dining room this evening?"

"I think that would be fine," Father said. "I think your mother would think it's fine, too, if she received a kiss on the cheek."

Thomas scooted off their father's lap and quickly onto Maud's where he promptly kissed her cheek. "Can I, Mama?"

Giving him a solid hug, Maud replied, "Yes, you can."

"Thank you, Mama. I promise to use my best manners and to wear a jacket."

"Oh, dear, I do hope we still recognize you," Father said.

"You will," Thomas assured him, "because I won't have a hat on. People always look different when they have a hat on. I think it's because you can't see their hair and…"

While Thomas was still explaining his reasonings about hats, a knock sounded on the door. Rosemary couldn't imagine who would be calling at six on a Sunday evening without an invitation, but neither her father nor Maud appeared surprised or confused.

A moment later, Rosemary's heart leaped into her throat and then sank to her stomach when Richard, their butler, announced the Duke of Turnbill was here to see her father.

"Show him in, Richard," her father replied.

As Michael passed through the massive front entranceway of Havenshire, he couldn't help but look up, past the chandelier to the small balcony two stories up where the two curving staircases met. He could imagine Rosemary standing on that balcony, looking down at who was entering. Perhaps because that had happened more than once when he visited the home with his family years ago, when her mother had been alive. Upon seeing them, Rosemary would let out an excited squeal and come running down the steps.

How could he remember her as such a young girl and now think of her as a woman? It seemed like it should be impossible, but it wasn't. She had grown into a beautiful lady.

"Right this way, Your Grace," said Richard, the same butler as back then, with a wave of his hand indicating the left hallway as they passed under the balcony. "They are in the main parlor."

"I remember the way," Michael said. "Thank you."

With a nod, the butler bowed and stepped aside.

Michael continued down the hall to the first room on the left and paused in the doorway. The family—the earl, his wife holding her young son on her lap, and Rosemary—were all seated together and looked to be enjoying their first evening home.

Had he expected otherwise?

Yes, he had.

"Your Grace," the earl said, rising to his feet and giving a slight bow. "Please come in. You remember my son, Thomas. He was just telling us how people are unrecognizable when they wear a hat."

Michael grinned at the boy, who, with his corn-colored hair and big brown eyes, was as adorable as Rosemary had proclaimed. "I do remember Master Thomas, and may I say that I'm glad I'm not wearing a hat, for I wouldn't want to be unrecognizable."

"It would have to be next time I see you," Thomas explained, "because I've never seen you before." A frown overtook his entire face as he asked, "Have I?"

"I believe it was when you were a small baby." Michael stepped into the room. "Now you've grown into a striking young lad, and I am happy to make your acquaintance again this evening."

Maud whispered something in Thomas's ear and Thomas crawled off her lap, clicked his heels together and performed a very straight-backed and stiff bow. "Your Grace."

Michael gave a bow of acknowledgment. Then he acknowledged the others in the room by saying, "Lady Havenshire, Lady Rosemary."

Both ladies responded with a dip of their chins, before the earl asked, "Would you care for a drink, Your Grace?"

"No, thank you," Michael replied, doing his best to keep his gaze from lingering on Rosemary.

"Very well. If you ladies will excuse us, the duke and I have something to discuss," Havenshire said. "We can speak in the study."

Michael gave a parting nod to the others and followed the earl from the room. "I'm glad to see Thomas appears to be in the best of health," he said as they walked farther down the hallway.

"Oh, yes, he's just fine. He would have enjoyed being in the country for the weekend as much as the rest of us did."

"Do you not visit your country estate?"

"My schedule doesn't allow that more than a couple times a year. Just enough to remember what it looks like. I have an excellent land steward who oversees the property."

"I recall Rosemary enjoying your country estate," Michael said.

"She does." Havenshire entered a room and waited for him to enter before closing the door behind them. "I've suggested that she go stay there, for I know she misses the country, but, well… She's quite committed to Thomas. Which is why I insisted that we attend your event this weekend and was so delighted to see her enjoying herself."

This room was much like Michael remembered, with heavy wood and leather chairs, a large table and shelves of reading material. His father and the earl had played many friendly games of poker in this room and had often included him in the games.

He paused near the table that the earl gestured toward. "We enjoyed having all of you at Turnbill this weekend, and please don't feel an invitation is necessary for you to visit."

"Thank you." The earl stopped near the long credenza and uncorked a crystal container. "Please, take a seat."

Michael sat and considered the best way to broach the subject of his visit while the earl poured amber liquid into two glasses and carried them to the table.

Setting one in front of him, the earl then sat in an adjacent chair and set his own glass down. "Dare I say, I'm quite honored by your visit, Michael."

The earl had always called him by his given name in private. "I'm honored that you agreed to see me, Ralph," he said in return, letting the man know they were meeting as friends.

"Your father and I discussed this, as did Amelia and Beatrice. Many times."

Michael was confused. To what was Ralph was referring? His mother and father had been close friends with both the earl and his wife, and no doubt would have talked about many things. "This?"

Ralph nodded. "Of course, we would never have forced anything upon either of you."

Confusion deepening even further, Michael said,

"My apologies, I'm not quite following what you're referring to."

"Forgive me," Ralph said, frowning. "I was assuming you were here to discuss Rosemary."

"I am," Michael said.

They sat in a stilled, thick silence for a few moments, before Michael felt a shiver coil around his spine. His preoccupied mind had completely overlooked, or perhaps ignored, exactly what his visit could appear to be to Ralph.

It appeared as if Ralph had just figured out the same thing. Relatively the same thing. The same subject anyway. "You aren't here to—"

"No, I'm not," Michael said. "My apologies."

"No, I'm the one who needs to apologize. Call me an old man who had gotten his hopes up too quickly."

"I was not aware that was something you and my father spoke of," Michael said, fully understanding the two couples had discussed their children, he and Rosemary, one day marrying. He'd never heard a word of such an expectation.

"Quite often. You were always so protective of her and generous in granting her every wish. Obviously, I misread your attention to her this weekend as something more, and I shouldn't have, considering it's been years since the two of you saw one another." Ralph took a sip from his glass. "So, why are you here? Did she do something to upset you this weekend?"

"No, not at all. Quite the opposite. I saw her as the

young girl I remember, now grown up, of course, full of life and adventure."

"That's what I saw, too," Ralph said. "Hence the reason why I really put my foot in it by assuming too much."

"I can understand how, as friends, you would want to see your children..." Michael couldn't say the word. It was sure to conjure up more thoughts about her, more visions, and he had more than enough running wild inside his head right now.

"Married," Ralph supplied. "We did. But have no fear, we never created a formal betrothal. We just hoped the two of you would fall in love and marry someday. Since that is clearly not the case, what is it that you want to discuss about Rosemary?"

"Well, I do not wish to raise your ire, but to be completely frank, over the weekend I witnessed her stepmother, Lady Havenshire, embarrass Rosemary on two separate occasions in ways that were quite unseemly."

Ralph sat back in chair and rubbed his clean-shaven chin with one hand. The man's once blond hair was now completely gray, and his brown eyes, which Rosemary had indeed inherited, didn't once blink as he stared across the table. "Would you care to elaborate?"

"Once she scolded Rosemary loud enough for many to hear about getting a smudge on her dress, and another time she informed several people that Rosemary can't carry a tune." Michael realized that neither incident sounded as crude as they'd truly been, therefore he added, "Because I understand she is your wife and do not wish to insult her or you, I will not describe either incident further, but want you to know, they were not slight reprimands."

Ralph nodded as he leaned forward and placed both hands on the table. "I have lived in this house for over seven years with Maud and Rosemary. Do you truly believe that I am not aware of the tenuous relationship between the two of them?"

Michael's spine stiffened. "I would hope not, but question why you would let it continue."

Ralph shook his head. "Trust me, it's been the most difficult situation I've ever encountered. Maud entered a home that a twelve-year-old girl had been running for a year and half. After Amelia's death, Rosemary took over all aspects of household management, overseeing everything, ensuring it continued to run smoothly and efficiently. Not wanting to upset Rosemary, Maud let that continue, except for when it was obviously necessary that she be seen as the lady of the house. Then, I'm afraid that Thomas's birth made it worse. Since about the day he was born, Rosemary has hovered over him like a mother hen."

Havenshire paused to take a sip from his drink, before continuing, "Now, don't get me wrong. Just as we all do, Maud has her faults, too. She could have tried a more assertive, more mothering approach, which is what I encouraged, and she tried, but that only alienated Rosemary further. When Rosemary refused a coming-out party two years ago and refused to attend social events unless I'm in attendance, both Maud and I grew worried that she would never be interested in marriage. Never have a life of her own. Maud believes that Rosemary is afraid, afraid to love anyone beside me and then Thomas, because she's fearful of losing someone she loves again, and I must say, that makes the most sense."

Michael felt some of his anger wither, yet was still quite put out by the insults he had heard from Maud. "That doesn't explain Lady Havenshire's behavior this weekend."

"Perhaps not to some, but in her own way, Maud is hoping that if she can make Rosemary defiant enough, she will seek a different life. One of her own. Where she's not taking care of her father and stepbrother, but of her own husband and child. I can see where that might appear harsh on Maud's part, but she's willing to let others believe that she's the evil stepmother that Rosemary has always cast her as, if it will help. We've tried everything else."

Rosemary did believe that Maud was an evil stepmother and had led others to believe it as well. Michael could make sense of what the earl was saying but still felt a strong need to defend Rosemary. "I believe Lady Havenshire may have been behind whoever knocked on Rosemary's door the other night."

"You would be correct."

"Why?"

Ralph's face grew a bit sheepish. "To create a touch of jealousy. We had high hopes for the weekend, and when Bellview was the one to come to Rosemary's defense so quickly earlier in the evening…" He shrugged. "We didn't realize that there was a budding romance between Bellview and your sister until the following day."

Michael's mind was on one word. "Jealousy?"

Ralph nodded, and like before, they stared at each other for a moment before the truth struck Michael. They'd wanted to make him jealous. He hadn't needed any help, had managed that all on his own.

"A foolish idea, I know," Ralph said, "but, Michael, the girl has practically made herself a prisoner in this house. It's heartbreaking. Like every parent, I want to see her happy and living life to the fullest, like she used to, like she did this weekend. That's the first time I've seen it in years. After Maud and I were married, Rosemary refused to visit Turnbill alone, and I believe that was because she thought I'd quit loving her if she wasn't here to show me how badly I needed her. I've tried to assure her that I'll always love her, but she turns it around as if I'm the one worried about losing her love and tells me that she'll never marry. Never leave Thomas and me. How can I fight a love that strong? If you know, please tell me, because I'm about at my wit's end. So is Maud. Despite how it appeared to you, Maud cares about Rosemary. Deeply. She wouldn't be living in this house if I didn't believe that with all that I am. Maud was the one who insisted that Thomas remain at home this weekend, for if he hadn't, Rosemary would have spent all weekend seeing to his needs rather than enjoying herself. Maud also suggested that we leave early this morning, hoping that Rosemary would refuse, especially after how well the two of you had got along during the ball last night. We would have then allowed her to stay and travel back to London with your family. But she didn't oppose the idea at all."

"I guess that now I'm the one who has put my foot in it," Michael said, beginning to understand things differently than he'd assumed. Embarrassed by his assumption that Ralph wasn't aware of what was happening, or doing anything about it, he admitted, "I truly was seeing only one side." In truth, he'd been the one who was unaware and had made things worse by his protective actions over Rosemary.

"Life isn't simply black and white. There are many shades of gray mixed in, and sometimes, depending on whose side we are standing, we don't see the same shades as the other side. I commend you for coming to Rosemary's defense. It shows you're as protective of her now as you were years ago. I appreciate that. For she truly has a heart of gold. I just wish she'd think of herself, her own future, as much as she does mine and Thomas's, because for years, she hasn't."

"You could be right," Michael admitted aloud.

"I believe I am, but I don't know how to fix it. Now that I am aware that I've jumped to conclusion over your reason for us to meet, my only hope is that while Nora's in town the next few weeks, perhaps she'll convince Rosemary to attend some social events. The only places she goes is to the zoo and park with Thomas. She needs friends her age. A beau."

Michael felt a familiar stirring in his stomach at the word *beau* and told himself to stop it. He had no right or reason to be jealous. "I happen to know that Nora will be inviting Rosemary to join her for several social events. She's already mentioned a few."

"If Rosemary will go," Ralph said. "She's good at finding excuses. Earlier this year, Maud thought a trip to Paris might help them grow closer, but at the last minute, Rosemary refused to go because Thomas's governess announced she was leaving. The woman was willing to stay until they returned, and a new one was hired, but…" He shook his head. "It's difficult, Michael. I'm responsible for this entire situation. I let Rosemary become the lady of this house as a child. Was proud of the way she took over after Amelia died. I praised her constantly, thinking I was doing the right thing. It was Maud who made me see that Rosemary was still a child and should be allowed to be one. I'm afraid that by then, the damage was already done. No matter what we've tried, things have gotten worse."

Michael struggled with the thoughts bouncing

around his head. If not for the fact that he, too, wanted to see Rosemary happy, he might have wished Ralph well and left. As it was, it was clear that Ralph didn't know what to do and that he blamed himself. Add to that the fact that Michael could see how Rosemary saw things one way, that he'd seen things her way as well, that he'd finally seen Rosemary enjoy herself this weekend and that he had already asked her for his help, he had but one option.

Before giving himself time to weigh the consequences, he said, "Perhaps if I was to invite Rosemary to attend events with Nora and the Viscount of Bellview, she would be more inclined to agree."

The flash of hope in Ralph's eyes was impossible not to see. "I believe she would. I know it's a lot to ask, but considering you have no interest in her in that way, perhaps you could introduce her to some well-stationed men. Even if you just made her aware that there is a life outside of this house. A life she could enjoy if she'd let herself. I would be forever in your debt if you could manage that."

"I can't make any promises," Michael warned, "but I do plan on being in town for a few weeks. I have some things to see to."

"I won't ask for promises, Michael, but do hope with all that's in me that you can succeed where both Maud and I have failed."

Michael felt the sincerity coming from Ralph, yet also wondered if this was how a man felt when he'd just shot himself in the foot, because he knew this could put him in a precarious position. "I hope so, too."

"With that settled, I would like to mention one other matter," Ralph said.

Michael nodded, wondering what more there could possibly be.

Chapter Eleven

Though it would take little more than a few minutes, and she easily could have asked Joelle to see to the task, Rosemary had ushered Thomas upstairs to dress for dinner shortly after her father and Michael had left the front parlor. She couldn't fathom a reason for Michael to need to speak with her father, other than to inform her father of her behavior this morning. How she had practically begged him to kiss her. She couldn't believe that was something Michael would do, but even searching into the furthest recesses of her mind, she couldn't come up with another reason for him to be here.

Now, after redressing Thomas from chin to feet, combing his hair and washing his face and hands, there was still half an hour before dinner would be served, and she questioned what she could find to busy herself with until she was sure that Michael had left.

"Can I go downstairs now?" Thomas asked, still overly excited to be eating in the dining room.

"Yes, you may," she replied.

He ran to the door of his bedroom, then stopped and turned around. "Aren't you coming?"

"I'm going to speak with Joelle for a moment. I'll be along soon."

"All right!" he shouted, disappearing out of the door.

"He certainly is excited," Joelle said, picking up the pile of clothes that Thomas had removed to carry downstairs for cleaning.

"He is," Rosemary agreed. "How was he this weekend?"

"As delightful as ever," Joelle replied. "He's such a well-behaved little boy, and he certainly loves animals. The dog was quite intriguing to him."

Rosemary asked a few questions—concerning the dog and about how Thomas slept and what he'd eaten—until she couldn't come up with any more. Thoughts of Michael were still too strong, along with how she'd behaved over the weekend. Maud had yet to mention the purple gown and most likely wouldn't during dinner, not with Thomas in attendance. It could happen afterwards, but perhaps she could excuse herself to speak with the kitchen staff concerning the weekly menu as soon as dinner ended.

With a plan in place, she took her leave of Joelle and spent a few moments in her own room, making sure her hair was still pinned in place. Then, she took the tiny flower out of the drawer once more, just to examine it, before she placed it back in the drawer and left her room.

Surely Michael was gone by now.

She practically held her breath all the way down the staircase, listening for voices. It wasn't until she entered the hallway that she heard any, and then she smiled. It was only Thomas she heard, and he was talking about Hugo.

However, when she arrived at the doorway to the parlor, her smile faded, and her breath locked in her lungs. Thomas was talking about the elephant to Michael.

Her father and Maud were in the room, too.

"Michael has decided to join us for dinner."

Her heart was echoing so loudly in her ears, Rosemary barely recognized her father's voice. "Very well," she managed to say. "I'll inform the kitchen to set another place."

"I already have," Maud replied. "Come sit down, dear. Thomas was telling Michael all about Hugo."

Rosemary didn't have time to sort through all the questions bouncing about in her head because Thomas had run across the room and grabbed her hand.

"Come sit," he said. "Michael said he can go to the zoo with us tomorrow. He's seen an elephant, but he hasn't seen Hugo."

Michael was sitting in the chair nearest the small settee, which was the only place left. Cheeks burning, Rosemary took it. There would have been plenty of room for Thomas next to her, but he was clearly too excited to sit anywhere.

"Did the elephant you saw have tusks?" he asked Michael, but gave him no time to respond, before saying, "Hugo doesn't. Someone cut them off when he was little. That wasn't very nice."

"I agree," Michael said. "It wasn't."

"Do you know what they eat?" Thomas asked, and again continued talking before Michael could answer. "Grass and hay, leaves and twigs, bark and roots, and fruits and vegetables, the same ones we eat. They also drink water. Lots of water." Spinning about, Thomas then asked Rosemary, "Do you know where Michael lives? Can Mr. Adams drive to his house?"

Mr. Adams was their driver, but this time, it was Michael who spoke before she had a chance to respond.

"I can have my driver come here, to your house, and he can drive all three of us to the zoo," Michael said.

"Does he know where the zoo is?" Thomas asked.

"I'm sure he does," Michael replied.

Finding her voice, Rosemary said to Thomas, "Remember how we talked about the weather? We'll have to wait and see if it rains."

"It's not going to rain," Thomas said.

"We'll bring along some umbrellas," Michael said. "Just in case."

Luckily, Richard entered the room and announced dinner was ready to be served. Or maybe it wasn't so lucky, because as her father stood to escort Maud from the room, Michael rose, stepped over to the settee and held out a hand to assist Rosemary from her seat.

Thomas was already heading for the door, slowing down only when Father reminded him to walk.

Laying her hand on Michael's, she said, "Thank you."

Once they were walking towards the doorway, he said, "I hope you don't mind that your father invited me to dine with you tonight."

"Of course not. I'm happy that you can join us, but I should explain that Thomas has been granted permission to eat with us in the dining room this evening."

"Maud explained that, and that it was a special treat that he really enjoys. I can relate to that. I enjoyed becoming old enough to eat with my parents."

She couldn't think of a reply. Actually, she couldn't think at all. His hand was on her elbow, and after dancing with him last night, one would think that wouldn't affect her. One would be wrong.

However, by the time the meal was over, Michael's friendly, natural way had made her forget the qualms and fears that had plagued her all day. He easily led conversations that included Thomas, and often had everyone laughing. It had made the meal progress so quickly, she was almost as sad as Thomas when it was over, they'd returned to the parlor, and he had to tell them all good night.

Thomas was happy though, when Michael said he would be there at one o'clock tomorrow, rain or shine.

Thomas then left the room holding Joelle's hand with a wide smile on his face.

"You have made him one happy boy," her father said to Michael.

"I look forward to seeing Hugo," Michael said. Then, with a nod in each of their directions, he said, "Thank you for the wonderful meal. I really must take my departure. My family will have arrived in London by now."

"Rosemary, would you care to walk Michael to the door?" Maud asked.

Knowing there could only be one answer, Rosemary rose from her seat. "Of course." She was no longer nervous and appreciated that. They had been friends for so long, and she truly didn't want that to change. Maybe she'd only imagined that he'd known what she had been thinking this morning. If that had been the case, she might have stayed at Turnbill to see the magician. Then again, she wouldn't have wanted Thomas to worry when his parents had arrived home without her. Now that she was back home, all those silly thoughts she'd had over the weekend would cease, because there were so many other things for her to focus on. Important things.

There were a few more parting words from her father, then she and Michael left the room.

"I do hope I won't be intruding tomorrow," Michael said as they entered the hallway.

"No, not at all. I just hope you won't regret offering to join us." Her own words surprised her, yet it was the truth.

"Never. It's been years since I was at the zoo. I used to love going there as a child. You did, too."

His smile not only filled his face, it made his eyes sparkle, and she could remember the trips they'd taken there with his family. Suddenly, she was as excited to go with him tomorrow as Thomas. "I still do."

"I know."

"How could you know that?"

"Because I'm clever," he said.

She laughed.

"You don't agree?"

"I agree, but I also remember how much you disliked the reptile house."

He shook his head. "I believe that was you."

"No, it wasn't. You wouldn't let Nora and me go inside the building because you were afraid."

His sideways glance included a wink. "I didn't let the two of you go inside, because I had been in there and didn't want you to get scared by the snakes and lizards."

"Likely story," she said, yet a faint memory was forming which said he could be telling the truth, because that was exactly the kind of thing he would have done. "We'll find out tomorrow, won't we?"

He nodded. "If you want to enter the reptile house, I won't stop you."

They had arrived in the entranceway where Richard was standing ready to open the door. Stopping in the center of the room, she asked, "Will *you* enter?"

With a grin, he said, "We'll see tomorrow. I'll arrive by one."

"We'll be ready," she said, and watched as he walked to the door with her heart beating faster than it should. There was a happiness inside her again, like she'd experienced while at Turnbill.

She and Thomas were ready when Michael's coach arrived precisely at one o'clock the following day. While Thomas raced down the stairway, clearly ecstatic that the waiting was over, Rosemary held her composure and stood at the center of the two stairways, on the small railed balcony that overlooked the entrance way.

A sense of pride rose up in her when Thomas, despite his excitement, clicked his heels and gave a bow when Michael entered the house.

"Good day, Master Thomas," Michael said. "Are you ready for our outing?"

"Yes, Your Grace," Thomas replied.

"And your sister," Michael said, glancing up at her. "Is she ready?"

"I am," she replied, turning to proceed to the stairway. She'd questioned the rationality of having him join them today, because she didn't want to damage their friendship again. This morning, she'd concluded that now that she was aware of the danger, she simply wouldn't let it happen again. Never again would she think about kissing him.

"I am happy to say we won't need umbrellas," Michael said. "The sun is shining brightly."

"I had noticed as much," she said, slowly making her way down the steps.

Michael was waiting at the bottom step, with a hand extended out for her to take. A thrill shot through her from head to toe. But his attention, even just the smallest of actions, had always made her feel special, so that wasn't anything to worry about.

"Nora sends her regards," he said as she stepped off the last stair. "She was not able to join us today but asked if we could make a short stop at our house after our visit to the zoo."

A wave of something she couldn't quite explain—perhaps a mixture of panic and regret—washed over her. Although she would like to see Nora as much as possible, she had duties here at home that couldn't be disregarded due to social events. Thomas needed her, as did her father. "I don't—"

"Excuse me," Maud said, stepping into the entranceway. After a slight curtsy, she continued, "I simply want to say goodbye." Maud lowered herself and held her arms out towards Thomas, who quickly ran over to give her a hug.

"I had just mentioned that my family would like us to stop off at our house after we've completed our visit to the zoo," Michael said to Maud.

"Oh, how nice," Maud replied. "It's a lovely day to be out and about."

Rosemary wasn't sure if Maud was mocking her for saying it might rain today or if she was hinting to join them. Either way, Rosemary said, "That will depend on how tired Thomas is."

"I won't be tired," Thomas immediately piped up. "I never get tired."

"We know you don't," Maud said, patting his head. "You be a good boy and mind Rosemary."

"I will."

"Shall we?" Michael asked.

Rosemary nodded and took a hold of Thomas's hand as they walked to the door.

Moments later, the carriage was filled with questions from Thomas, everything about the coach and the horses pulling it to the many different animals they would see at the zoo. Rosemary was impressed by how patient Michael was in answering and providing thoughtful questions to Thomas in return. She was thankful, too, because Thomas's constant chatter kept her mind from roaming.

That didn't stop when they arrived at the zoo. As soon as they were through the main gate, Thomas became a miniature expert on animals, exotic and domestic, including those in the reptile exhibit.

"We can leave anytime you are feeling uncomfortable," she said to Michael while Thomas was busy touching a snake that a zoo worker was holding.

With a devilish gleam in his eyes, Michael asked the employee, "Could the lady hold the snake?"

Rosemary gasped. "Absolutely not."

"Are you sure?" he asked, with a brow raised.

"Yes," she replied.

"Never mind," he told the employee before asking her, "Scared?"

"No, I'm not scared, I simply wouldn't want to scare the snake."

He laughed and then laid a hand on Thomas's shoulder. "What are we going to see next?"

"The hippopotamus!" Thomas replied.

"Lead the way," Michael told Thomas.

As they left the reptile exhibit, which she tolerated for Thomas's benefit because some of the creatures did make her quiver, Rosemary accepted that this visit would rank as one of her favorites. Not only was Thomas having the time of his life in sharing all he knew with Michael, she was enjoying Michael's companionship. He acted as if he'd forgotten their encounter in the great hall, and she sincerely hoped it stayed that way.

"I assumed the elephant would be the first animal we visited," Michael said as they walked along the stone pathways between exhibits.

"He saves that for last, so he can spend the most

time there," she explained. "He's quite fascinated with Hugo."

"He's quite fascinated with all the animals, and knowledgeable. I must say, you've taught him well."

"Thank you."

"Do his parents ever join him on his zoo excursions?"

"No, Maud doesn't care for animals, and Father is too busy." She said no more but once again was reminded of just how bored her younger brother would be without her.

The hippopotamus was submerged in his pond, so it wasn't long before they made their way to the elephant house. The large enclosure behind the house was surrounded by a tall fence made of sturdy metal pipes, and as they approached, Thomas exclaimed, "Hugo's outside today!"

"Would you like me to lift you up so you can see better?" she asked.

"Yes!"

"Allow me," Michael said and hoisted Thomas not into his arms but onto his shoulders. "How's that?"

"Perfect! I can see everything from up here!" Thomas exclaimed. "Look, Rosemary, Drake is here! Drake! Drake!"

Michael couldn't say exactly what he felt as he saw Drake Taylor. His coal black hair was as recognizable as his happy-go-lucky grin. He'd missed the friendship they used to have, but considering he was the one to ruin it, he couldn't blame Drake for never wanting to talk to him again.

"If it isn't Mr. Thomas and Lady Rosemary," Drake said, approaching the fence. "Except Mr. Thomas has gotten a whole lot taller."

"No, I haven't. I'm just on Michael's shoulders!" Thomas explained.

The boy had an answer for everything, and nearly every one of his answers had made Michael smile, including his one. "There's no one on my shoulders," he said.

"Yes, there is." Thomas squirmed and bent down to look him in the eyes. "It's me, Thomas. Up here."

Michael laughed. "Someone *is* up there!"

"I do believe that is Thomas on your shoulders." Drake climbed through the sturdy pipes that made up the fence. "I'd recognize that towheaded little scamp anywhere."

"And I'd recognize you anywhere, Drake Taylor," Michael said, holding out a hand in friendship.

"As I would you." Drake gave his hand a solid shake and slapped his shoulder. "It's been too long, my friend."

"You're friends?" Thomas asked. "Drake's my friend, too!" After a pause, the boy added, "Isn't he, Rosemary?"

Michael's stomach sank as he noted the smile on Rosemary's face as she looked at Drake. He refused to acknowledge any other feelings. He couldn't warn off Drake as he had Rafael, because Drake and Rosemary obviously knew each other. His question quickly became, how well did they know each other?

"Yes, Mr. Taylor is your friend," she told Thomas.

"I have two friends!" Thomas proclaimed excitedly. "You're my friend, too, aren't you, Michael?"

"Indeed, I am," he answered. "I only let friends ride on my shoulders."

The elephant had followed Drake to the edge of the fence and had lifted its long trunk over the rail to rub Drake's back. Michael stepped closer so Thomas could touch the elephant as he asked Drake, "What are you doing here?"

"Well," Drake said, turning to rub the elephant's trunk, "technically, I still own this big boy here."

"Mr. Taylor is in the process of donating Hugo to the zoo," Rosemary said, "but hasn't agreed to it until he knows Hugo is comfortable here."

She was still smiling, and there was definite admiration in her tone and eyes, which Michael was doing his damnedest to not notice or react to. "How'd you end up with an elephant?" he asked. "Or do I not want to know?"

Drake laughed. "Saw him in Africa being used at the docks to unload cargo. I didn't like the way he was being treated, so I bought him. It wasn't an act that I clearly thought through. He eats upwards of two hundred pounds of food a day and drinks fifty gallons of water. Neither of which are readily available while a ship is at sea. Then, when we finally arrived in England, it became quite obvious that he couldn't live in my town house."

Knowing Drake, Michael didn't need to have him elaborate on the town house living. An elephant wasn't the first animal he'd hauled across the ocean, then needed to find a new home for.

"The trouble is, Hugo here took a liking to me and wouldn't eat for anyone else," Drake said. "He's improving. I only need to stop by every couple of days now."

"Makes being a sea captain difficult," Michael said.

Drake shrugged as he smiled and glanced at Rosemary. "I'm in town for a while."

Michael had questions but withheld asking them. He'd broken his friendship with Drake once over a woman and would never do that again. Not with any friend or over any woman. The past had taught him to be aware of his shortcomings and how to control them.

Mostly. He just needed extra restraint when it came to Rosemary.

"Come here, Mr. Thomas." Drake reached up and pulled Thomas off Michael's shoulders, then he climbed up to the second rung of the pipe fence and set Thomas on Hugo's back.

"Oh, Mr. Taylor, I don't think that's a good idea," Rosemary said. "Please lift him down."

"Aw, Rosemary, I'm fine!" Thomas disagreed.

So did Drake. "He's fine."

She looked at him, and the concern in her eyes had Michael putting his arm around her. "Drake wouldn't put any child in danger. Let him sit there."

"It's an elephant," she said.

"I know, and I know Drake."

Her fears seemed to settle as Hugo didn't move, other than his trunk which kept roaming over Drake's back. Drake stood on the fence, with his hands on the elephant's side, right below where Thomas was sitting.

"Have you known him long?" she asked.

"Who? Hugo or Drake?" Michael asked in return.

"I'm being serious," she said. "If something were to happen to Thomas—"

"Nothing is going to happen to him," he assured. "How long have you known Drake?"

"Only the past few weeks, since he brought Hugo here."

Michael appreciated that answer and tugged her a bit closer to his side. "I've known him for years. We attended school together, and he wouldn't put Thomas up there if he didn't completely trust Hugo."

"It still makes me nervous."

"It wouldn't have made you nervous when you were that age." An idea came to him, and without giving it a second thought, he grasped her behind the knees and lifted her into his arms.

"Michael! Put me down!"

"I will."

She wrapped her arms around his neck as he climbed up on the fence next to Drake. "You wouldn't dare!" she hissed.

"I dare," he said and set her on the elephant's back next to Thomas.

The boy was laughing and cheering, though she was still holding on to Michael's neck. "Scared?" Michael asked.

"No." She eased her hands off his neck and sat up straight, then grinned at Thomas.

"Isn't this grand?" Thomas asked with a beaming face as he looked around as if he was a king sitting on a throne.

"Just grand," she replied.

The smirk she flashed his way, her nose crinkled, made Michael laugh. He'd been awake half the night wondering if he'd made the right choice in agreeing to escort her around London, but now concluded that teaching her to have fun again, to think about herself, wasn't going to be so bad after all.

More than once since collecting her and Thomas from their house today, he'd witnessed her attempting to come up with excuses to avoid activities, even visiting his family, which was much like Ralph had said.

With that on his mind, he said to Drake, "Interested in coming to dinner one night this week?"

"I could be talked into that," Drake answered.

"Good." Now he'd just have to talk Rosemary into

it. Starting out small seemed like the perfect plan. Rather than worrying about her having a beau, maybe finding her one would be better. That could solve his problem, hers and her father's.

Chapter Twelve

Michael had always liked when a plan came together, but that wasn't the situation this time. Rosemary gave him every excuse under the sun as to why they couldn't stop at his house after the zoo and why she couldn't attend a dinner party tomorrow night. Every excuse was around Thomas. He could understand how much she cared about, loved, her younger brother, for the boy was a charmer and adored her as much as she did him, but Michael was very close to coming to the same conclusion as her father. Taking care of Thomas and the household was Rosemary's only focus.

"Fine," she finally said, casting him a look of frustration that was followed by a smile towards Thomas who was sitting beside her. "We can stop but only briefly. Thomas has lessons to see to yet this afternoon."

"I'd think riding an elephant was a good lesson for today," Michael replied.

Thomas nodded enthusiastically. "Me, too."

Rosemary frowned at him. "Riding an elephant is not educational."

"But it was enjoyable," Michael replied. "Even for you."

She pursed her lips, but he could tell that she was trying to hide a smile. "I would appreciate if you didn't tell people about that," she said.

"About you riding an elephant? Why not?"

Clearing her throat, she glanced at Thomas, then whispered, "Someone's mother would be very upset to hear about it."

"Well, I'm quite sure she will hear about it," he replied, glancing at Thomas. They both knew the boy was going to tell everyone about sitting on an elephant and that Rosemary had, too.

The visit with his family was brief, and as Michael delivered her and Thomas home, he was sure that she thought she'd convinced him that she couldn't attend his family dinner tomorrow evening. He was convinced that she could. And would.

Which was why at six o'clock the following evening, when she was summoned to the front parlor of her father's house, Michael was seated in a chair, smiling as she paused in the doorway.

"Michael," she said, glancing at her father, then her stepmother and then back to him. "What are you doing here?"

He stood, greeted her by saying, "Hello. You look

lovely, as always." She did look very beautiful. The gown she was wearing was silver in color, with white lace, and he couldn't ignore the reaction inside him every time he saw her.

In truth, those same reactions showed themselves when mere thoughts of her entered his mind. As did other reactions. The thought he'd had yesterday, about a possible connection between her and Drake had been diminished today when he'd sought out Drake and invited him to dinner this evening. Upon mentioning that she would be in attendance, Drake had been blunt in his assurances that he had no intentions towards her. That, although he found her pleasant and beautiful, he was as committed to his shipping company as ever, which also meant that other than an occasional encounter, there was no place for a woman in his life.

Drake had also commented that he wished Michael well in his pursuit of Rosemary. Michael had denied any pursuit. Once again, Drake had been blunt. Stating that was too bad, because she was the exact type of woman a duke would seek for a wife.

Michael had to admit that Drake was right, and seeing her now, looking so elegant and poised, that was confirmed even stronger.

Glancing at her family again, she crossed the room, stopped close to him and whispered, "I explained that I'm busy this evening."

"Doing what?" he whispered in return.

"You do look lovely, dear," Ralph said. "That's one of the dresses Maud brought you from Paris, isn't it?"

She pinched her lips together and briefly closed her eyes before looking at her father. "Yes, it is. Helen just completed the alterations and asked me to try it on." She then turned back to him. "That is what I'm busy with. Dress alterations."

"I don't see how that dress could fit you any better," he said. The shimmering material drew his eyes again, and his gaze followed the delicate lines of lace that were sewn down the front of the silver material, over her breasts, down her stomach, stopping at her trim waist. Even though he pulled his eyes off her exquisite curves as quickly as possible, a rush of heat was already shooting through his veins.

She was biting down on her bottom lip when their gazes met again, and she shook her head. "I've promised Thomas that I will eat in his room with him this evening."

"Don't let that stop you from going," Ralph said. "You don't want to disappoint Lady Nora."

"I don't want to disappoint, Thomas, either," she replied.

"He can eat with us again," Maud said. "In the dining room."

"I'm sure he'd enjoy that," Michael said. "Is he still talking about sitting on Hugo?"

"Hugo? The elephant?" Ralph asked.

Rosemary's eyes had grown as wide as saucers,

and Michael didn't pretend to hide his smile. "Yes, the elephant. It was perfectly safe. Hugo's owner was there the entire time."

"I can't believe he didn't tell us about that," Maud said.

"I'm sure he'll enjoy telling you about it at dinner," Michael said, staring at Rosemary, who was glaring back at him. "We really should be leaving now. We wouldn't want to keep the others waiting on our arrival."

"Most certainly," Ralph said. "Enjoy yourselves and say hello to your family from us."

Steering Rosemary around and towards the doorway, Michael said, "I will."

Once they were in the hallway, she whispered, "I can't believe you told them about that."

He knew she was referring to Thomas sitting on Hugo. "Why hadn't you? Or should I ask, why didn't you let Thomas tell them? It was the highlight of his day."

"Because they may not let him go back to the zoo again," she replied, still whispering and still mad.

Probably about as mad as he'd ever seen her, yet she continued to walk along beside him. "I highly doubt that," he replied. "They know how much he loves the zoo, and he wasn't in any danger."

"You don't know them like I do."

"Granted, that is true." He didn't want to push her too far, but she was never going to see what she was doing to herself if it wasn't pointed out. He knew that from experience. From when Drake had been courageous enough, or simply a good enough friend, to point out the truth to him about Martha. He'd apologized to Drake today, and they both confirmed it was in the past and held no bearing on their renewed friendship. "But they are Thomas's parents."

She clearly had a response to that but didn't say it because they'd entered the entranceway where a maid was waiting with a short cape that matched the dress.

Thanking the maid, he took the cape, draped it around Rosemary's shoulders and fastened the clasp beneath her neck.

The butler was there, too, and opened the door.

Michael thanked him as they stepped outside.

Once the door was closed behind them, and they were walking down the outside steps, she said, "I am his sister, and just like you protected your sister, I protect him."

"I never protected Nora from our parents."

"You had a very different situation."

"True again," he said, nodding at the footman holding open the coach door. He took ahold of her elbow as she stepped inside the coach, then climbed in and sat on the seat across from her.

She was purposefully not looking at him, staring out the window instead.

"I'm sorry," he said, deeply meaning it. "It was not my intent to upset you."

Arms crossed, she said, "It was not my intent to join you for dinner tonight."

"I'm well aware of that, but I don't understand why not. I thought you were looking forward to spending time with Nora while we are in town."

She let out a long sigh. "Things are different here than in than in the country."

Figuring he'd pushed her hard enough, he said, "Well, let me say again that you look very pretty. Your dress is lovely."

"It's gray," she said.

"I'd call it silver."

Turning from the window, her gaze settled on him. "Did you tell my father that you'd invited me to dinner tonight?"

"I sent a message to the house stating that I would arrive at six to pick you up."

"I didn't get a message."

"I addressed it to your father, seeking his permission."

Her expression didn't change, other than her cheeks puffed as she let out a sigh. "That explains why Helen brought this dress to me a short time ago, insisting that I try it on after she'd completed the alterations."

"You said you were still in the middle of the alterations."

Sighing again, she turned back to the window. "I know what I said."

He grinned, knowing that the alterations had been

nothing more than an excuse. He chose to be content with the silence between them, while wondering if he'd made the right decision in forcing her to come to dinner. He'd never known her to be one to hold a grudge but would know for sure soon enough.

He hoped that wouldn't be the case, because he did want her to have fun. To see that she was a young woman who should be enjoying this time in her life rather than committing herself to nothing more than running her father's household and seeing to the needs of her younger brother. Ralph was completely invested in her finding her own life and had agreed to pressure her into leaving the house, attending every function Michael had suggested. Maud had agreed, too, and the more he saw of her, the more he believed Maud was the evil stepmother in Rosemary's eyes only, because that was what Rosemary wanted her to be.

The other subject that Ralph had brought up for discussion the other night was Bellview and how the rumors circulating, that were damaging his reputation, were not true. Ralph had that on good authority, including his wife. As Bellview's aunt, Maud had known Geoffrey for years and insisted he was nothing like his father had been. Ralph had offered to help in any way possible to stop the naysayers.

Michael had told him that was why he was in town, and Ralph had agreed that attending social events with Geoffrey and Nora was the best way for people to learn the truth. He'd said Michael would be killing two birds with one stone.

Michael just wasn't sure if it was only two birds.

The more he learned, the more his feelings for Rosemary increased. A mixture of feelings. He'd spoken to Bellview today concerning Maud, and Geoffrey had confirmed that he'd been shocked by his aunt's actions at Turnbill, claiming he'd never known Maud to be anything but kind. He'd truly thought that it must have been too many glasses of wine to cause such a change in her.

Michael had also spoken to his own mother about Maud, who had also stated that despite Nora's beliefs, she'd personally never seen Maud's behavior towards Rosemary be unkind until at Turnbill last weekend.

Even Aunt Lettice had a fresh opinion on Maud. She'd stated that she'd listened to Nora's descriptions of Maud, which had all come from Rosemary, and that she should have known better, because Ralph had always been a good man and wouldn't have tolerated anyone mistreating his daughter.

All in all, he was as convinced as Ralph that Rosemary was seeing things the way she wanted to see them because she was afraid of seeing things any other way. Afraid of losing someone she loved again.

That left him wondering exactly what he was feeling towards Rosemary. Empathy, concern, worry or something deeper. Something he'd sworn to never feel towards a woman ever again.

* * *

Rosemary did her best to calm her shattered nerves as the coach rolled along the streets towards the Knight home. Michael wasn't making it easy. Being near him confused her. Confused so many things inside her. It made her question everything she knew about herself. That was what had happened at Turnbill, and she couldn't afford to let it happen again. The girl she'd remembered, and wanted to be again as soon as she'd entered Turnbill last weekend, didn't exist. She'd died along with her mother. That was when she'd had to grow up, learn to take care of her father, because he needed her. More than one person had told her that, including her own mother the night before she'd died.

Why didn't Michael understand that? Understand that she was needed at home.

She'd told him yesterday that she couldn't join his family for dinner this evening. The fact that everyone in the household had known he'd arrive by six explained why Helen had barely been able to hold in her excitement over how perfectly the gray dress fit.

The dress had been hanging in her wardrobe since Maud brought it home from Paris. Rosemary hadn't known the maid had taken it from her room, let alone made any alterations to it. She'd never tried it on before, yet had to admit that the dress did look prettier on than she'd imagined.

All in all, that goaded her. Maud had to have been

behind Helen's actions. As usual, she was trying to marry her off, get her out of the house. That had been her goal since she'd married her father. Maud had admitted as much. After the wedding, Maud had told her that she could now be a child again, that Maud was there to take care of both her and her father.

Rosemary had seen it for what it really was—Maud's plan for her to no longer be needed—and now Michael had fallen right into her trap.

Wouldn't that be the last laugh, if he fell in love with her and they did get married? That, of course, would never happen. The house would fall into disarray without her overseeing the management of it.

Furthermore, Michael would never think of her that way nor would she want him to, because, well, because she could never leave her father. Not even for Michael.

She couldn't believe that he'd mentioned that Thomas had sat on Hugo yesterday. Out of necessity, she'd told Thomas that was a secret for just the two of them to know. Maud could try to stop their visits to the zoo if she thought Thomas was in danger. He hadn't been and would be so upset if he wasn't able to visit the animals he loved so much.

Maud had tried to stop it before. Of course, she'd used the excuse that a young woman should be more interested in doing things with her own friends rather than only with her younger brother.

The more she thought about it, the more it saddened

Rosemary that Michael had betrayed her. It was almost as if he was on Maud's side.

By the time they arrived at the Knight home, she couldn't believe that she'd ever wanted Michael to kiss her. Now, she never wanted to see him again.

Her body didn't seem to agree with her mind, because as soon as he cupped her elbow to escort her into the house, heat ran up her arm straight to her heart, and it started beating erratically.

Nora opened the door as they reached the porch and rushed forward. "I knew Michael would convince Maud to let you come tonight."

Rosemary's cheeks grew warm. Nora would believe Maud would have been the reason for her not attending. Well, Maud *was* the reason, in a sense, but not in the way Nora meant.

"Yes, I did," Michael said, gesturing for them both to enter the house before him.

Nora kissed his cheek. "Thank you." Then, hooking her arm with Rosemary's as they walked over the threshold, she told Michael, "Drake and Geoffrey are in the front parlor with Mother and Aunt Lettice. We'll join you shortly."

The entranceway was as lovely as the rest of the house, with cream-colored silk wallpaper, ornate, molded trim and two large gilded mirrors, one on each wall, which was where Rosemary caught her reflection. She hadn't tried on the cape before, and noted that in the mirrors, the material did look silvery the way it shimmered in the light from the overhead chandelier.

"I love your dress and cape," Nora said. "It's gorgeous. Where did you get it?"

Rosemary had to admit, "Maud brought it home from Paris."

Nora looked shocked. "She let you borrow it?"

Unhooking the clasp on the cape, Rosemary shook her head. "No, it's one she brought home for me."

"Well, I'm thoroughly jealous," Nora said. "It's exquisite."

"I must admit that it didn't look this pretty until I put it on. It just looked like a gray dress." She removed the cape, which exposed the short, puffed sleeves made completely of white lace and lined with tiny pearls. The pearls also ran across the neckline that went from shoulder blade to shoulder blade.

"That can't be possible, it's far too pretty," Nora said, taking the cape and draping it over a chair for a maid or the butler to put away until it was needed again.

Rosemary glanced in the mirror again and wondered if it was truly possible that she hadn't noticed how pretty this dress was before today.

Resting her chin on Rosemary's shoulder, Nora met her gaze in the mirror and with sparkling eyes asked, "Did Michael tell you about tomorrow night?"

Turning away from the mirror, Rosemary shook her head. "What's tomorrow night?"

"We are all going to the theatre! Well, you and me and Michael and Geoffrey." Nora held up a hand. "Don't fret. Michael will convince Maud to let you come, because you *have* to join us. I can tell you this now, because Geoffrey's told Michael. There are rumors about Geoffrey keeping young women at his country estate, for his own pleasure. But they are all rumors. It's actually his cousin, Sarah, who lives there and helps young girls who have nowhere else to go. They've kept it a secret to keep the girls safe. I know you'll keep it a secret, too. But the greatest news is that Michael, all of us, are in the city to clear up the rumors about Geoffrey, because once that happens, Michael will give us his approval to marry!"

Rosemary was still processing all she'd just been told when Nora wrapped her in a solid hug.

"Isn't that just the best news ever? I'm so happy!" Nora eased the hug and took a step back. "Thank you for helping! Despite his views on marriage, Michael still draws women to him like bees to flowers, so you have to come with us. That way, they'll leave him alone, and he can focus on making others see what a wonderful man Geoffrey is and forget all about the rumors."

Rosemary tried to smile, just to appease Nora, but it felt much more like a grimace. Searching for an excuse of some sort, she went for her most common one. "Thomas will worry if I'm gone two nights in a row."

Nora frowned. "He has a governess. One you hired

and adore. Furthermore, if you ask me, Maud needs to be more responsible for her own son. You're his sister and deserve to have your own life. Not one dedicated to taking care of him." Once again hooking their arms together, Nora then said, "Come, we've kept the others waiting long enough."

A moment later, Rosemary was all too aware of Michael's gaze as she entered the parlor and did her best to keep her gaze from meeting his. He knew it had been her and not Maud protesting her attendance tonight and would know the same thing about tomorrow night, yet a few moments ago he had made it sound otherwise to Nora. It wasn't right that he'd lied on her behalf, and she didn't want it to happen again. The guilt inside her was already compelling her to apologize to him.

It was just that no one seemed to understand the situation she was in, how she had to abide by the promise she'd made to take care of her father. She was the only one who knew how to do that and how to take care of Thomas properly.

She accepted a glass of sherry from Michael and took a seat in one of the chairs, smiling as if all was right in the world—which it clearly wasn't. Not with the way her insides seemed to be at war. A part of her wanted to be here, having fun, and another part of her said she should be at home, fulfilling her duties there.

Due to Drake's presence, the conversation quickly became focused on Hugo and his trip to England.

His colorful tale of acquiring the elephant and then stopping at ports, large and small, along the way to purchase hay and water, had the room filled with laughter, including hers, right up until dinner was announced.

The delicious meal, consisting of seven full courses, starting with a creamy vegetable soup and ending with a sponge cake pudding for dessert, lasted well over two hours. Those hours were also graced with laughter, and Rosemary hadn't even realized the length of time that had passed until they once again entered the parlor and the mantel clock said it was after nine thirty.

When Nora suggested a walk in the park, Rosemary wanted to decline. No, that wasn't completely true. She was having a wonderful time, and just as during the ball at Turnbill, she didn't want it to end. It was that knowledge that scared her and signified that she *should* decline. But she couldn't, in any case, as she was at Michael's mercy for a ride home.

"As much as I regret these words," Drake said. "I must decline. I have a meeting at ten."

"A meeting at ten at night?" Michael asked.

"Yes. This was the only time the man had available," Drake said. "I'm looking for a business partner, and he's interested."

"What sort of business partner?"

"Shipping," Drake replied.

"Is this something we should discuss?" Michael asked.

"Another time, my friend." Drake nodded towards her and Nora. "Right now, you have two beautiful woman who want to walk in the park, and there's a big old full moon to light your way."

"You are correct," Michael replied.

Moments later, the four of them—her and Michael, Nora and Geoffrey—walked out of the house and across the street to a section of Hyde Park. Being over three hundred acres, the park was massive, and it wasn't unheard of for people to get lost there. Therefore, Rosemary was always careful to stay on the pathways and only walk in the areas that were well-known to her when bringing Thomas here. She'd instructed Joelle to do the same.

"I told Rosemary about the theatre tomorrow night," Nora said, looking over her shoulder as she and Geoffrey walked along the trail ahead.

"I was sure you would," Michael replied.

"You'll make sure she can attend, won't you?" Nora asked.

"I will," he replied.

"Thank you!" Nora said. "We will take the left pathway, you two take the right, and we'll meet at the bridge." Pointing at the bundled napkin that she'd handed Geoffrey before they left the house, she continued, "I saw a dog in the bushes earlier today and have a little something for him to eat. He appeared quite frightened, and I don't want to scare him away by there being too many of us."

"Very well," Michael said.

"It could be the same one that Thomas saw," Rosemary said. "That is the path that Joelle said they were on."

"It could be," he replied. "Would you like to go that way, too?"

Between the moon and the gas lamps, the pathways were well lit, and Rosemary shook her head. "No, I agree with Nora, too many people could scare him."

"Well, knowing Nora, he could be living in our backyard by the week's end."

"That's true," Rosemary replied.

She attempted to focus her attention on the surroundings, for the flower beds, manicured hedges, clusters of trees, and open areas of thick grass, were all truly beautiful, but her mind simply wouldn't allow it.

After they'd walked a short distance, the need to apologize that had been plaguing her had grown too large to ignore. "I'm sorry that you had to lie for me earlier this evening." When he remained silent, she added, "When you had to say that you'd convinced Maud to let me come to dinner tonight."

His hand took ahold of hers and gave it a tiny squeeze. "Would you care to share why you didn't want to attend?"

"It's not that I didn't want to. I just worry about Thomas when I'm not there."

"He is with his parents and his governess."

"I know."

"He was fine while you were at Turnbill."

They were slowly walking along the pathway, and the way he was still holding her hand was making her feel things and confusing her mind. "Yes, he was. Joelle said he was his happy little self all weekend."

"When Nora was born, my father told me that it would be my job to protect her. That girls and women needed protection, and that it was the job of the men in their lives to do just that. Protect them. Sometimes I wonder if I took that more seriously than I should have."

"Why?"

"Because I've never forgotten it. Not for a single moment."

Rosemary's mind went to how she'd wanted a big brother just like him, but she couldn't say that, nor could she verbalize her other thoughts, about her promise to her mother. If anyone were to understand, it could be him. "You're worried about Nora now. About marrying Geoffrey."

"Yes, and no," he said.

"She told me about Geoffrey's reputation, about the rumors and his cousin Sarah. Not a lot, but enough to know that it must be true. That it's all rumors, and that's why you are in town, to stop the rumors."

"Rumors can't be stopped," he said. "All we can do is allow people to see the truth and make their own conclusions. As the Duke of Turnbill, and Nora's brother and guardian, my opinion of him will override what a few disgruntled former employees of his father's are saying about him."

"Once you've done that, you'll grant them permission to marry?"

"Yes, I will. He's a good person, and from what I've seen, I believe he will protect Nora as thoroughly as I have all these years."

"That's why you will be attending events that you normally don't, to help her, to protect her from untrue rumors."

"Yes."

"You're a very good brother, Michael. The best."

"You are a very good sister," he replied. "And a very good friend."

A sigh built in her chest, and she let it out slowly so he wouldn't hear it. "I will go to the theatre tomorrow night with you."

"How about the Duckworths' Ball on Friday night?"

This time she didn't hide her sigh, simply let it flow freely, because she couldn't say no to him. "Yes."

"Thank you."

"You're welcome."

Chapter Thirteen

Michael was torn between releasing Rosemary's hand or using it to pull her closer for a long hug. He felt as if she could use one. She was afraid of her life changing, and he could understand that. Though he'd been much older than she had been when she'd suffered her loss, he'd been just as afraid of the changes that had happened when his father had died. Not the duties or responsibilities that had then fallen upon his shoulders, but the fact that everything would be different. In some ways, he'd held on to certain aspects of his life as strongly as she was holding on to running her father's household.

One of the things he'd held on to had been his unrelenting protection over Nora, because that had been something he could control. If he had trusted his sister's ability to protect herself, he wouldn't be in the predicament he was right now.

A horse and rider coming down the path made his decision concerning Rosemary's hand for him. Although the walkway was fairly wide, he guided her onto the grass and positioned himself between her and the oncoming stranger.

When the man had trotted by, Michael didn't step back onto the walkway. Instead, he stared down at the features of Rosemary's face. Her thickly lashed eyes, the curves of her cheekbones, the petal shape of her lips. Light from a nearby lamppost was casting a golden glow upon her, emphasizing that she had grown into a strikingly beautiful woman, yet he still saw traces of the girl he'd always known. The one he'd self-determined to protect as strongly as he'd promised to protect his sister.

While doing all of that, had he prevented her from learning how to protect herself? Was that why she was afraid to leave her father's house?

She was looking at him with just as much scrutiny, and he wished he could read her mind. He also wished he could kiss her.

"I made a promise to my mother," she whispered. "Like you did your father."

"You did? When?"

"The night before she died. She told me that it would be my job to take care of my father. That he was going to need me. That he would always need me."

Knowing the weight of such promises, Michael pulled her into a hug. A long hug. He pressed his lips to the top of her head, then said, "You've done that. Just as you promised."

"He still needs me," she whispered.

Michael took a moment to find the right way to say what he felt she needed to hear. "He will always need you, but he needs you as a daughter, not a housekeeper or a governess. He has a wife to do those things for him."

The way she stiffened in his arms told him that he hadn't found the perfect words. He just couldn't seem to get anything right when it came to her. Although he'd probably regret it, he chose to push further. "I can only imagine that he wants to see his daughter living life to the fullest, wants her to come to him for advice about men, the right man, and eagerly awaits her wedding day and the time when she will provide him with grandchildren."

Her hands slipped off his back and then pressed against his chest as she took a step backwards. "Why would you say that? You have been talking to Maud."

Shaking his head, he grasped her arms. "No, I have not been talking to Maud. I say all of that because that is what *my* father wanted. He told me so more than once. Not just pertaining to Nora but to me. He liked when I'd go to him for advice, and he told me to wait for the right woman but not to wait too long, because he wanted to see his grandchildren. Sadly, that never happened. I'm sure your father thinks of that. He and my father were as good friends as our mothers were."

The look on her face said she wanted to break loose of his hold and run. He tightened his grip on her upper arms to make sure that didn't happen. "I don't believe your mother would want you to give up your own life for a promise that you've already fulfilled."

She shook her head and twisted as if to break his hold on her upper arms.

His goal had been for her to see things differently, and it appeared as if he was failing, as well as running out of ideas. She should be experiencing things that other women her age were, things that Nora was getting to enjoy right now, while she was falling in love.

What struck Michael next might not have been the best idea—or maybe he had simply quit thinking altogether and decided to just act. Pulling Rosemary close, he lowered his head and brought his lips against hers.

The touch, the connection, filled something inside him that he hadn't known had been empty. It was as if the kiss emanated from his very soul as their lips fully melded together, creating a combination of pleasure and satisfaction that he'd never experienced. Her arms wound around his neck, and she pressed herself harder against him, all the while moving her lips in time with his as if they'd done this before.

It was only possible for him to fight the desire to part her lips and take the kiss further because he didn't want to frighten her. And he wanted to prove that he still had some semblance of control when it came to her.

"Michael! Rosemary!"

The sound of his sister's voice was like a bucket of cold water. He snapped his head up and drew in a deep breath in preparation to face Nora. After a glance left and right, he met Rosemary's eyes.

Gazes locked, breathing hard, they both grinned as the shout came again. It was clear that Nora was shouting from around the corner of the pathway.

Michael grasped Rosemary's hand, and together they ran towards the corner.

"There you are!" Nora said as they rounded the corner and came face to face with her. "It's not a he, it's a she, and she has puppies! Hurry, we need your help!"

"Help with what?" Michael asked.

"The dog," Nora said, running ahead of them.

He glanced at Rosemary. She shrugged, and together they ran along the path.

Geoffrey was standing by a thick set of bushes a short distance off the pathway. "The pups aren't very old," he said. "Maybe a few days."

"There's eight of them," Nora said. "It's going to take all of us to carry them home."

Michael looked at Rosemary. "Told you."

She laughed. "Yes, you did."

It took the better part of an hour to carry the puppies and mother dog home, to find and modify a crate to fit Nora's specifications, and to get the canine family settled on the back porch. All the while they listened to Nora's explanations and various reasons as to why they couldn't leave the dog in the park.

White with brown splotches, the dog had short hair and legs, and the puppies themselves weren't much bigger than mice. The mother dog appeared grateful as she snuggled down on the blanket inside the crate and curled her little body around her babies.

"Aren't they just the sweetest?" Nora said, kneeling beside the crate.

"They are," Rosemary replied, kneeling beside her. "I'll have to bring Thomas over to see them. I'm sure this is the same dog he told me about seeing in the park this weekend."

"I'm so happy that nothing had happened to her between then and now," Nora said.

Half expecting Nora to repeat her list of all of the possible dangers the dog could have encountered *again*, Michael glanced at Geoffrey, who was smiling and shrugged.

He'd already come to the conclusion that Geoffrey was the man for Nora, but that moment solidified his decision. The man understood and accepted his sister's need to help others, something he clearly already undertook himself in his work with his cousin Sarah.

Michael nodded, then gestured to the women. They both stepped forward to assist the ladies to their feet.

"I've asked for the coach to be brought around," Michael told Rosemary as they entered the house through the back door.

"Thank you," she said.

"We'll have an early dinner here before going to the theatre tomorrow," Nora said.

"I think it would be better if we dined at a restaurant near the theatre," Michael said.

"Oh, that would be wonderful," Nora said.

His gaze was on Rosemary, who nodded.

She then bid Nora and Geoffrey good night, and together they walked through the house. They stopped in the parlor for her to say goodbye to his mother and aunt before making their way to the front door.

Due to Nora's arrival and the transportation of the dog and her puppies, they hadn't had a chance to address the subject of what had occurred in the park. Michael knew it needed to be discussed before it became a barrier between them. He hadn't stopped thinking about it and, all in all, knew that he shouldn't have done it.

For more than one reason. Reasons on both sides, his and hers. He'd never forget how sweet she tasted or how amazingly perfect her lips had felt, melded with his. Or how he wanted a repeat of it. That alone should be enough of a reason. He'd vowed to never let the want of a woman override his common sense ever again. There were too many consequences that went along with that.

Consequences that included her. He knew how much she trusted him. Kissing her like that could have destroyed that trust. Destroyed their friendship.

Destroyed her chances of finding the happy life that her family wanted for her. That he wanted for her.

She sat across from him in the coach. It barely started to roll when she asked, "Why did you kiss me?"

He might have been surprised by her boldness if he hadn't remembered this was Rosemary. The girl he remembered had never shied from speaking her mind. "Because I wanted to," he answered honestly.

She nodded and sat silent for a moment, then asked, "Because you wanted to or because you knew that I wanted you to?"

That did surprise him a touch. Or maybe the surprise was the way his heart lurched inside of his chest—something he tried to ignore, knowing that her confession shouldn't thrill him like that. "You wanted me to?"

"Yes, I'm quite embarrassed to admit that I did."

Other than intermittent splashes of passing light from gas streetlamps, the interior of the coach was dark, making it difficult to tell if her face was flushed or not. She wasn't smiling, though, if that was an indication. "Why would you be embarrassed to admit that?"

"It's not something I should have wanted or expected."

"Why?"

"Because I know that you would never think of me in that way."

"What way?" Before she could answer, he suggested, "As a beautiful woman, whom I admire?"

"You admire me?"

"Yes, I always have." That truth struck him. He had always admired her and still did. In this moment, he admired her for questioning him and his actions. The protectiveness he'd always felt for her was still there, too, and he wondered if the person he should be protecting her from was himself.

She was innocent when it came to men, and though she should understand that kissing was a normal occurrence when a man and woman were getting to know each other more intimately, he was *not* someone she needed to get to know. She'd known him her entire life.

"I've always admired you, too," she said.

"There you go," he said, trying his best to sound as if nothing between them had changed. "It's perfectly normal for two people who admire each other to kiss." It occurred to him that he wasn't the best person to provide her with advice on the subject, but what else could he have said? If he apologized for kissing her, she'd think that something had been wrong, and nothing about that kiss had been wrong. Other than him and how he shouldn't have given into his desires. Desires that he desperately needed to get back under control.

Smiling, she leaned back in her seat and asked, "What time should I be ready tomorrow evening?"

"Five," he said the first number that fluttered across his mind, and quickly determined that he needed to get Geoffrey's reputation cleared up as fast as possible. He was enjoying Rosemary's company too much. Simply too much. He'd enjoyed that kiss too much, too, and ultimately needed to make sure it never happened again.

Rosemary twisted and turned, looking for the smallest malfunction in her appearance. The gown was another one that Maud had brought home from Paris. It was an olive green color, which had seemed so dull until she'd put it on, and then, like the silver gown, a shimmer in the fabric had been revealed, one that made the gown light up. The layered skirt was adorned with both black and cream-colored lace, and the bodice had tiny black pearls sewn around the waist. Trimmed with black lace, the sleeves came down to her elbows, and the neckline made a V, not too low, enhanced by one large, black, pearl-shaped button.

This one had a cape, too. It was black velvet, with the same cream-colored lace sewn all along the bottom, and there was a matching velvet hat, adorned with a single olive green flower.

A good splattering of guilt roiled in her stomach over how she'd thought the gown was dull and drab until now. She'd wanted to hate every dress that Maud had brought home to her, and she had, until forced to wear them.

She hadn't been forced to wear this one. Nor the one she'd worn last night, not really—merely tricked, and she was no longer upset over that, either.

Every part of her filled with happiness when she thought about kissing Michael. It had been spectacular. So spectacular that she felt as if she was walking on air all day.

Her father and Maud had been in the parlor when she'd arrived home last night, and Michael had accompanied her inside to explain the lateness, telling them about Nora finding the dog. Even Maud had smiled about that and had readily agreed that Thomas would enjoy seeing the puppies once they were a bit older.

At breakfast this morning, her father had mentioned that he regretted he wouldn't be home in time to see her leave for the theatre, then had kissed her forehead and said that he was sure she'd enjoy it immensely.

She was looking forward to going out with Michael, to the whole evening. She'd never been to a restaurant in the city, just wayside inns while traveling. Nor had she ever been to the theatre. Nora had invited her several times over the years, but she'd always declined. Just as she'd always declined invitations to Turnbill, always stating she wouldn't be given permission. The truth was, she'd never asked for permission because she'd known it would be granted.

Last night, she'd accused Michael of talking to Maud when he'd mentioned marriage and grandchildren. He'd said that he hadn't. That he'd said those things because it had been what his father had wanted, and he was sure that her father wanted the same things. Could that be true? Michael wasn't one to tell falsehoods. He was in town to put a stop to falsehoods about Geoffrey.

If that was true, was what he had said about her mother true, too? That she had already fulfilled the promise she'd made to her mother?

It was all so confusing. The opposite of what she'd always believed. Just like the gowns she'd once thought were dull and drab, but in truth were beautiful.

Maud had been the one who had suggested the green gown today, which wasn't the first time; she had suggested several of the gowns from Paris when they'd been packing for their weekend at Turnbill.

Rosemary had refused to even consider them and felt yet another bout of guilt at the memory. Why now, after all these years, was she starting to see the faults in her behavior? The faults in her beliefs?

Because of Michael. He was making her see things differently.

She had to believe what he'd said about what her father wanted for her, because if she didn't, then she couldn't believe that he'd kissed her because he wanted to or that he admired her.

She wanted those things to be true with all of her heart.

Maybe she was thinking about all of this too much.

Too hard. Michael just needed her to attend events with him while he corrected the rumors about Geoffrey.

Twisting about, she touched her hair as she stared directly into the mirror. Helen had used a curling wand and then painstakingly had pinned each lock into an elaborate style that was quite stunning. She'd also left two long curls hanging free, one in front of each ear.

Much like at Turnbill the night of the ball, she hoped that Michael would appreciate how she looked. She wouldn't hope, nor expect that he would kiss her again this evening, just would enjoy being in his company again. Enjoy collecting a few more memories that she could hold dear.

A knock on her bedroom door sent her heart into a tailspin. Taking a deep breath, she let it out slowly, then walked to the door. Opened it to a smiling Helen.

"The Duke of Turnbill has arrived, my lady," the maid said. "I will collect your cape and have it ready for your departure."

"Thank you, Helen," she replied. "And thank you for all your help in my preparations this evening."

"You are welcome, my lady."

Rosemary left her bedroom, walked along the hallway and then down the stairs. Truly, she wanted to race down them as quickly as Thomas often did. Every part of her was tingling with excitement when she walked into the parlor.

Michael was holding Thomas on his lap and instantly stood, placing her brother on the floor and rose from his seat. She not only felt his eyes on her but noted the way he swiftly scanned her from head to toe before catching her gaze again. "Good evening, Lady Rosemary."

"Good evening to you, Your Grace," she replied, feeling almost as elegant as she hoped she looked to him.

"Rosemary, Michael said as soon as the puppies have their eyes open, I can go see them, and Mama said that would be fine," Thomas said, smiling from ear to ear. "That's fine with you, too, isn't it?"

"I think that sounds perfect," she replied.

"Speaking of perfect." Maud rose from her chair and walked forward. "I picked these flowers from the garden." She held up a small bouquet, tied together with a cream-colored ribbon. "May I?" She nodded towards the large black button on Rosemary's dress.

Rosemary nodded. She'd seen other women wearing bouquets on their dresses, including Maud at times. Her stepmother tied the ribbon around the button, arranging it so the flowers were all upright and the ends of the ribbon hung down evenly.

"There," Maud said. "They look beautiful, as do you."

"Thank you, Maud," Rosemary replied, unable to find anything to dislike about the flowers or Maud's behavior. "They are lovely." The arrangement was very pretty, and something about her stepmother's thoughtfulness struck her deeply. So deeply her eyes stung.

"Doesn't your sister look pretty, Thomas?" Maud asked.

"Yes, Mama, as pretty as I've ever seen her." Still looking up at her, Thomas shook his head. "You're going to need a lot more paper for that many flowers, Rosemary."

Instantly knowing he was referring to the small flower in her drawer, she knelt down and kissed his forehead. "I will." Needing to leave before she started thinking too deeply all over again, she rose and looked at Michael. "Shall we?"

He gave her a nod, but it was the appreciation in his eyes that she really noticed and had a distinct feeling it wasn't just because of her gown.

After bidding Thomas and Maud goodbye, they paused in the entranceway for her to collect her cape. Michael draped it over her shoulders, and carefully tucked the front corners beneath the flowers.

"You do look beautiful," he said. "And the flowers were a nice gesture on Maud's part."

"Yes, they were. And you look very handsome," she replied. It was the truth. His frock coat was dark gray, fitted at the waist, and the hem ended mid-thigh. Beneath the coat was a black vest, embroidered with white swirls, a high-collared white shirt and a blue silk ascot. His pants were ankle length and black. The suit enhanced his handsomeness, but that was only a small portion of what made him so appealing. He was kind, too, and intelligent and honest. Far more honest than she'd been, even with herself.

"Thank you," he replied, both to her and to Richard who held the door open for them.

Once inside the carriage, he explained, "We will meet Nora and Geoffrey at the restaurant."

"Very well," she replied with a nod. "How was your day?"

"Long."

"Why is that?"

"Because I was waiting to see you."

It might have been the words or his heart-stopping smile, but either way, Rosemary knew she was as close to swooning as she'd ever been. He just, well, did things to her. Unusual things.

"How was your day?" he asked.

Then, perhaps because she was feeling dizzy, or maybe it was that his honesty was wearing off on her, she replied, "Long."

A moment of silence was followed by laughter from both of them, and then they discussed what they each had accomplished that day. He'd visited Geoffrey's business and then a gentlemen's club, and she told him about going over the kitchen shopping list and Thomas's lessons and how much she was looking forward to the performance this evening.

Nora and Geoffrey hadn't arrived yet by the time the coach stopped near the restaurant, and Michael suggested they take a walk while waiting. Street vendors were still selling their wares, and shops were open, enticing people to step inside their establishments by having their doors propped open.

They took turns pointing out unique and unusual items in windows, fine-looking horses pulling coaches and wagons and anything else that caught either of their eyes. They laughed over some things, had more serious discussions about others and merely looked at each other and shrugged over a few oddities.

Rosemary rarely went shopping and was intrigued by all that she saw, but it was more than that. It was if her eyes were being opened to a much larger world than the one she had been living in.

That happened again at the restaurant. Part of the reason she'd never been to a restaurant was because it had only recently become more acceptable for women to dine out in public. If Rosemary was being honest, she had to silently admit that Maud had suggested that the two of them go shopping and dine out more than once, but she'd declined, stating she had other things to do.

The restaurant was quite lavish, with round tables that didn't host more than four chairs, covered in linen clothes with small lit candelabras in the center. Huge potted plants were placed amongst the tables, and male waiters dressed in red uniforms with brass button were everywhere.

She lost track of the courses of food that were delivered to the table and didn't recognize some of the foods, but it was all delicious. Several people stopped by the table, recognizing Michael, and he introduced each visitor to everyone. There, too, she lost track of names, but it was clear that the Duke of Turnbill was well-known, well-liked and respected.

The theatre was but a few streets away, but their coaches were waiting when they departed the restaurant and drove them to the double front doors of the massive building. Captivated by her surroundings the moment she stepped inside, Rosemary couldn't look fast enough to see everything that she wanted to see. The tiled ceilings, massive chandeliers, ornate woodwork, marble floors were all eye-catching, as were the massive works of art hanging on the walls.

Here, too, people recognized Michael, and introductions were made, but what she noticed most were the wide-eyed onlookers, mainly woman with their gazes locked on Michael as if he was a horse they were considering buying.

"See what I mean?" Nora whispered in her ear. "If you weren't here, the flock of women around us would be so thick we wouldn't get as far as the stairway."

The staircase Nora was referring to, which they were now walking up, made almost a complete circle, so those walking up the stairs could see the entire room below at one point or another. Or maybe it was made that way for those below to see the people who had the best seats in the house. Rosemary wasn't sure, but she had to agree with Nora when it came Michael. Women were drawn to him like bees to flowers. "I do see what you mean," she whispered back. "Has it always been like this?"

"It's became worse since he became the Duke of Turnbill," Nora replied.

Rosemary had but one thought: With all these women so eagerly interested in him, how would he ever choose the right one, as his father had instructed him to? There were simply too many.

They arrived at the upper gallery and entered the private curtained box maintained by the Knight family. There, they settled upon four chairs and were served champagne by a uniformed theatre attendant.

"Will there be anything else, Your Grace?" the attendant asked.

"No, thank you," Michael replied.

With a bow, the man said, "Very well, enjoy the performance."

Sipping from her glass, Rosemary scanned the other boxes, noting the number of eyes cast their way, and then the floor below, where more people didn't shy from staring directly at their box.

"Does it bother you?" she quietly asked Michael.

Leaning close, he whispered, "Does what bother me?"

"All the people staring at you."

"They are not staring at me. They are staring at the beautiful woman with me."

She frowned at him.

He winked at her. Then, to her disbelief, he lifted her hand and kissed the back of it, with a good portion of London's elite still staring at them.

Her heart would never be the same, she was utterly convinced of that.

Chapter Fourteen

The moment the lights had been extinguished, Rosemary's eyes had gone to the stage and never left. The props, the costumes, the music coming from the orchestra pit, and the actors themselves were all captivating, but it was the way that Michael was still holding her hand that affected her the most. Their hands were below the railing, but even if they hadn't been, it was too dark for anyone to see, so she had to assume he was holding her hand because he wanted to. She wanted it, too.

Sometime later, when the curtain fell, indicating an intermission, Rosemary let out a sigh, for she had been following the storyline and wanted to know how it ended.

"Enjoying the performance?" Michael asked as the lights came on.

"Yes, very much."

"Good," he replied, glancing down at the floor below their balcony seats where people were rising to their feet. "For most in attendance, their goal is to be seen rather than enjoyment."

Whether he meant it to or not, his comment reminded her that that was the reason they were there, too. To be seen and to let others know that the Duke of Turnbill didn't believe the rumors that had been spread about his soon-to-be brother-in-law were true. Her reason for being here was so that Michael could do that without being flocked by women who would be very interested in becoming his duchess. It was an understandable desire. They would be a member of the *ton's* highest-ranking members with an arsenal of privileges and money that would make others jealous. Even in her early years, while dreaming of kings and queens and knights in armor coming to the aid of damsels in distress, social status had never been in Rosemary's dreams. Falling in love with a *hero*— whatever his background—had been what she'd imagined in her make-believe world.

Make-believe. That was what it had been, and despite those silly thoughts still flitting about in her mind more often than not, she would do far better to remember that being needed was her station in life. A station she'd accepted and enjoyed many aspects of…yet sitting here made her wonder if she was missing out on things.

Nora and Geoffrey had already risen from their seats, so, accepting the role she'd just silently acknowledged and knowing that was how things needed to be, Rosemary asked, "Shall we stretch our legs?"

There was some Turnbill business that Michael needed to complete while in London, meetings concerning several major investments and properties, and contracts to renew with buyers and suppliers. His hope had been that spending a few days focusing on the family enterprises would get his mind off Rosemary.

Off kissing her. An act he swore would not happen again. So far it hadn't.

And it wouldn't.

It had been two and a half days since they attended the theatre. Now, as he sat behind the large mahogany desk in the room that had once been his father's office, it was so easy to remember how beautiful she'd looked, how much the theatre performance had attracted her attention, how she'd enjoyed the restaurant and exploring the shops and scenes of the street. Her enthusiasm must have been contagious, because he had never enjoyed such activities so greatly.

He also had to admit to the pride he'd felt at having her on his arm. The swivel of heads their way and the look of admiration on men's faces.

The problem with all that was that he was intelligent enough to know the true reason he'd enjoyed everything was because of her. Not merely her enthusiasm but just her company. She simply made everything enjoyable.

To complicate things even more, he regretted not kissing her again. There had been ample opportunities. It was as if he was challenging himself to see exactly how much control he had. It was the hardest battle he'd ever fought, because if he was winning, there was no joy in it.

It wasn't just a physical attraction that he felt towards her. Although he knew he wasn't looking for a wife, a duchess, he couldn't stop himself from recognizing how perfect she would be in the role. She cared nothing about a title or prestige. Her focus would be on his house and family. Like him, she enjoyed being in the country, yet as she'd proven the other night, could fit in at any event. She'd been cordial and welcoming when he'd made introductions to those they had encountered at the restaurant and the theatre. He could see her hosting luncheons, garden parties and afternoon teas with other ladies while they were in town, whenever parliament was in session or he had business matters to conduct.

He could see so many things, including children, whom she would adore as much as she did Thomas. Although he tried hard to blot out such thoughts, it was becoming practically impossible.

He could see a future full of happiness being married to her, and that was a problem. He would need to marry someday and had to admit that the idea wasn't as undesirable as it once had been, but the truth was, he couldn't marry Rosemary. That wouldn't be fair to her. She still needed to see there was more of a life out there than she'd currently been living. He had to let her have that opportunity.

Furthermore, his goal for this trip to London had not been to dream about his own future but to secure Nora's.

Things were progressing well on that front. The rumors were not only being squashed, but Geoffrey was also receiving invitations to private clubs and events that were only extended to men of reputable backgrounds. Nora was beside herself with excitement and was anxious to know when a formal announcement could be made about their engagement. Geoffrey had also received invitations to a long list of balls and parties, and Nora would only be able to attend them with him once their engagement was official.

It was up to Michael as to when that would happen, and once he did make the announcement, he could return to Turnbill. He should be looking forward to that, but he wasn't. He was concerned that Rosemary hadn't yet been convinced that she wasn't responsible for her father, his household or her younger brother. That she could have more in her life. Much more.

He would know more after tonight. After the Duckworths' ball.

At that thought, he closed the ledger book and rose from the chair. His father's office was one of a suite of rooms on the upper floor of a bank building. On his way downstairs, he stopped in the bank's office, discussed a few future investments and then made his way outside to await his coach which was being brought around.

The street was flush with vendors and street callers advertising their wares. Foods such as fruits and vegetables, fried fish, baked potatoes, coffee, muffins and breads. Others were selling clothing, and more still were selling meat and bones for those who had pampered family pets.

Michael made his way to that cart and purchased a meaty bone for Nora's stray dog. As he was walking away, a young boy waved at him from where he stood near an upside-down crate.

"I got bones, too, my lord, if you need another one," the boy said.

The mud lark couldn't be much older than Thomas, and Michael walked over to investigate his wares.

"Right here," the boy said, pointing at two small bones lying amongst an assortment of rocks, pieces of glass and a few chunks of coal.

"Have you sold anything today?" Michael asked. It was common to see mud larks on the streets. The children, far too young in his eyes, wandered the banks of the Thames, scavenging for anything they could find to clean up and hopefully sell to supplement their family's income. If they were lucky enough to have a family. He knew from his philanthropic endeavors that there wasn't enough room at the orphanages for all the mud larks in the city. It was an all-around sad situation.

The boy had a mop of black hair and mud streaked his face, clothes and bare feet. "No, my lord," he replied.

Michael picked up a small piece of brown glass that the jagged edges had been ground to a smooth finish. "I happen to be looking for a piece of glass just like this, but I have one worry about it."

"I rubbed the edges smooth myself," the boy said. "And scrubbed it clean. If'n you hold it up to the sun, you can see through it."

Michael held the piece up to the sun as if he needed to confirm what the boy said. "It's a fine piece," he said. "That's for sure, but I worry that if I pay you for it, someone older than you will get that money off you before you get home."

The boy hung his head, confirming exactly what Michael had known. For every young lark, there was an older one who made money by robbing the more vulnerable one.

"How about you let me give you a ride home, and I'll give the money to your mother?" He'd done such a thing on more than one occasion.

"I don't have a mum," the boy replied. "She died when I was a babe. And my papa died last year. He was a dockworker. That's what I'm going to be when I get older."

The boy didn't have much, but still had pride. "Who do you live with?" Michael asked.

"My sister."

"Well, then, I'll give the money to your sister."

"How much money?"

"I'll buy everything on your box."

Though his green eyes filled with hope, the boy still hesitated.

"You can sit up on the seat with my driver, to show him the way," Michael offered.

That seemed to convince him, yet while nodding, the boy said, "It's a distance from here."

"Then it's a good thing that we won't be walking," Michael said. "My name is Michael, what's yours?"

Gathering up all the items off his crate with both hands, the boy held them out. "Ned. Ned McCay."

"Well, Ned McCay," Michael said while taking the items and dropping them in his pocket, "my coach is right over here."

Ned picked up his crate—a coveted possession for a mud lark—and carried it to the coach. After the boy was seated on the driver's seat, Michael told Arthur, his driver, that he'd be right back. He visited a few of the other stands, purchasing as much food as he could carry, and then handed an apple to Ned before climbing into the coach.

Ned had been right: it was a distance, all the way to East London, where the smoke from the industrial area hung heavy in the air and everything was covered with a dark, filthy soot. When the carriage finally stopped, Michael opened the door and climbed out.

"We have to walk now," Ned said, scurrying down from his seat, holding his crate in one hand.

Michael surveyed the area, quickly noting that neither man nor beast could be safe here. Buildings that had been reduced to nothing but dilapidated shells lined the street on both sides, and the people mingling about looked as if their souls were as empty as the buildings. "Stay with the horses," he told Arthur.

His plan had been to carry the food to Ned's sister, but Michael changed his mind and left it all inside the coach. People had lost their lives over less. Staying vigilant to his surroundings, he followed Ned down long, narrow alleyways until they came to an area filled with piles of rotting lumber, discarded milling machines and various other rubbish.

Along the way, Ned pointed out a building and said they used to live in it, until Clara, his sister, had gotten hurt.

"Is she better now?" Michael asked, his mind formulating a plan because he couldn't leave this child and his sister in a place like this.

"I think so. She doesn't cry as much."

Ned led him through and around the piles of scrap, including the hull of an old boat, to a place where boards had been laid over the open space between two rusted machines of some sort. More boards made up a makeshift door that Ned instantly disappeared behind. A moment later, he poked his head out.

"Clara says go away."

"Please ask Clara to come out here," Michael said. "Tell her that I didn't lie to you, and I won't lie to her. Nor will I hurt either of you."

There was mumbling and pleading, and finally the makeshift door was slid aside and a young girl stepped out of the makeshift shelter. A girl too young to be in the family way. Michael's hands balled into fists, knowing exactly how Clara had been hurt. The plan he'd been formulating came to completion.

Feeling too tall and overbearing, he lowered himself onto a pile of debris; he wasn't sure what but didn't care, either. "Clara, my name is Michael, and I know of a place where you and Ned will be safe. You'll have food to eat, clean clothes to wear and beds to sleep in."

"We can't go to an orphanage," she said, wrapping an arm around Ned. "They won't take us."

"I know," he said. "It's not an orphanage. It's a place in the country."

Her hair was as black and unkempt as Ned's, her clothes were rags tied together with twine, and she was so thin, there was no possible way she or the baby she was carrying would survive childbirth in her current condition. "How old are you?"

"Fifteen," she answered. "Ned is eight."

"I know you're scared," he said. "To be honest, this place scares me, but if you can trust me just a little bit,

I promise, you'll both be taken care of. I will make sure of that."

"He gave me a ride here," Ned said, looking at his sister. "Let me ride with the driver. And he gave me an apple." Digging in his pocket, he pulled out half of the apple and held it out to his sister. "I saved some for you."

The moment Rosemary stepped into the parlor, dressed in a gown of dark blue silk with a matching lace overlay that she'd purchased yesterday while shopping with Nora, along with a white loosely crocheted shawl draped over her shoulders, she knew something was different about Michael. He rose from the chair and greeted her amicably, but there was a dullness in his eyes that she'd never seen before.

Her father and Maud had waited for Michael to arrive, before leaving for the ball themselves, so there wasn't time to ask him anything until they were in his coach.

"What is troubling you?" she asked. "And don't tell me nothing, I know you too well for that."

Being close to nine o'clock, it was already dark, so she couldn't see his face clearly but heard his heavy sigh.

"I'm not going to stop asking, so you might as well tell me sooner than later," she said.

"I think I've seen the worst thing I've ever seen in my life today," he said.

She reached out to touch him but then changed her mind. Leaving her shawl on the seat, she gathered her skirt and maneuvered across the small space of the coach so she was sitting beside him. Then she wrapped an arm around his. "Tell me about it."

"I met a mud lark today," he started, "and…"

By the time he'd completed his story about Ned and Clara, Rosemary had tears streaming down her face, and her head was on his shoulder, with his arm around her, holding her close. The tale was tragic, but she hoped Michael saw promise in his actions. She certainly did. "From what Nora has said, I know they'll be well taken care of at Bellview."

"I know that, too," Michael said. "Geoffrey said there was sure to be room for two more, but there are others just like Ned and Clara out there."

"I know there are," she said, feeling his anguish. "But you saved those two today. You, alone, saved their lives. That's something to be proud of."

"They were nearly starved to death," he said.

"And you fed them."

"It's not enough. There should be more that I can do," he said.

Nora had told her more about Geoffrey's cousin, Sarah, and the girls she helped and how they would soon be moving onto another piece of property. Michael knew all of that, too, so repeating it wouldn't make him feel any better, and that was all she wanted. Some way to help him…

"What if you helped Geoffrey renovate and extend the new place that Sarah is moving to?" she asked, thinking aloud. "That way more mud larks, more girls, could go live there. Away from the streets of London. I know that my father would donate money for materials and such, if we told him about it."

He stiffened, and she lifted her head to look at him. He was staring at her, shaking his head.

Her stomach sank. "I'm sorry, it was just a thou—"

"You are a genius," he interrupted. "We don't have to threaten anyone's safety by revealing their location to raise money to help them. Plenty of money to make it bigger, make sure they are all fed and clothed."

"No, we don't," she replied, feeling his excitement.

"We could start right away. Tonight!"

"Yes, we could!" she agreed.

He grasped her face with both hands and kissed her. Although she knew it was a kiss of gratitude for her suggestion, it still thrilled her to the bone. She wrapped her arms around his neck and kissed him in return.

Something changed then. The meeting of their lips became more ardent, more purposeful. His hands were roaming up and down her back, her sides, and her breasts tingled, as if wishing his hands would roam up a bit farther and touch them. An irrational thought for sure, but she could feel her breasts straining against the scooped neckline of her dress, wanting more than just his gaze.

His lips were moving, too, touching hers, then moved to place small kisses on her cheek and chin. It was so delightful that she released the tiny moan tickling the back of her throat.

At the same time his lips returned to her mouth, his hands reached her breasts, and his thumbs brushed across her nipples. The sensation was so breathtaking she opened her mouth to suck in air. His tongue slid across her bottom lip, then over her teeth and into her mouth, and there, too, the sensations he evoked were all she could think about.

She touched her tongue to his, and almost immediately, they were swirling together, and she couldn't get enough of tasting him, kissing him. An ache grew deep inside her, one that had her body growing overly sensitive. Every part of her wanted to be touched by him, kissed by him.

Her back arched, giving him greater access to her breasts, and she moaned again as each of his hands cupped a breast and his thumbs rubbed the bare skin above her dress. She arched her back more and leaned her head back, which broke the kiss, but she didn't mind because his lips planted small kisses on her chin, then her neck.

His mouth moved downwards, kissed the swell of her breasts, while his hand still caressed them, making heat swirl in the very core of her womanhood.

She found herself cursing the material of her dress, wanting his lips to go farther down.

As if reading her mind, his fingers slipped beneath the neckline of her gown and pulled it downward, exposing her chemise. He kissed her there. On the chemise and the nipple directly beneath it. She clutched his shoulders as an amazing tingle shot down from her breasts to her stomach and below, to where the heat was growing into a swirling storm of need.

He pulled the chemise down, exposing her nipple to the night air and the heat of his breath. Enticed, thrilled and wanting more, she watched as he rubbed her nipple between his finger and thumb. The pleasure was so great that she whispered, "Yes. Oh, yes."

His gaze caught hers, and she smiled. He did, too, before he dipped his head and licked her nipple with the tip of his tongue. The sensation had her thrusting her body forward, her breast firmly against his mouth. His lips parted, and he took her breast into his mouth, twirling his tongue around her nipple.

His other hand was still caressing her other breast, and she didn't want any of it to stop. Not ever.

She bent forward, laid her forehead atop his head, and lost herself in doing nothing but basking in the most wonderful feelings in the world.

Eventually, he kissed his way back up to her neck, then chin and her lips, all the while tugging her chemise back into place, and then her dress. Although the kiss was wonderful, her entire body was aching, and her nipple was missing his attention.

When the kiss ended, he leaned back. "Let me see."

Opening her eyes, that she hadn't realized had been closed, she asked, "See what?"

His hands slid beneath her arms, and his palms cupped the sides of her breasts and pressed them inwards, an action she did herself to get everything in place at times.

"Oh, yes, perfect." He kissed her nose. "And perfectly in place."

She looked down, amazed that it looked like her dress had never been tugged down. Another amazing thing was that she was able to think and breathe. Her body felt as if it had melted right into the leather of the seat.

Leaning over her, Michael pushed aside one of the heavy curtains over the windows, to peer out, and she wondered how or when the curtains had been untied, for she was sure they'd been tied back when she'd climbed in the coach. At that same moment, she realized they were no longer moving. That the coach was no longer moving.

"We're here?" she asked, with a sense of panic filling her. "At the ball?"

"We just arrived," he said. "But there is a long queue of coaches." Reaching across to the other seat, he picked up her shawl and then draped it around her shoulders. "Shall we walk from here? It'll cool us off."

Considering the way her body was still throbbing, she doubted any amount of *cooling off* was going to help. "If you want."

"It's not what I want, it's what I need," he whispered, then unlatched the door.

He climbed out first and lowered the step, then held her hand as she exited the coach.

Her knees were weak, and it was a few steps before she felt as if she had control over her movements.

"Are you doing all right?" he asked quietly, for there were others walking the final stretch to the large, brick mansion.

The overwhelming sensations he'd evoked were diminishing but also leaving an afterglow that was nearly as wonderful. "Yes, are you?"

Smiling, he nodded. "More than all right."

Returning his smile, she replied, "Me, too." And she was. She was feeling as if she'd just been granted a wish.

Perhaps she had.

He'd said that it was perfectly normal for a man and woman who admired each other to kiss, but that had been more than a kiss. More than she'd ever imagined. It was simply impossible to believe that Michael would kiss her like that if he didn't think of her as more than a friend. She couldn't imagine letting another man kiss her like that.

What if he was falling in love with her? And her with him? What if her childhood fairy-tale dreams were all coming true? She would be the happiest person on earth.

Truly the happiest.

Which was exactly how she felt right now.

She glanced up at him, caught his gaze, and the smile they shared filled her with even more happiness.

That feeling and more stayed with her throughout the night.

She'd never known such pride as the moment the Duckworth's butler formally announced, "His Grace, the Duke of Turnbill, and Lady Rosemary Crofton." Of course, the heart-stopping smile that Michael again bestowed upon her at that same time was part of it.

Though she'd never consider herself an overly boastful person, she did feel quite conceited when the other women in the room looked at her on Michael's arm, then turned away as if they knew they'd lost any chance of gaining his attention that night.

Or perhaps any other night.

The thought made Rosemary giddy. She simply couldn't stop herself from believing in fairy tales, hoping one might come true. Surely it could. Something deep inside her said so.

To become Michael's wife, his duchess, would be a fairy tale come true. The best one ever.

She tried to quell such silliness but found it impossible, because every time she glanced his way, Michael was smiling.

The Duckworth mansion was beautiful, and the ballroom was lavishly decorated with silk streamers hanging from the paneled ceiling. Large potted plants, including a lemon tree complete with lemons, and massive flower bouquets lined the walls, and an ornate wrought iron railing surrounded the raised platform where an orchestra played a wide variety of music.

One of the first things they did was find Nora and Geoffrey and shared the idea that Rosemary had mentioned in the coach.

Geoffrey was shocked at first and questioned if Michael truly wanted to become involved in such an undertaking.

"I'm already involved," Michael proclaimed. "My question to you is whether I may involve others. We could fund an estate large enough to accommodate a great number of young women and mud larks. There are details to be worked out, but I'm convinced that with a few additional backers, we can have everything in place in a relatively short amount of time."

With Geoffrey and Nora's consensus, the next couple they sought were her father and stepmother. Tonight, for whatever reason, although she was convinced it was related to the man standing beside her, Rosemary didn't question the sincerity of the tears that welled in Maud's eyes when Michael related his experience of finding Ned and Clara. Her father, wrapping an arm around Maud and kissing her temple, simply asked where he should send a check.

For once, Rosemary found a place in her heart for a small amount of joy at the fact that her father had remarried. In all honesty—since she was being honest with herself tonight—there *had* been times when she'd seen her father and Maud truly happy. She'd just always ignored them.

Now she wondered whether that was because she'd never been truly happy herself.

"Is something wrong?" Michael asked.

"No," she assured him. "I'm so happy that Geoffrey agreed to our idea." That was the truth, just not the whole truth.

"I am, too," he replied. "Your idea was perfect."

"Our idea," she said. "I didn't come up with it all on my own."

He winked at her. "I guess we make a good team."

Her heart doubled in size. "Yes, we do."

They continued making their way around the room, discussing the topic discreetly with a few other people who were just as touched and just as willing to help in any way, including Michael's mother and Aunt Lettice.

After securing a plethora of support for their plan, they danced. Several times. Then they ate and laughed and danced some more.

During one of their dances, they discussed another topic, and Rosemary was in total agreement with Michael's suggestion.

Therefore, at midnight, to Nora's surprise, Michael made the official announcement of the engagement of Lady Nora Knight to Geoffrey Burrows, the Viscount of Bellview.

It truly was a night for wishes to come true.

Because, oh, yes, Michael kissed her again on the way home in the wee hours of the morning.

By the time she laid her head on her pillow, Rosemary had no doubt that she would become the Duchess of Turnbill.

Chapter Fifteen

"Do you mean it, Mama? Papa?" Thomas asked from where he sat on the back porch, holding two puppies in his lap and petting another that was still in the crate with its siblings and mother. "Do you really mean that I can bring one of these puppies home with me, to live with me forever and forever?" His face was aglow with anticipation as his gaze bounced between his parents.

"Yes, son, we mean it," Ralph said, patting Thomas's head.

"But not today," Maud said. "They need to get a little bigger before they can leave their mum."

"I know," Thomas said. "And they have to decide which one wants to live with us."

Michael frowned at that logic. "How will a puppy decide that?"

Thomas shrugged, yet his smile never faded. "It just will. Like Hugo decided he wanted to come to England with Drake."

Michael nodded, knowing that when Drake had told Thomas about finding Hugo at the docks in Africa, he would have left out the components of his story about the elephant being mistreated. His first instinct was to glance at Rosemary, who was standing beside him, and her nod confirmed that was exactly what had happened.

It was Sunday, and his mother had invited the entire Crofton family to an afternoon luncheon. Michael was grateful for that. He had been looking for a reason to see Rosemary since the Duckworths' ball on Friday, all the while knowing that he shouldn't. Things had gone further than he'd intended in the coach on Friday night, and though he dreamed of it happening again, it couldn't.

There was no excuse for his reckless behavior. He'd tried to find one. Tried to justify it, but there was no justification. Yes, they had gotten caught up in the excitement of finding a way to help Ned and Clara and others like them, but a simple kiss would have been celebration enough. He'd not only practically compromised her, he'd let his foolish behavior continue all night.

Throughout the ball he'd cherished every moment of her being at his side. Relished the looks of admiration he'd received from others at having such a beautiful woman on his arm and had basked in the way she'd looked at him. That glorious shimmer in her eyes had made him feel as if he was on top of the world.

He'd crashed back down to earth after dropping her off that night. After kissing her again.

There was no excuse for that, either. He was supposed to be protecting her, protecting himself, and had failed.

He'd worked himself into a corner and needed to find a way out. There was only one reason he would have allowed himself to become so entrenched in a relationship with Rosemary, and he was quite outraged at himself for letting it happen. He was supposed to be immune from love. He'd sworn to himself that he'd never open his heart up again. Sworn he'd never lose another friend over love, and here he was, doing just that, because he did consider Rosemary a friend.

At the same time, he didn't want what he'd found with her to end—even while knowing that was selfish on his part. Rosemary was an innocent, had no experience with men other than him, and he'd pushed her into all of this. Hadn't given her a choice to say no to anything. Hadn't given her a chance to see the life she'd been missing.

"Could we speak privately for a moment?" Ralph asked him.

"Of course," Michael agreed, assuming it was pertaining to either the dog or a donation for the construction of a larger facility for Sarah and her waifs. That had been a topic of discussion earlier today while they'd eaten, and several good ideas had been shared.

He led Ralph to the second floor and his study there.

Once they were settled in leather chairs near the fireplace, unlit during this time of year, Ralph laid a piece of paper on the table between them. "Here is my pledge for the endeavor. Once you know where the funds will be accepted, just present that to the bank and monthly payments will be made in that amount."

Michael didn't need to look at the note to know it would be a generous amount. "Thank you. Geoffrey will be making those arrangements this coming week."

"I'm assuming with the announcement of their wedding that you have completed the business which brought you to London."

"I have," Michael agreed.

"Quicker than you'd assumed," Ralph said.

Michael nodded. Uprooting the defamatory rumors had been easily accomplished, partly because those rumors hadn't been nearly as catastrophic as he'd once imagined. His need to protect his sister had loomed larger in his mind than it had in reality. He understood that now.

"And you'll now be returning to Turnbill," Ralph said.

"I will," Michael replied, although he hadn't decided exactly when.

"I wanted to take the opportunity to thank you," Ralph said. "In a small window of time, you instilled changes in Rosemary that I feared I'd never see. She's not only been willing to leave the house for a variety of reasons, she's shown interest in things besides running the house and Thomas. Her attitude has altered, too. Just yesterday, she and Maud had a lengthy discussion about mud larks and other social issues. It warmed my heart to see them in agreement and to recognize how similar their beliefs are to one another. I've even witnessed times of laughter between them, a true rarity."

"I've seen changes in her, too," Michael said. "I believe it wasn't your love she was afraid of losing, but your need for her. Her own capacity to be needed."

Ralph nodded. "That is an interesting observation, one that amplifies the new concerns I'm facing."

"What are those?"

"I fear Rosemary may be very disappointed."

"Disappointed?" Michael asked, not following the man's line of thinking.

"Yes. She may have seen helping you as something else. Understandably, considering you're the first man to pay her that kind of attention. You were clear a marriage was not of interest to you, and I don't want to you to be put in an uncomfortable position, but after the ball the other night, other people may assume there is more than friendship between the two of you. Therefore, I am requesting that you end things with her. I know it's only been a week and merely a few outings, but it's been a transforming week for her, and

I simply don't want her to harbor hope where there isn't any. Once she knows the truth, she may be open to other offers."

A flood of emotions washed over Michael. He was fully aware that Ralph was protecting his daughter and rightfully so. In truth, he hadn't needed any of that pointed out to him, because he'd already come to those very same conclusions. One thing the man had said, however, stuck him like a knife. "Other offers?" he asked.

"Yes, she's merely on the brink of seeing what her future could hold, and I wouldn't want to see that stymied."

Michael nodded, dazed. He'd already determined that Rosemary deserved the opportunity to experience things she'd missed out on by being so committed to her father and brother. Deserved to meet other men, perhaps including one she would fall in love with. Would consider marrying someday.

What he hadn't realized was how much his own emotions were coloring his perception of Rosemary's feelings. The way Ralph had put it struck him hard. Rosemary just wanted to be needed. And that was exactly the position he had put her in. He'd asked her to help him, and she had helped.

Was that all it had been for her? Had his concerns about fostering an impossible love, about ruining their friendship, been unfounded? Was he once again seeing love where it wasn't? Like he had with Martha?

Because that was what he wanted from Rosemary, what he felt, and therefore perhaps he'd assumed things on her part that he should not have.

"Nor would I," he said, forcing himself not to flinch at the reality sinking in fast and hard.

Ralph appeared to be relieved. "Thank you. I knew you would understand. The role of a duchess is one that many seek to acquire, but few foresee the complex duties of a station that is best suited for those far more experienced."

Michael had no response, other than to agree because it was true. He'd almost married a woman once because he'd been thinking with his heart instead of his mind, and rather than learn from it, he'd almost done it twice.

Almost. He hadn't crossed the line yet.

More importantly, he hadn't compromised Rosemary. Ralph was right in many aspects but one very main one. She was on the brink of seeing what her life could become, and when she did, she would have many options. Many were far less complex than becoming a duchess. Michael could stand in her way no longer. "With your permission, I will provide Rosemary a ride home this afternoon and speak with her during that time."

"Granted," Ralph said, standing and extending a hand.

Michael shook the man's hand, wondering if he should be grateful that Ralph had just given him a way out of the corner that he'd blocked himself into. He didn't feel thankful. He felt wounded and questioned if he'd ever have the ability to protect anyone ever again. Including himself.

He'd never expected the genuine affection he'd always felt for Rosemary to turn into something more, but the turmoil he'd felt since being reunited with her at Turnbill had been intense enough to create warning bells right from the start. He had heard them, but he hadn't heeded them.

It was time to do that.

Less than half an hour later, as he held Rosemary's hand while she stepped into the carriage, Michael had another deep realization. He was going to miss her. Everything about her. There simply wasn't a thing about her that he didn't admire. He'd never enjoyed someone's company as much as he did hers. Had never looked forward to seeing someone as much as he had her and had never missed someone the way he was already missing her. There was already an emptiness inside him.

He waited until she was seated and had smoothed her skirt before he climbed in and sat down across from her, pulling the door closed behind him. "I believe Thomas is quite excited over acquiring a puppy."

"Yes, he is. Maud and I discussed it yesterday. It will give him the opportunity to develop responsibility."

He nodded. "It will and provide him with companionship."

"Yes, that, too."

"Companionship is important," he said, using it as a bridge to the topic he'd promised to discuss. "I've appreciated your companionship this past week, and all of your assistance. I'm glad that everything worked out so quickly."

She blinked and a small frown formed between her brows. "I am, too. Nora has already started planning the wedding."

"I believe that she's been planning it for some time already," he replied, "and will appreciate your help in that, too."

"I'll be glad to help her." Her gaze had become thoughtful. "You'll be going back to Turnbill, now, won't you?"

He held in a sigh. "Yes."

"When?"

"As soon as possible."

She pinched her lips together and glanced out the window. "Well, that was the plan, wasn't it?"

"Yes, it was." He leaned forward and touched her hand. "I will always consider you a very dear friend." Good Lord! Dear friend? That was all he could think to say? Yes, because this was about her, not him. Not the hollow numbness that was already consuming his body and mind.

"As I will you," she said.

"And we'll see each other again soon." Why the hell had he said that? He couldn't promise her that. Couldn't promise her anything. He had to put distance between them. For as long as she needed. "Whenever you visit Turnbill," he added, trying to clarify his statement.

She nodded, and for a length of time, he couldn't do anything except stare at her face, mesmerized by her beauty and memorizing it at the same time. Storing away visions of it for the days, weeks, months and years ahead.

Returning his gaze with a hint of scrutiny, she asked, "Why didn't you marry Martha Grossman?"

Though the question caught him off guard, he wasn't surprised that she knew he'd considered marrying Martha. Though only a handful of others did, one of them was his sister, and Nora would have told Rosemary—told her as much as she knew, that was. He hadn't shared much with his family. He couldn't claim it had been out of respect for Martha. It had been out of embarrassment. His embarrassment over his failure to discover Martha's true character, to see through her lies. He'd been so focused on the next step in his life that he'd failed to see what was right before his very eyes, to the point he'd lost a good friend over his blindness.

That was exactly what he'd done this time, too. Been so focused on his own goals and on Rosemary's father's goals that he'd overlooked *her* goals, believing he knew what she needed. Believing she needed his protection, when in reality, what she needed was freedom. And that included freedom from him.

"We had different goals when it came to marriage," he said. "When I eventually decide to marry, I will expect my wife to be fully committed to being the Duchess of Turnbill in every way. She will need to understand the complexities that come along with the role besides the title and prestige. Martha did not."

"Did you love her?"

"No." He paused briefly, because he had thought that he had loved Martha but was now aware that he hadn't. She'd made him believe he loved her. She'd told him that he loved her, and he'd believed her because he'd wanted to believe her. Wanted to believe he was making the right choice. "Love can easily be mistaken. Miscalculated." He wanted to believe that he was making the right choice this time, too. "I'd like to ask a favor of you."

"Certainly," she replied. "What is it?"

From her expression, the tone in her voice, he didn't know if his leaving wasn't affecting her or if she was hiding it so that he didn't feel bad. He felt awful. He felt as if he was letting her down, as a friend, abandoning her, but her father was right. Not only would people assume that there was more than friendship between them if he didn't stop seeing her, but beyond that, she would never experience the freedom she deserved to with him around.

"Don't stop attending events," he said. "You've enjoyed yourself this past week, and there is still so much more for you to explore. To enjoy."

I will not cry, Rosemary repeated to herself. A vow that was turning out to be extremely hard to keep. She'd clung to it several times since climbing in the coach, ever since the excitement she'd felt at spending a few moments alone with Michael had turned into despair.

He was leaving. Their time together was over. Her fairy tale was just that, too. Over. And it would never, ever come true.

She swallowed against the burning in her throat and the stinging in her eyes. "Well," she said, doing her best to sound like she wasn't falling to pieces on the inside.

It was her own fault. She knew the only reason he had escorted her about town had been to help Geoffrey and Nora. That was how it had started out for her, too, and it was no one's fault but her own if she'd temporarily forgotten. Now that it had been proven that Geoffrey was everything that Nora had claimed him to be and that their wedding had been announced, their scheme was done. Everything was over.

"That will be an easy request to complete," she lied, because going anywhere without him was sure to be a disappointment. "Just this afternoon, Nora mentioned that the Whitehalls will be hosting an event next weekend and asked me to attend."

Nora had said the four of them would go, but she must not know yet that Michael was leaving for Turnbill as soon as possible. That was what he'd said. As soon as possible.

For the briefest of moments, after he'd said that, Rosemary had considered telling him that she loved him. Had loved him for a very long time. Thankfully, that brief moment of what had to be lunacy passed as soon as he'd said that they'd always be friends. Dear friends.

She didn't want to be just his friend, but he clearly didn't want more than that. He didn't want marriage.

That much had been clear from his answer about Martha and his following comments. Everything he'd said about the complexities of being a duchess and how love can be mistaken felt all too pertinent—as though he was talking about *her*, not about Martha Grossman. And if she'd been in any doubt on that score, he had asked her to continue to attend events. Without him.

A bout of fortitude struck—or perhaps it was mere stubbornness. Either way, she told herself that she would do just that: she would attend events, and she would enjoy herself.

And she would not cry.

Not in front of him.

Holding true to that promise, she dedicated the rest

of the ride to talking about Thomas and how he'd likely be begging to visit the puppies on a daily basis, how that might override his demands to see Hugo and anything else she could come up with to say. The trip home seemed to take forever.

Michael walked her to the front door of her father's house, and she wished him God's speed on his journey to Turnbill. Then she kissed his cheek and hurried inside, swiftly closing the door behind her.

She ran up the stairs and along the hallway to her bedroom, fully prepared to throw herself onto the bed and cry her eyes out, but once she entered her room, she determined that wouldn't do her any good. Once the tears started flowing, they might never stop.

Instead, she removed her hat, put it in a hatbox and put the box on the shelf in her wardrobe, all with remarkably steady movements. It should have been impossible, because inside she was far from steady. Her very soul was being ripped apart as if it was an old bedsheet, being shredded into rags.

The thing was, she recognized that feeling. It was part of losing someone. Someone she'd loved.

That was what it had felt like when her mother had died. The pain had been overwhelming, and she hadn't known how to make it stop, until she had remembered her mother's request to take care of her father. She'd discovered that in many ways, taking care of him and the household had superseded the pain, most of the time.

When her father had married Maud, the memory of losing her own mother, the pain of it, had still been fresh enough in her mind that she'd decided she would never feel that way again. In deciding that, she'd determined that if she didn't like Maud, didn't ever learn to like, let alone love her, she'd never experience that pain again.

Thomas, though, when he was born, she had to love. It had been impossible not to, so she'd committed herself to never let anything happen to him.

Rosemary sank down onto her bed, contemplating all the things she'd always known but only now accepted as truths. Michael hadn't died, but he had made it clear that he would never love her, would never consider her suitable to become his duchess. Only his friend.

The single tear that streaked down her cheek burned. So did the next one and the many that followed thereafter.

Over the next month, she tried finding things to consume her time and thoughts. She went shopping so many times that her wardrobe and the drawers of her bureau were overflowing. She searched for mud larks, but they quickly concluded that she had to be from an orphanage and ran as soon as she got close. Last week she had traveled to Bellview with Nora and the dowager duchess.

Sarah was a true angel on earth, and every one

of the young women she housed were all sincerely grateful to have been saved by her, as they worded it. Rosemary met Ned and Clara during the visit, who were doing wonderfully well and made her miss Michael even more.

Because she did. Miss him. It was impossible not to. Telling herself not to was useless.

Almost as useless as trying to stay busy.

She attended every event possible. All of them were boring. As boring as the ones that she used to attend with her father and Maud before going to Turnbill that weekend and dancing with Michael.

That was the way she now thought about things, how she'd started to chronicle time—before Michael and after Michael.

The pain was still there. Some days it was sharp and poignant; other days it was dull and achy.

She took Thomas to see the puppies regularly and hoped each visit to hear news that Michael was coming to town. There was no reason for him to; she was just hoping. And every night she'd tell herself that her hopes now were just as foolish as her fairy-tale wishes had been years ago.

The only difference between now and then was that she had indeed fallen in love with a man who would never love her in return.

Not only that, falling in love with him meant that she compared every other man to him, and they all came up lacking.

Even Rafael Williams. He'd been at several events she'd attended, and though she was happy to see and speak with him, she had no desire to dance with him. Or anyone else.

Rafael had been at the Creswells' party last night, and Willette had been with him. It had actually been an event to raise money for Sarah's waifs. Therefore, her father and Maud had attended, as well as Nora and Geoffrey and other members of the Knight family.

Not Michael, of course.

That could be the reason the pain was strong and poignant this morning. Then again, there truly didn't need to be a reason. It just was that way some days. All she could hope for was that the passage of time would lessen the pang at some point during the day.

She made her way downstairs and then towards the dining room. For some reason, the sound of her father's voice made her pause. He sounded frustrated, and she moved closer to the doorway but didn't step into the opening.

"I know, I know," her father was saying. "I'm just worried."

"I know you are, dear," Maud said. "You just need to give her time."

"She wouldn't even dance with Rafael Williams. He's a nice young man. When I asked Michael to stop seeing her, I thought—"

Rosemary went momentarily deaf. Either that, or she couldn't believe what she'd just heard. Her father wouldn't have… Shaking her head, she leaned closer to the doorway, needing to hear more.

"Stop seeing her?" Maud asked. "Why, when?" Maud didn't wait for her father to answer, instead her voice grew higher pitched as she said, "Ralph Crofton! I agreed with you when you suggested to let her manage the house and to let her be so overprotective of Thomas. I even agreed to be the mean stepmother, saying and doing things that I'll forever regret, while hoping she'd get so furious that she'd want her own life, but I will not agree with this!"

Rosemary flinched at the sound of a teacup rattling.

"Why on earth," Maud continued, now almost shouting, "would you want to ruin her chance at true love?"

"Love?" her father said.

"Yes! Love! She and Michael were falling in love."

"Michael would never think of her that way. I spoke with him about it when he came to London. Told him how our families had always hoped that, but he wasn't interested in marriage between them."

Rosemary slapped a hand over her mouth to cover a gasp and felt the warmth of her tears running down her cheeks. She hadn't needed confirmation of how Michael felt, but she'd got it nonetheless.

"He came to London because he was already falling in love with her!" Maud said. "I saw that at Turnbill. That's why I suggested that we leave and let Rosemary stay. Please tell me that you aren't that blind?

Never mind, don't tell me! I don't want to know. What I know is that though I love you, I also love Rosemary, and I will not let her go on suffering."

"What are you going to do?" her father asked.

"Never you mind!"

Rosemary didn't have the opportunity, or perhaps the wherewithal, to move. Therefore, when Maud exited the room, Rosemary was standing there and fell into her stepmother's outstretched arms, where she cried. Cried like a baby in their mother's arms.

Chapter Sixteen

It had been a long day, and Michael pushed Atlas a little hard, hoping to get to the stable before dark. Between the mine and Lettice's harvest, he'd been burning the candle at both ends all month. He appreciated the work that was keeping him busy. In reality, he could leave it all to the mine and land managers, who were capable men, good men, and he was doing his best not to get in their way. It was just that he needed something to do. If not, he'd have already left for London.

Weeks ago.

And while there, he'd have told Rosemary that he loved her. Loved her deeper and more strongly than he'd known he was capable of loving, because it continued to grow rather than weaken. Every day it grew.

He couldn't do that of course. Couldn't tell her that he loved her. Maybe in a year or so, after she'd experienced life—and hopefully hadn't fallen in love with anyone else. In that respect, he was in total disagreement with her father. He didn't want her to fall in love with anyone but him.

That was the difference between hope and expectations. Michael hoped that Rosemary wouldn't fall in love with someone else, and her father had expectations that she would. But Ralph had also once had expectations that the two of them would marry someday, and it was that expectation that Michael hoped the earl would be able to resurrect.

Dear Lord, he hoped that was possible. He also hoped that he was doing the right thing by letting Rosemary have time to experience life.

He'd also come to a conclusion about what it took to become a duchess. It was simple. While many women might seek the role, Rosemary *was* the role. As he lay in bed every night, he recalled moments in time when she'd shown grace and beauty, but also when she'd been so willing to assist him. The moment she'd come up with the idea of providing Sarah's waifs with more funds.

Furthermore, she knew how to manage a household, take care of children and love. She knew how to love.

Michael hadn't.

He did now.

How could he not? She was the most lovable person he would ever know. Had been from the time she'd been a young girl chasing fairies, looking for ghosts and awaiting her knight in shining armor to rescue her.

Oh, how he wanted to be that knight.

Waiting until that might happen was torture, and it had only been a month.

His thoughts about Rosemary had made him forget that he was in a hurry to get to the stable. Left to his own schedule, Atlas had slowed the pace to a walk, so they didn't arrive until after dark.

Michael turned the horse over to the stableman and made his way to the back door of the house. A letter from his mother had arrived yesterday, stating they wouldn't be returning to the country for a few more weeks. She'd written that between plans for the wedding and raising funds for Sarah, there was much to accomplish, and that couldn't be done from Turnbill.

Her letter had also said that she'd traveled to Bellview and met Sarah, as well as Ned and Clara, who were doing well and shared their gratitude for his help.

She'd also mentioned that Rosemary had accompanied her and Nora to the estate. He'd reread that part more than once, simply taking a bit of solace from reading her name, all the while wishing his mother had said more about her. Told him if she was doing well.

He truly hoped she was doing well and that she was happy. He'd suffer through months of unhappiness if it meant she was happy.

Entering the house, he encountered Horace and handed the man his hat and coat.

"Dinner can be served immediately, Your Grace," Horace replied.

"Thank you, and please apologize to the kitchen for my tardiness," Michael said, knowing the kitchen staff would have kept the meal hot and ready for whenever he arrived, which he did appreciate.

"Yes, Your Grace."

Something about Horace's expression, almost as if he was trying not to smile, made Michael frown, but he quickly dismissed it. Horace was a happy sort of man, and there was nothing unusual about him smiling.

Michael entered the small room off the hall where there was warm water waiting for him to use. He washed his hands and face and was handed a towel by Gilbert.

"Thank you," he replied.

"I have a clean shirt for you, Your Grace," Gilbert said.

"That's not necessary," Michael replied. Eating alone didn't require him to dress for dinner. However, it was decidedly lonely.

He was decidedly lonely.

"Might I suggest a fresh waistcoat?"

"Thank you, Gilbert, but I will simply eat my dinner and retire for the night, and you may do the same." He didn't want to be rude, but this was one of those times when he wished he wasn't a duke with people waiting on him hand and foot. He'd much rather just be a man. A man who could marry the woman he loved with no worries about the pressure he'd be putting on her by becoming a duchess.

Rosemary fit the role, but she had to want it and wouldn't know whether she did until she'd discovered what other options were available to her.

"Very well, Your Grace," Gilbert said and left the room.

Michael exited the room as well, and the echoing of his footfalls reminded him of how alone he was, even in a house full of people dedicated to providing him with his every need—well, almost every need.

For a moment, he considered skipping dinner altogether and just going up to his room where he could wallow in his own misery, but the kitchen had laid on dinner for him. Furthermore, he could just as easily wallow in his own misery in the dining room.

Catching movement as soon as he entered the dining room, he lifted his head, assuming it was a servant and wanting to acknowledge their attendance. What he saw brought his feet to a dead stop and sent his heart beating like a drummer in a parade.

For several long seconds, all he could do was stare, questioning his eyesight. Finally, needing to know if he'd lost his mind or not, he asked, "Rosemary?"

"Hello, Michael."

His ears couldn't be playing tricks on him, too.

Yet, not daring to move lest she disappear, he asked, "What are you doing here?"

"I thought I would join you for dinner, if you don't mind."

"Mind?"

She nodded.

Still questioning his senses, he asked, "Are you a ghost?"

Her giggle, though soft, reverberated the room, and his ears. Made him fully understand that he wasn't seeing things that weren't there.

"No, I'm not a ghost. Why? Are you afraid?"

Hell yes, he was afraid. Afraid that he'd lose all control. Lose any ability to ever let her out of his sight again. "No, not of ghosts. Just surprised." He forced his feet to walk rather than run and flattened his hands against his hips because they badly wanted to touch her. "Where's the rest of your family?"

She was standing next to the table and smiling. God's teeth, but he loved her smile. Loved her. There wasn't a single part of him that wasn't rejoicing at her presence.

"At home," she replied. "In London."

He arrived at the table, close enough to touch her, but he didn't dare. He was still half afraid that she might disappear. "How did you get here?"

"A coach."

He cautioned himself against conjuring up possible reasons for her to be here. Especially one possible reason, one that pertained to him. And to love. "Who traveled with you?"

"Helen, Maud's maid, and her driver. She lent me her coach and driver."

"Why, is something wrong? Your father? Thomas? Maud?" Why hadn't he asked that earlier? Rosemary would only be here if something was wrong! Until this moment he hadn't thought of that possibility because he'd been so busy hoping for something different. Hoping that she'd sought him out for the very same reason that had prevented him from going to London.

"Thomas, my father and Maud are all fine. They send their greetings."

He nodded, still staring at her, at her calm demeanor, then shook his head. "I don't understand, why are you here?"

"We will discuss that," she said, sitting down in her chair, "after we eat. The kitchen staff has been awaiting your arrival."

He sat. "We can discuss it while we eat."

She nodded at him and then towards the door that led to the pantry where the food would have been kept warm. A servant entered, carrying two plates already full of food and set one before each of them. Normally, the food was served in covered dishes to be dished up at the table, but he cared little about that.

Picking up her fork, she asked, "Shall we eat before it gets cold?"

He nodded and picked up his fork, but as he aimed

it towards his plate, he set it back down. "Why are you here?"

No longer smiling, she set her fork down and met his gaze with one filled with seriousness. "I am here to apologize."

The hope he'd been harboring fizzled. "For what?"

"My father. He will apologize himself the next time you see him, but I decided that it wasn't something that could wait until you were next in London."

The joy at seeing her, and the confusion, were slowly turning into apprehension. There was something here that he didn't understand, and for the life of him he couldn't figure out what it might be. His befuddled mind simply couldn't concentrate on anything except for how much he'd missed her. How badly he wanted to collect her in his arms and hold her tight. How badly he wanted to spend the rest of his life holding her, loving her.

"He regrets having told you to stop seeing me," she said. "I regret that he chose to interfere in a matter that you and I had yet to determine for ourselves."

His joy returned, but he contained it, as well as the smile that wanted to overtake his lips, lest he was jumping to conclusions. "What had we yet to determine?"

"Whether we were falling in love with each other," she said.

The shine in her brown eyes told him all he needed to know, yet he asked, "Were we?"

"That is my conclusion," she said, "because what I feel cannot be mistaken for anything else. I have loved you for a very long time."

He'd never experienced such a rush of happiness. It literally shot him to his feet.

Her startled expression said that hadn't been the reaction she'd expected, and he extended a hand towards her. The moment she laid her hand in his, he tugged her to her feet and into his arms.

"Yes, we were falling in love," he said. "I, too, know that what I feel for you cannot be mistaken for anything expect love. A love so deep that it will last a lifetime."

Her eyes glistened as she whispered, "Oh, Michael, I have missed you so."

"As I have you," he replied, a moment before their lips met. The meeting, the depth of the kiss they shared was so deep it not only filled his soul, it confirmed all he'd concluded over the past month. She'd captured his heart long ago. He'd just been too blind to see it.

As the kiss ended, she laid her head upon his chest. "I've been wrong about so many things," she said. "Maud isn't the horrible person that I made her out to be. I was just afraid of losing another mother. Afraid of losing someone I love again, but in clinging to my fear, I was missing out on life. You showed me that." Lifting her head, she looked at him with glistening eyes. "Showed me that there are real life fairy tales."

He touched her cheek. For years he'd mistaken what he was truly feeling for a need to protect her. He'd confused his promise to his father with a number of things. "I, too, was wrong about several things, and it took you to open my eyes. Rather than believe Nora could make her own decisions for her own future, I took it upon myself to decide for her. I did the same to you by asking for your assistance and by leaving London. Neither time did I ask what you wanted. I promise never to do that again."

Her smile grew. "I believe my father was involved in your leaving."

"He is your father."

"Well." She nuzzled his chin with her nose. "Would you go along with something else he has suggested?"

He leaned back to look her in the eyes. "What?"

"Being the commanding officer for the Royal Army does include a few privileges," she said. "If you are interested, we can be married in the chapel at Buckingham Palace."

His heart soared. "Is that what you want? To marry me? Become the Duchess of Turnbill?"

"Yes, more than anything in the world."

He pulled her into another hug. "That is what I want, too." He kissed the tip of her nose. "Whenever, wherever you want, I'll be there."

"Day after tomorrow?" she asked.

"That may not be possible, we need to get a license and—" He stopped at how she was shaking her head.

"We already have special permission from the Queen." She shrugged. "Again, privileges for those who protect the Royal Family."

He lifted her off her feet and spun in a circle. "We'll leave for London first thing in the morning." Setting her back on her feet, he kissed her in a way that said he couldn't wait and was overjoyed that it would only be two days before they were husband and wife.

"You look positively radiant," Maud said, fussing with the flower blossoms attached to the veil that was pinned to the crown of curls Helen had expertly arranged.

"Thank you," Rosemary replied, looking at herself wearing the long white gown made of silk and lace. "Do all brides feel this happy on their wedding day?"

"They should," Maud replied. "But this is your day, and you don't need to think about anyone but yourself and your husband."

"It's all because of you," Rosemary said, appreciating how close she and Maud had become over the last month. "I wouldn't have had the courage to go to Turnbill if you hadn't convinced me."

"Nonsense," Maud said, wiping the corners of her eyes. "It's all because of you. Michael fell in love with you, and it's no wonder why."

"I just can't believe you're getting married before me," Nora said. "Nor can I believe we are going to be sisters! It's a dream come true."

"It is," Rosemary agreed. It was all so perfect that she kept wondering if she really was dreaming. She'd been afraid upon arriving at Turnbill but had been determined to convince Michael that they had fallen in love. It had turned out to be a simple task, because they were deeply in love. The two of them had talked through most of the night, about the past, the present and the future.

They'd kissed several times, and though she had wanted more, she'd known consummating their love would have to wait until tonight. A night Maud had fully prepared her for with a deep, motherly discussion.

The wedding itself was small, with only family in attendance, but when she and Michael stood face to face at the altar, it was as if they were the only two people in the world. When she looked into his eyes, the love she felt was too great for her to hear or see anything else.

The marriage was sealed with a kiss that held so much promise she wished they could forgo the wedding breakfast that her father's household staff had been preparing yesterday and this morning.

As they rode together in his coach to her father's house, Michael held her close. "It's too far to travel to Turnbill, and wanting as much privacy as possible, I have booked us a stay at the Langham Hotel."

He'd shared that while kissing her neck and cheek and chin, instilling memories of the night of the Duckworth ball, which had her body heating up with a sweet, powerful need.

"The most luxurious and expensive hotel in all of London," she said. "What will people think?"

He laughed. Kissed her. "That nothing is too good for the Duchess of Turnbill."

"Nor the Duke of Turnbill," she said, catching his mouth for a deep and resounding kiss.

Hours later, after the celebratory meal that contained toasts of well wishes, lively conversations and great bouts of laughter, Rosemary kissed her father's cheek, as well as Maud's, and then Thomas's as she prepared to leave. Foreseeing how the change in the household might affect her son, Maud had seen that the new puppy had been brought home yesterday, and once again, Rosemary acknowledged how mistaken she'd been about her stepmother.

She'd once feared the day she would leave her father's house. Now she knew how foolish that fear had been, for today, she felt nothing but great joy and anticipation of a wonderful life yet to come.

A short time later, as they walked inside the massive six-story hotel, she admitted, "I've never stayed at a hotel."

"It's a day of firsts for you," Michael replied with a devilish grin. "You've never been married before, either."

"True," she whispered in his ear. "Which means

I've never had a husband before. I may not know what to do with him."

He laughed. "Life with you is going to be an adventure."

If she wasn't so excited to get the adventure started, she might have noticed the glamor and glory of the hotel that was favored by royalty and the wealthiest of the wealthy around the world. As it was, she only had eyes for her husband as an electric lift took them up to a suite of rooms where she and Michael would share secrets and dreams. Some that would never be shared with anyone but each other, and others that they would build together.

Tears of joy stung her eyes as she waited for the door to close and for Michael to turn the key in the lock. Then she waited for him to turn about and walk towards her. Maud had told her that she had every right to love Michael to the fullest and to enjoy herself while planting the seeds of future, and hopefully of babies.

She planned on doing just that and flung herself into his arms. Looping her arms around his neck, she kissed him until she was dizzy, and then within the warm embrace of his arms, kissed him some more.

In no time, she found herself lying on a bed stripped down to the bare skin and biting down on her bottom lip as a searing hot need surged through her system, needing Michael in the most basic way.

He'd kissed her, teased her and loved her in every

way except the very one she was nearly dying to receive. The rest of him was as gorgeous and perfect as she'd imagined, and feeling quite smug at capturing his heart, she grasped his shoulders, asking, "Now?"

"Yes, now," he answered, positioning himself atop her.

A soft gasp escaped as she felt him entering the innermost recess of her body, and another as he slid in deeper, then deeper still. If there was any pain or discomfort, she didn't feel it. Only blissfulness at knowing this was exactly what her body was craving. What her life had been craving. To love and be loved. To need and be needed.

Michael slowly began to move, creating a rhythm that her body instantly responded to. It was a dance as old as time, where the beats of the music were created by their bodies, and the tune was pleasure-filled sighs and moans that conveyed she'd never felt anything so wonderful in her life.

She could feel her body straining at an ever-increasing acute yearning that overtook her in entirety—her body, heart, mind and soul.

Her first bout of insecurity struck unexpectedly when it felt as if she might explode on the inside, and she gasped, trying to speak. "Michael?" she managed to say.

"I know, darling," he whispered. "Just let it go."

She wasn't sure what he meant, what she ought to let go, until a moment later when an intense burst of pleasure struck. "Oh, my!" The intensity had eased, but the pleasure remained, and she closed her eyes, focusing on nothing but the waves of bliss washing over her.

Until she felt Michael's entire body stiffen, and as he made a final thrust deep inside her, she sensed that he'd reached the same pinnacle she had. A second bout of pleasure struck, making her toes curl, and she grasped onto his shoulders, riding the waves all over again.

For a length of time, neither of them moved, just lay there, united as one, basking in the bliss of their love. She felt as if she'd just reached a place where she'd always belonged and always would. A place where fairy tales came true.

Michael lifted his head. Kissed her. "I love you, Lady Rosemary."

"And I love you." She cupped his face with both hands. "My very own Knight, who saved me from my ivory tower."

Epilogue

A faint stream of light shone in through a gap in the drapes, and Rosemary rolled over to snuggle up against Michael but found the space empty. She reached up to touch his pillow, but it too was bare.

Groggily, she opened her eyes and found the bedroom altogether empty. Smiling, she knew why.

She climbed out of the bed, lifted her robe off the chair beside the bed and shrugged it on as she quietly made her way to the door. The hallway was dark and deserted, for it was still early in the morning, except for the far end of the hall, where faint morning light was just beginning to shine through the stained-glass windows, casting tiny, almost invisible, dancing points of light onto the floor.

Fairy lights.

Happiness welled inside her, and she couldn't imagine ever not being captivated by Turnbill. Inside and out. Beyond the window, the lush green grass was now winter brown, the trees stripped of their leaves and the flower beds long ago cut back and covered with straw, yet it was still beautiful. Still magical.

As magical as her life.

She made her way down the hall and found the door she was seeking already cracked open, and there was her husband, sitting in the rocking chair.

Walking up behind him, she wrapped her arms around his neck and kissed his cheek. "We have a nursemaid," she whispered.

"I know," he whispered, grasping her hands that were rubbing his chest inside his robe. "I couldn't sleep."

"Because it's his birthday?" she asked, her gaze going to the babe sleeping in his crib. "His first birthday." Their son, Donavan Michael Knight, was as handsome as his father, and as loveable.

"You should still be sleeping," he said. "It will be a busy day with your family and others arriving to celebrate this evening."

Her family would be arriving, as would Nora, Geoffrey and their son, Andrew, who was six months younger than Donavan. Rosemary was sure the two were to be best friends as well as cousins. Drake and his wife, Meridith, were coming, too, as were Rafael and Willette. "I would still be sleeping if you had been in the bed," she said.

"I'm sorry."

"Don't be," she answered, feeling desire growing inside her. Stepping around the chair, she sat down on her husband's lap and laid her head on his shoulder. "It is amazing. This little life that we created is already a year old. Yet, in many ways, I feel as if we were just married yesterday."

He kissed her. "Donavan is proof that we weren't." Rubbing her back, he added, "Though I know the feeling. A day doesn't go by when I don't love you more than the one before."

"The feeling is mutual," she said, drawing a line on his chest with one finger. "You know, now that I'm no longer nursing him, the chances of Donovan having a sibling are greater."

His smile caused a plethora of wonderful shivers to issue forth over her body. Without saying a word, he slipped one arm under her knees and stood with her in his arms.

"Where are we going?" she asked, as if she didn't know.

"Back to bed," Michael said.

"I thought you couldn't sleep," she said, nibbling on his ear.

"I couldn't, but I didn't want to wake you." He carried her out the door, pausing so she could reach back to quietly close it. "That is no longer an issue."

"I never complain when you wake me."

"You never complain, period."

"I have no reason to complain," she said. "I'm living in a fairy tale where all my dreams come true."

"Is one of your dreams for Donavan to have a sibling?"

"Yes," she admitted.

"Your wish is my command," he said as he strolled into their bedroom and kicked the door shut.

She expected no less from her knight, and he never disappointed her.

* * * * *

Whilst you wait for the next instalment of Brides for Sworn Bachelors, make sure to check out other captivating reads by Lauri Robinson

A Dance with Her Forbidden Officer
A Courtship to Fool Manhattan
The Cowboy's English Lady

And why not check out Lauri Robinson's The Redford Dukedom miniseries?

Captivated by His Convenient Duchess
Winning His Manhattan Heiress

MILLS & BOON®

Coming next month

RESCUED BY THE RAKISH LORD
Sarah Mallory

'It is a rather delicate matter. It concerns Lord Graddon's guest, the one with the roguish epithet Devil Blackbourne.' Lady Kenton declared. 'You will recall we all thought he had quit Graddon Hall.'

'But he has returned?' Selina replied cautiously.

Lady Kenton nodded.

'And now, I suppose, it is all over the town and all the poor mamas are once again anxious for their chicks. But is this all, ma'am?' Selina asked, still anxious. 'I cannot think it warrants you driving here especially to tell me.'

'You are quite correct, if it was only the rake's return I would have left it until we met, or you heard it from one of your other friends. As it is, Sir Alfred came home today with the most alarming report and as soon as I heard it, I came to warn you.'

Selina was now thoroughly alarmed. Was news of her masquerading as a serving maid all over Torrisford now? She waited anxiously while Lady Kenton tapped her fan against her palm, clearly struggling to find the right words to express herself.

'Oh, my dear Selina,' she exclaimed at last, 'The rogue has made you the subject of the most outrageous wager!'

Continue reading

RESCUED BY THE RAKISH LORD
Sarah Mallory

Available next month
millsandboon.co.uk

Copyright © 2026 Sarah Mallory

COMING SOON!

We really hope you enjoyed reading this book. If you're looking for more romance be sure to head to the shops when new books are available on

Thursday 23rd April

To see which titles are coming soon, please visit
millsandboon.co.uk/nextmonth

MILLS & BOON

TWO BRAND NEW BOOKS FROM
Love Always

Be prepared to be swept away to incredible worldwide destinations along with our strong, relatable heroines and intensely desirable heroes.

OUT NOW

Four Love Always stories published every month, find them all at:

millsandboon.co.uk

FOUR BRAND NEW BOOKS FROM
MILLS & BOON MODERN

Indulge in desire, drama, and breathtaking romance – where passion knows no bounds!

OUT NOW

Eight Modern stories published every month, find them all at:

millsandboon.co.uk

OUT NOW!

Available at
millsandboon.co.uk

MILLS & BOON

LET'S TALK
Romance

For exclusive extracts, competitions and special offers, find us online:

- **f** MillsandBoon
- **X** @MillsandBoon
- **◉** @MillsandBoonUK
- **♪** @MillsandBoonUK

Get in touch on 01413 063 232

For all the latest titles coming soon, visit
millsandboon.co.uk/nextmonth